PENGUIN BOOKS

UNDERSTANDING INFLATION

John Case obtained a B.A. in social studies from Harvard University in 1966. He did graduate work in political science in Bordeaux, France, supported by a Fulbright scholarship, and at Harvard. In 1969 he joined the Cambridge Institute, an independent think tank directed by Gar Alperovitz and Christopher Jencks, where he helped found the magazine *Working Papers for a New Society*. He has also co-edited two anthologies on social change. He lives in Cambridge, Massachusetts, with his wife and two children.

UNDERSTANDING INFLATION

by

John Case

PENGUIN BOOKS

Penguin Books Ltd, Harmondsworth,
Middlesex, England
Penguin Books, 625 Madison Avenue,
New York, New York 10022, U.S.A.
Penguin Books Australia Ltd, Ringwood,
Victoria, Australia
Penguin Books Canada Limited, 2801 John Street,
Markham, Ontario, Canada L3R 1B4
Penguin Books (N.Z.) Ltd, 182–190 Wairau Road,
Auckland 10, New Zealand

First published in the United States of America by
William Morrow and Company, Inc., 1981
Published in Penguin Books 1982

LIBRARY OF CONGRESS CATALOGING IN PUBLICATION DATA
Case, John, 1944–
    Understanding inflation.
    Reprint. Originally published: New York:
Morrow, 1981.
    Includes bibliographical references and index.
    1. Inflation (Finance). 2. Inflation (Finance)—
United States. I. Title.
[HG229.C35   1981b]   332.4'1   81-15797
ISBN 0 14 00.6082 0   AACR2

Printed in the United States of America by
Offset Paperback Mfrs., Inc., Dallas, Pennsylvania
Set in Baskerville

For Quaker

Foreword

This book is for people who want to know why prices keep going up.

It is not—rest assured—an economics textbook. It contains no equations, one graph, and only a few statistics. Nor is it a book for specialists. Economists interested in the fine points of business-cycle theory or monetary policy will have to look elsewhere. So don't worry if you never (or haven't yet) made it through Economics 101. You don't need to know a thing about supply and demand curves or the theories of John Maynard Keynes in order to read what follows. You may not know much about these matters when you're through. But you should understand inflation.

That of course is no idle ambition. Every morning the papers report some new development on the "inflation front," as if the economy had been transformed into a battlefield. Nearly every day a public official offers a pronouncement or a promise about the high cost of living. Inflation regularly tops opinion-poll lists of Americans' major concerns. If you can understand the subject, you will find the nightly news a good deal less puzzling than it used to be, even if the day's top story is about floating exchange rates or changes in the money supply. You will also find that a considerable amount of what is said about inflation in the press or at the lunch table is confused, misleading, or untrue. Everyone *can* understand inflation, even without a background in economics. But not everyone does.

Inflation is also a useful point of entry into the puzzling behavior of the modern economy. A rapid, continuing rise in prices with no end in sight—the kind of inflation we have experienced since the late 1960s—has never occurred before in American history. For decades, even centuries, prices rose and fell with predictable if not perfect regularity. Since World War II they have moved in only one direction: up. Since about 1967 the rate at which they move up has increased dramatically.

What happened? We like to blame inflation on greedy unions, businesses, or oil sheikhs, on spendthrift governments or chickenhearted politicians. Greed, profligacy, and chickenheartedness are all no doubt widespread. But inflation creates these attributes as much as it is created by them. Moreover, there's no reason to think that these traits were invented ten, fifteen, or even thirty-five years ago. The important chapters in the story of inflation reflect not human vices but human inventiveness. Our own resourcefulness has led us, as through a maze, to a world of apparently permanent inflation. The pages that follow will explain how this came to be.

Three cautions. First, don't expect a simple answer to the problem of inflation. There isn't one. The ways of controlling inflation discussed in the last chapter are messy and imperfect. By the same token, though, the problem is not beyond solution. As with most economic issues, it's a question of what—or who—should be sacrificed.

Second, remember that the American economy is enormously varied. Most of the generalizations in this book allow of exceptions. But don't let the exceptions blind you to the way things work most of the time. Similarly, do not be distracted by what happened to inflation the month before you read this book. Inflation may be getting worse or it may be easing up. But even a temporary improvement is not a sign that the problem is disappearing. Inflation has been with us for some time now. Unless something changes dramatically, it will be with us for a long time to come.

Finally, keep in mind that this is a book about inflation as a social phenomenon and political issue. It is not about inflation as a personal financial problem. There are many books available that treat the latter subject. Some may even contain good advice. But this one discusses what we as a nation ought to do about inflation, not what a few individuals can do to beat it. Only so many people, after all, were able to fit into the *Titanic*'s lifeboats. Better that someone should have told the captain to watch out for icebergs.

Acknowledgments

Thanks to James Campen, Christopher Jencks, Nancy Lyons, and Robert Zevin, all of whom read portions of this book in manuscript form. Most of their suggestions were gratefully accepted. Thanks also to John Brockman, who helped me get started.

Special thanks to my parents, Everett Case and Josephine Young Case, who offered advice and support of many kinds.

Contents

1. The Mixed Curse:
Inflation in Perspective

The cost of living has gone up another dollar a quart.
—W. C. FIELDS

Back in 1965, prices did not seem inordinately low.

A dime would no longer buy a cup of coffee in most restaurants, and three dollars wouldn't pay for a copy of the hit new album by a young singer named Bob Dylan. Volkswagens could be driven out of the showroom for less than $2,000, but a fully equipped Pontiac Bonneville station wagon might run as high as $4,700. Ten gallons of Texaco premium cost $3.20, up from $3.10 a few years earlier. A typical new home sold for about $20,000, and mortgage rates had climbed to almost 6 percent.*

People complained about the high cost of living, and the complaints seemed justified. Prices had jumped nearly 75 percent since the end of World War II. And though high annual inflation rates hadn't been seen since the late forties

---

* Sources for these and other statistics, quotations, and so on, will be found in the Source Notes section at the back of the book.

and early fifties, prices nevertheless kept inching upward a percent or two every year.*

The complainers, of course, didn't know what they were getting in for. But then neither did anybody else.

In 1966 inflation began to heat up a little. Both that year and the next, prices rose more than 3 percent. In 1968 the rate neared 5 percent and in 1969 it topped 6 percent. By the end of the decade a typical item that cost $10 in 1965 was going for $12.05—a 20 percent jump in just five years.

Maybe, people thought, inflation was only temporarily bad—a result of the war in Vietnam. Every other war in America's history had brought hefty price increases. Americans over forty could remember the period right after World War II, when wartime controls were lifted and prices shot up. Even more could remember the inflation brought on by the Korean conflict in 1950 and 1951. But the hope that things were so simple soon vanished. U.S. troop levels in Southeast Asia peaked in 1969. Inflation stayed bad. By 1973 the war was essentially over. Inflation got worse.

Between January 1970 and late October 1979, prices exactly doubled. Inflation during the seventies averaged a little over 7 percent annually—more than triple what it had averaged in the previous two decades.† Nearly every year prices went up faster than they had gone up in *any* year during the fifties and sixties. As the 1970s ended, inflation was well into double digits. In the 1980s the outlook is for more of the same. In all probability prices will double again before another ten years pass.

Most of this book is about where inflation came from, why it has been with us so long, and why it got so much worse

---

* See the Appendix for an explanation and discussion of the various measures of inflation. Throughout this book, "prices" will refer to the Labor Department's Consumer Price Index and "inflation" or the "inflation rate" to percentage changes in the index (unless otherwise specified).

† An average rise of 7 percent a year leads to a cumulative 100 percent rise over ten years because of compounding.

during the seventies. The book will also discuss what can be done about inflation. Before these mysteries are unraveled, though, it helps to consider the nature of the beast. Like all objects of fear and loathing, inflation has grown larger than life, and in the process has engendered a set of cautionary tales. Inflation, it is said, is making us poorer by the day. It saps our economic strength, discourages hard work, undermines thrift, eats away at earnings. There is enough truth in these charges to make them credible.

The whole story, however, is not so simple. Like the Lord, inflation giveth and inflation taketh away. Also like the Lord, inflation gets blamed for the negative side of the ledger, while the positive side is chalked up to our own intelligence and hard work. The analogy ends here: inflation is beyond doubt a curse. But its effects, which this chapter will scrutinize, are mixed.

Inflation is not making us poorer

During the 1970s, prices doubled. Yet most Americans were making more than twice as much at the end of the decade as they were making at the beginning. Most families' purchasing power rose. The purchasing power of some of our society's most vulnerable groups—the elderly, for example—rose even faster than the average. Some people are better off than they were, some worse off. But in general the poor are no poorer, the rich no richer. Some goods and services are relatively cheaper than they used to be, some relatively more expensive.

Economists calculate these changes in what they call real terms—real wages, real prices, and so forth.* To figure real changes, all you need is a standard of comparison, like last year or 1970; then you adjust your figures for the effects of inflation. If you made $100 a week in 1970 and $200 a week

---

*Another phrase that means the same thing is "constant dollars." If two prices are calculated in constant dollars—1970 dollars, for example —then the later price is discounted by the amount of inflation that occurred in the interim.

in 1980, for example, your real wages (or your purchasing power) hardly changed at all. If you got a 12 percent raise in 1979, when inflation was running at 13 percent, you wound up making 1 percent less in real terms than before.

Between 1970 and 1979, average after-tax income rose about 25 percent per person in real terms. Except for the economic downturn of 1974–75 and the beginnings of recession in 1979, it rose steadily throughout the decade. Average income rose almost as fast in the 1970s as it had in the boom years of the 1960s.

In real terms, a lot of things are easier to afford now than they were in 1970 (see box, p. 19). Nearly everything is cheaper in this sense than it was in the Depression, despite what those who lived through it tell their children and grandchildren. Eggs, for example, went for about 38¢ a dozen in 1935. To earn that much, a typical worker (if he or she had a job) had to work nearly three quarters of an hour. In 1980 eggs cost about 88¢ a dozen. That took the typical wage earner about seven-and-a-half minutes to earn. By the same measurement, a color television set "cost" perhaps eighty-six hours of work in 1970. In 1980 a similar set cost only forty-two hours.

Sometimes, of course, real prices rise. If the world really is running out of oil, for instance, the price will eventually go up with or without the Organization of Petroleum Exporting Countries. And a hospital with a lot of modern sophisticated equipment in it will cost more per day in real terms than a hospital of the 1950s. As long as the economy is growing, though, most of the things we buy will be easier to afford every year. Inflation drives up prices, but in a growing economy people's income rises even faster.

Where the money went

A moment's reflection will convince you that it would be hard for inflation to be making *everyone* poorer. You and I and everybody else are spending a lot more money than we used to. But the stores, landlords, and banks that get the

TEN ITEMS THAT WERE EASIER TO AFFORD IN 1980 THAN IN 1970 . . .

Item	Price Increase
Potatoes	69%
Rent (residential)	79%
Clothing (men's & boys')	40%
TV sets	3%
Whiskey	29%
New cars	67%
Public transportation	81%
Refrigerators & freezers	57%
Telephone services	31%
Property taxes (residential)	56%

Consumer Price Index, same period up 110.7%

After-tax income, per person up 136%

& A FEW OF THE ITEMS THAT WENT UP THE FASTEST . . .

Fish & seafood	174%
Gasoline	257%
Hospital room	180%
Soft drinks	234%
Home maintenance services	141%

NOTE: Price increases for each item reflect changes in individual components of the Consumer Price Index. They compare the index figure for May 1980 with the 1970 annual-average index figure for the item in question. "After-tax income" compares the per capita disposable income figure for 1970 ($3,348) with the Census Bureau's figure for May 1980 ($7,894).

money don't just sit on it. They spend it—on wages, supplies, dividends, investments, and so forth. So do the governments that are collecting more and more of your money in taxes. Every dollar that comes in goes out—to pay a teacher or a tax collector, to provide benefits like social security, to build roads or cruise missiles. You may not like what businesses and governments do with your money, but you can't accuse them of not spending it. And one person's expenditure is another person's income.*

Money, of course, may be ending up in other people's pockets instead of yours. If stock dividends skyrocket while real wages fall—and you don't own any stock—then all the averages in the world won't convince you that you're better off than you used to be. The issue of who's getting the income may therefore be just as important as whether average income has kept up with inflation. And indeed, some specific groups have gained economic ground during the last ten years while other groups have fallen behind.

Welfare recipients—despite all the rhetoric about America's overgenerous welfare programs—have done badly. Average benefits under the Aid to Families with Dependent Children (AFDC) system dropped about 20 percent in real terms between 1970 and 1978. Single-parent families in general didn't do so well. Families headed by a single woman —about a sixth of all families, at last count—just about maintained their purchasing power in the last decade while other families' real incomes were increasing. Workers dependent on the minimum wage almost kept up but not quite: the federal minimum for most workers rose from $1.60 an hour in 1970 to $3.10 in 1980 while prices were a little more than doubling.

People employed in retail trade, finance, insurance, and real estate, on the average, lost ground. Librarians and college professors did too—full professors' real incomes dropped

---

* If a lot of money were flowing abroad, of course, Americans could be getting poorer while others were getting richer. And it's true that the United States' balance of payments has been getting worse, thanks in part to the rising price of imported oil. Still, the numbers are not huge. In 1977 through 1979, we imported about $30 billion a year worth of goods more than we exported, or roughly 1.5 percent of the Gross National Product. And the "current account" balance, which measures things like income from investments abroad as well as from exports, has actually been in surplus for much of the last decade.

nearly 10 percent between 1967 and 1978. Vacuum-cleaner salesmen, Avon ladies, household workers, and free-lance writers have all, by some reports, done poorly. So have cowboys. "Five, six years ago," one range rider in Arizona told a reporter, "the average cowboy in these parts made about three hundred dollars a month, along with room and board. Today he's still making about three hundred."

On the other side of the ledger, steelworkers have done well. Their average earnings rose from about $7,500 in 1967 to more than $19,500 in 1978—a gain, after inflation, of 35 percent. Most other blue-collar workers who belong to strong unions have more than kept up with rising prices. So have most federal employees, accountants, schoolteachers, police, and keypunch operators.

Among those who have more than kept pace—surprisingly, given the traditional belief that inflation hurts retired people most of all—are the elderly. The median income of those over sixty-five rose more than the average between 1970 and 1978. The proportion of old people under the government's poverty line fell from 25 percent in 1970 (about twice the national average) to 14 percent in 1977 (only a little more than the national average). One key to this unexpected development is social security, which accounts for roughly half of all the income going to the elderly. Benefits rose in real terms during the early years of the decade, and since 1975 have been increased yearly to keep up with the Consumer Price Index. Another key is private pensions. Since many private pension plans began after World War II, they cover a larger fraction of the elderly today than they did ten years ago. None of this, of course, means that the elderly have been handed the keys to Fort Knox. Their incomes, on the average, are lower than other people's, and many live perilously close to the poverty line. Those who counted on savings accounts or fixed-income pension plans to see them through have lost a good deal to inflation. On the whole, though, the situation of the elderly as a group has been getting better rather than worse.

Overall, the distribution of income has changed scarcely at all during the last decade. Neither the roiling inflation of the 1970s nor any other factor has made the poor significantly poorer or the rich significantly richer. Economists measure income distribution by dividing the population up into fifths (commonly called quintiles) according to how much money people are receiving. In 1978 you were in the highest quintile if your family's income was more than $28,632. Income under $8,720 put you in the bottom quintile. If your family brought in $17,640 you were right in the middle.

In 1970, the poorest quintile of families got 5.4 percent of the income, or a little more than one twentieth of the total. The richest quintile garnered 41 percent, or more than two fifths of the total. Thus the average family in the top group was bringing in nearly eight times what the average family in the bottom group was getting. In 1978 the bottom quintile's share was 5.2 percent and the top's was 41.5 percent. Everything else had stayed roughly the same too. Individuals may have moved up or down, but the economic ladder stayed put.

For the most part, different groups' winnings and losings cannot be blamed on inflation. Wage and other income variations depend more on politics and on changes in the marketplace than on changes in the price level. The elderly, for instance, have grown more numerous, and Congress has discovered that it is good politics to make sure that social security at least keeps up with inflation. Raising welfare benefits is not as popular, so those who depend on programs like Aid to Families with Dependent Children don't do as well. Oil-rig employees in Texas are likely to have done better in the last ten years than shoe-industry workers in Maine. People with skills that are in short supply and high demand—good corporate lawyers, for example, or electronic data-processing engineers—will do better than those who can more easily be replaced. Unionized workers will win wage gains more easily than unorganized workers, and so on.

Inflation's effects, moreover, frequently cut both ways. For

FALLING BEHIND INFLATION

• *Chief executive officers* of major American corporations saw their compensation increase only 9.7 percent in 1979 while inflation hit 13.3 percent, according to a study by Arthur Young & Company. The executives' salaries ranged from a low of $193,300 (CEO's in utility companies) to a high of $454,200 (CEO's in the petroleum and chemical industries).

• *Loan sharks* have maintained constant interest rates during the 1970s despite spiraling inflation, says an FBI special agent who supervises the Boston office's organized crime squad. The typical rate, the agent said, is about 5 percent a week, though it varies with the size of the loan and how well you know your neighborhood loan shark. The loan shark's business seems to increase with inflation: "investigators believe more persons may seek loan-shark money as inflation rises and credit becomes tighter," said one report.

SOURCES: "Executive Raises Trail Inflation Rate," *The New York Times*, August 26, 1980; Richard J. Connolly, "Loansharks Holding the Line on Inflation," *The Boston Globe*, May 19, 1980.

---

example, inflation is supposed to hurt those who work in industries like automobiles or electronics that must compete with imports. If the other country's prices are standing still, it does; U.S. goods get priced out of the market. But for most of the 1970s prices were going up faster in every other large industrial nation except West Germany than they were in the United States. So inflation "helped" those industries rather than hurt them. Similarly, inflation is supposed to hurt those who live on fixed incomes. It does. But most Americans do not live on fixed incomes. Those who do are as likely to be rich bondholders clipping their coupons as poor pensioners with no social security.

INFLATION IN THE NECESSITIES

One interesting notion making the rounds in the late 1970s was that inflation made the poor worse off because of what they spent their money on. The argument, first developed by economists associated with a group called the Exploratory Project for Economic Alternatives (later the National Center for Economic Alternatives) in Washington, was called the "four necessities" theory.

According to the theory, four basic necessities of life —food, fuel, housing, and health care—were going up in price faster than other goods and services. Since the poor presumably spend a larger fraction of their income than the rich on necessities, their purchasing power was going down faster than the purchasing power of those who were better off to begin with. The rapid rise in food and oil prices during the 1970s lent credibility to the argument.

Other studies, however, disagreed with its premises and its conclusions. Both the Cambridge (Massachusetts) economics magazine *Dollars and Sense* and Brookings researcher Joseph J. Minarik pointed out that the theory (as *Dollars and Sense* put it) "does not correctly identify the dividing line between luxuries and necessities." Clothing, for instance, is not counted in the necessities column—and clothing prices rose more slowly than most in the 1970s. And the "food" component of the Consumer Price Index, as Minarik noted, "includes not only basic food items but also sirloin steaks and restaurant dinners—hardly essential fare."

Moreover, calculations by *Dollars and Sense* and by sociologist Christopher Jencks showed that the actual market basket of goods that poor people spent their money on rose in price at about the same rate as everyone else's market baskets. The magazine reported its findings this way: "Dividing consumer spending into thirty different items, and calculating price indexes for each tenth of the population from the poorest to the richest, D&S found that from 1967 to 1978 the price indexes for each tenth increased between 93.4% and 95.0%. That is, the degree of inflation experienced by different groups varied only slightly." What about food and oil? The theory, *Dollars and Sense* said, "overlooks the fact that these prices move in spurts, whereas other prices rose steadily though less dramatically. From 1975 through 1978, food and gasoline prices rose more slowly than consumer prices as a whole."

In a sense of course this debate is beside the point. Some poor people have probably not lost ground to inflation during the last decade—thanks in part, as Minarik points out, to the "implicit indexing of medicare, medicaid, and various forms of rent subsidies, and [to] the explicit indexing of food stamps." Other poor people undoubtedly have lost ground. But the poor are in many ways more vulnerable to any economic reversal than are those with more to lose. A lost job or a rising fuel bill is hard to cope with if you have nothing besides welfare to fall back on. And the uncertainty of inflation will weigh more heavily on those who are barely getting by than on those with more of an economic cushion.

NOTE: The original study was published as "Understanding the New Inflation: The Importance of the Basic Necessities" (Washington: Exploratory Project for Economic Alternatives, 1977). The study's principal author, Leslie Ellen Nulty, developed a similar argument in "How Inflation Hits the Majority," *Challenge: The Magazine of Economic Affairs*, January/February 1979, pp. 32–38. The response by Jencks appeared in *Working Papers for a New Society*, September/October 1978, pp. 8–11 ff.; the *Dollars and Sense* critique is in the magazine's October 1979 issue, pp. 14–15; and the Minarik critique can be found in the *Brookings Bulletin*, vol. XVI, number 4 (1980), pp. 8–10.

Nest eggs and homes: inflation's effects on assets

"The only thing wealth does for some people," wrote the Comte de Rivarol in the late eighteenth century, "is make them worry about losing it." Inflationary times inevitably increase the number of worriers, for rising prices do have indisputable effects on assets. As with the income-expenditure balance sheet, though, the effects are mixed. And the question of who's really poorer because of inflation remains as obscure as before.

At the end of 1978, stock prices on the New York Stock Exchange were more than 30 percent lower (in real terms) than in 1970—and 1970 itself was an unusually poor year for stocks, with prices already nearly 25 percent below their 1965 level. The value of long-term corporate triple-A-rated bonds fell by almost half over the same period. In 1980 it looked for a while as if the bottom would drop out of the long-term bond market altogether. Though values subsequently recovered, it was no longer a place where the jittery investor could find a haven.

The reason for the decline in stock prices is the subject of considerable debate among economists, brokers, and the investors who lost at least the buttons off their shirts. Inflation is only one among several villains that commonly get blamed. With bonds, inflation's role is harder to deny. Rising prices in fact may have done in the long-term bond market all by themselves.

One undeniable effect of inflation is that it drives up interest rates—not the interest you get on your bank account, necessarily, since that's regulated by law, but the interest rates on bonds and other devices by which businesses and governments borrow money. Interest rates rise partly because nobody wants to lend money unless they can make a little profit over and above the expected rate of inflation.

Now suppose you own a $10,000 bond paying 5 percent, purchased, say, in 1966, and coming to maturity (that's when the bond issuer gives you your money back) in 1996. In stable times, your bond is worth essentially $10,000 because you can sell it for something approximating that figure on the open market. In inflationary times, though, you're in trouble. New bonds issued by corporations are paying 8, 10, or even 15 percent. No one wants your bond unless they can get it for substantially less than its face value. The bond's market price—its value to you right now—has dropped. The only way you'll get your $10,000 back is to hold the bond to maturity, and by that time your ten grand may buy you no more than a ten-speed bicycle.

So financial assets haven't done very well, thanks in part to inflation. Who's poorer? Banks, insurance companies, pension funds, and other institutional investors are. So are the very rich. At last count, about four fifths of the American people owned no stocks or bonds. About half of all the stock and three fifths of all the bonds owned by individuals were owned by people in the richest 1 percent of the population. Doubtless people in this category believe that hard times are upon us; doubtless too, some worthy individuals who are not rich have been hard hit by the drop in stocks and bonds. But their cries of anguish should not be allowed to obscure the silence with which most Americans greet the changes that shake Wall Street.

The main asset that a lot of people do own is a home. Here the trend has been exactly opposite. Between 1970 and 1978 the price of existing homes (as distinct from newly built homes) rose almost two thirds more than average prices. This rapid increase is usually reported in terms of the hardships it places on young families and others looking to buy a house. It can also be viewed as a dramatic rise in the value of the primary asset owned by the average American. According to economist Alan Greenspan, homes increased in value a total of more than a trillion dollars between 1974 and 1980. "Inflation is not all bad," California Senator Alan Cranston is reported to have said. "After all, it has allowed every

American to live in a more expensive neighborhood without moving."

Homeowners' equity undoubtedly rose even faster than home values. If you buy a house for $50,000, with $10,000 down and a $40,000 mortgage, you are said to have $10,000 worth of equity in the house. Suppose now that you can sell the house for $55,000. Your equity has risen from $10,000 to $15,000, an increase of 50 percent.

The cost of a house would have gone up in the 1970s with or without inflation, primarily because the baby-boom generation (born in the years after World War II) was getting to home-buying age and was bidding the prices up. But inflation played a part too. Investors and speculators saw early on that real estate values were consistently beating inflation, and so began to buy more property. As they did so, prices rose. More investors and speculators were then attracted to real estate, and more middle-income families stretched their budgets to buy a home because it looked like a good investment.

Also, for most of the 1970s, mortgage interest rates were low compared to the rate of inflation. If you borrowed money at 8 percent to buy a house while inflation was nearing double digits, your loan essentially cost you nothing. At the same time, inflation-induced wage and salary hikes were driving everyone into higher tax brackets. The tax breaks the government gives homeowners—you can deduct both mortgage interest payments and property taxes from your taxable income, which is a little like allowing tenants to deduct half or even three quarters of their rent—thus became ever more important. Both of these effects increased the number of potential buyers and made it possible for people to afford more expensive homes than they otherwise could.

The rise in the value of homes as opposed to stocks and bonds does not mean that the poor have been surreptitiously getting rich or the rich poor. Many of the poor don't own homes and many of the rich own a lot of them. Stockholders have lost some portfolio value, but the after-tax profits that pay their dividends have remained generally healthy for most of the decade. Those who sell houses are richer, but those who buy them are poorer; sometimes the same person does both, and winds up back where he or she started. On the whole, probably the very richest people (with the most financial assets) have lost some of their wealth and probably a lot of middle-income people have gained some wealth. How much these gains and losses might come to, no one knows.

The money illusion

Despite all these numbers, a lot of us feel that we're worse off than we used to be. If we didn't feel that way we wouldn't worry about inflation. And inflation is consistently near the top of the list when polltakers ask people what they think is America's number-one problem.

Why should this be? The very rich and the very poor, as we have seen, have good reason to be aggrieved with inflation. At the top, rising prices have undermined more than a few bond portfolios. At the bottom, welfare benefits have not kept up with the cost of living and thus have fallen in real terms. Yet if prices had remained stable, benefits probably would have too. Legislators are never overjoyed with the prospect of raising welfare levels, but they don't particularly like to cut them either.

Other losers, though, are in some ways deceived by rising prices. If prices remained stable, those who lost economic ground would have seen their incomes fall. Workers in declining industries or regions would have lost their jobs, or would have been forced to take wage cuts. Owners of failing businesses and partly vacant buildings would have seen profits drop off and rents dry up. In inflationary times, most of those who are losing ground see their money incomes rising—just not as fast as prices. The true villain is whatever has caused their real income to drop—new competition, business reversals, bad management, shifts in technology or in taste. But the only villain that shows its face is inflation. Everybody else is subject to a similar kind of money illusion, even when their real incomes are going up. Most of us feel entitled to a raise in pay as we grow older, gain seniority, advance in career or profession. These raises are supposed to enable us to take winter vacations in the Caribbean one year or buy a new motorboat the next. Most of us get the raises. But inflation makes us uncertain as to what the raises will be worth, and seems to eat up every additional dollar. MIT economist Lester C. Thurow, noting that real incomes rose 16 percent between 1972 and 1978 while money incomes went up 74 percent, describes the effect this way: "If the milkman were a moneyman, and you expected him to deliver $74 to your door in the morning but instead he delivered only $16, you would feel cheated. You are $16 better off than you were, but you can imagine what life would be like with the $74. You may even be able to convince yourself that your real standard of living has fallen." Thus does a rising price level camouflage what is really taking place.

In keeping with this role as smokescreen and scapegoat, inflation has concealed one real change in the economy that is helping us all feel poorer. This is the relatively sluggish growth in many people's real wages. In 1960 the typical worker in private industry was making $2.09 an hour. By 1965 this wage had risen to $2.46 and by 1970 to $3.23. Allowing for inflation, the increase worked out to an average gain of about 1.8 percent a year.

By 1975 the wage had gone up to $4.53 an hour, and by 1979 it was $6.16. This time, though, real gains amounted to only about 2 percent over the whole decade. The major reason was that in the 1973–75 recession—and again in 1979 —real wages for this group of workers fell, and the drops in those years brought down the decade's average. In 1979, the typical private-sector worker was making little more, in real terms, than he or she was making in 1970.*

To be sure, average incomes were rising: remember the

---

* Note that this comparison refers to hourly wages. Much has been made of the fact that average *weekly* earnings have stagnated or even fallen, depending on what year you start from. Weekly wage statistics,

average after-tax income figures mentioned above. Average incomes went up partly because many sources of income rose faster than the wages of rank-and-file private-sector workers. Social security benefits, government employees' wages, and many higher-level salaries all did better than inflation. Incomes also went up because a larger fraction of the population was working. If, for example, your spouse went to work for the first time during the 1970s, your family's real income undoubtedly rose regardless of how well you yourself were keeping up with inflation. But the improvement in your standard of living may not have given you much satisfaction for long. Spending the money proved easy—in fact you may have known what the money would go for (college educations, old medical bills) before your spouse went to work. And now you have to worry about whether both of you can keep up with inflation, because there's no one left to go to work. When both members of a couple are working, a family is as likely to feel strapped as it is to feel well-provided for. In that sense the relative prosperity of the 1970s was small comfort, and worries about keeping up with inflation persisted.

The trouble with inflation

This chapter's objective, so far, has been to relieve inflation of some of its extraneous burdens—to put it in perspective. Not all the economic hardships we feel are due to inflation. Not all are even as real as they seem. If the story ended here, the moral would be simply to

---

however, lump together full-time and part-time workers. Since part-timers are more numerous today than they used to be, the average can look low even when hourly wages are rising.

The hourly figures too are subject to interpretation. According to *The Wall Street Journal*, for instance, Labor Department economist Paul Ryscavage believes that the larger number of young people in the work force these days—because they typically earn less than older workers—may be pulling down the average wage, "even though all workers may individually be as well off as workers of their ages have ever been."

learn to live with the beast. Unfortunately it doesn't.

For one thing, America is not alone in the world. Americans are generally well protected against the proverbial ravages of inflation. So are the citizens of most other industrialized countries (even Israel, where the inflation rate hit 111.4 percent in 1979). Citizens of poor countries are not. In Ghana during the 1970s, the price of food rose almost half again as fast as average prices, to the point where a couple of pounds of fish or poultry cost the typical worker a full day's wages. In Peru, workers' purchasing power dropped by half between 1976 and 1980, and the price of bread rose tenfold. The noncommunist world's economy is highly interconnected, and America is in many ways at the center. When the United States sneezes, it used to be said, the rest of the world catches cold. Now the United States has a cold and the rest of the world is lucky if it gets off with double pneumonia.

Inflation's effects at home can't easily be ignored either. It may not be making us poorer, but it does make us uncertain. And uncertainty has effects of its own.

Suppose you knew that prices were going to go up 10 percent a year, inexorably and invariably. If you knew that your income was going to rise at least that much every year—plus whatever you could add through working harder, moving up the hierarchy, or bargaining for a share of your company's profits—you wouldn't be nervous at all. The 10 percent annual price hike would quickly be reflected both in interest rates on mortgages and other loans and in what you could earn on your money in a savings bank or other investment. You would mentally adjust to prices doubling about every seven years, knowing that the price increases weren't "real."

If you knew prices were going up 10 percent but didn't know how much your income would go up, you'd be considerably more nervous. The chances are you would do whatever you could—take two jobs, press for militant union activity, lobby for special treatment for your business, and so on—to ensure that your income would keep pace. It might not take too long before most workers got cost-of-living adjustments written into their contracts. (Slightly less than half of the unionized workers covered by major collective bargaining agreements now have these adjustments.)

The situation at present is even worse than this. You think prices will rise, but you don't know how much, and there's always the chance of inflation rates up around 20 percent or more. Unless you have an unusually good job (or happen to own a few oil wells, in which case you may not care), you have no way of knowing whether your income will keep pace. Most investments are uncertain. Even borrowing is risky, because the economy might take a sharp downturn. That, you think, might cure inflation, but you might be out of a job. Uncertainty is a fact of life. But inflation intensifies it, and before long the economy begins to look like a giant lottery, with winners and losers chosen at random.

Businesses face the same kind of uncertainty. Why build a new plant or modernize the old one if you aren't sure what's happening to the economy, or how much things will cost next year? On the other hand, maybe you should build or modernize right now, before prices go up again. Is it prudent to borrow money, even though interest rates seem unbelievably high? Maybe it's foolish *not* to borrow money. Interest rates may go still higher tomorrow, and if inflation gets worse you'll be repaying your loan in ever-cheaper dollars.

The results of this kind of uncertainty and the widely remarked "loss of confidence" it has apparently led to are by no means clear. At worst, as some economists believe, uncertainty makes businesses unwilling to invest, consumers unwilling to save, and everyone unwilling to work hard, innovate, and be productive. Economic growth thus slows to a crawl. At best, uncertainty makes for a highly volatile economic environment, in which every organized group is desperately trying to push its own interests to the exclusion of everybody else's. This may be the economic reality behind the "me decade" recently ended. It may also be the reason for the apparent stalemate of governmental initiative. When all are screaming loudly, the safest course for a politician is to do nothing that offends anyone. Ordinarily that means doing nothing at all.

Worst of all, inflation has a dismaying tendency to feed on itself. As long as it's mild, as in the 1950s and early 1960s, it can be tolerated and held in check. When it begins to get worse, as it did in the late 1960s and 1970s, presidents of the United States and chairmen of the Federal Reserve Board feel they have to do something before it gets out of control. Their attempts usually entail engineering a recession, as in 1974–75 and again in 1980. Recessions by definition lower our standard of living. Production falls and real incomes drop. If inflation weren't so bad, the measures employed against it might not have to be so drastic.

Before we examine how inflation got this far, it is worth remembering that what we're looking at is an unprecedented phenomenon. The American economy has always had periods of rising prices. Today's prices, however, have been rising consistently for more than forty years, and have doubled in the last ten. Inflation of this sort is new to history.

For most of the nineteenth century—except during wartime—prices edged downward. A basket of goods that cost $50 in 1800 was selling for $42 in 1820, $30 in 1840, $27 in 1860, $29 in 1880, and $25 in 1900. The first four decades of this century seemed little different. World War I brought inflation, but prices fell 10 percent in the recession of 1921 and 6 percent more in 1922. When the Great Depression hit, prices dropped an average of 6 percent a year for four years. They fell again in 1938 and 1939 after rising a little in the middle thirties. The pattern was clear: war and boom times brought inflation, and a slump then ended it. Prices returned to normal.

After World War II, prices stopped falling. Now they rose a little every year. If the economy was in recession they might stop rising momentarily, but when the recession ended they resumed their upward course. In the 1970s prices rose faster than ever and were harder to check. The recession of 1974–75, for example, was by all accounts the worst of the postwar era. It did what observers hoped it would: ended the threat of runaway inflation. Prices had been rising 12 percent in 1974; they rose only 5 to 7 percent in the following three years. But note the difference. In the old days, a recession made *prices* fall. Inflation disappeared altogether. Now only the *rate of inflation* fell. Prices kept on rising and, despite the recession, were still going up faster than they had in almost any previous year.

The way our economy works, in short, had changed. The next several chapters will trace these changes. Some go back to the late nineteenth century, before their inflationary effects were noticed. Some appeared in the Depression, and some in the years during and immediately after World War II. All these changes help account for the apparently irreversible inflation we have experienced since the war. Finally, some changes turned up only in the 1970s, and explain the virulence of inflation during the last ten years.

Many readers doubtless have a theory as to which change will turn out to be the villain. Some will blame the minimum wage, the disappearance of the gold standard, federal budget deficits. Others will look at the swollen Pentagon budget, corporate profiteering, the abuses of Big Labor, or the ineptitude of the Federal Reserve. For the moment, all such theories should be set aside. The story of inflation is not a potboiler, where the culprit will be revealed at the end. It is more like a jigsaw puzzle, with each piece fitting together in a particular way and at the end revealing a picture you didn't know was there.

The various pieces have historical roots, but understanding them involves looking at the present as much as at the past—and eventually at that enigmatic golden age between 1945 and 1965, which ended with people grousing about the high cost of living. The starting point, inevitably, is prices, for without rising prices there is no inflation.

2. The Inflationary System:
Big Business

Prices, we generally assume, are set by supply and demand. "Demand" means how much consumers are willing to spend for something—how badly they want it, and how much they can afford to pay for it. "Supply" means how much is available for sale at various possible prices. If consumers want more of something than is immediately available, the price rises. If they want less, the price falls. The moving price, in turn, attracts more buyers or sellers as the case may be.

This introductory lesson in economics is not entirely useless. It explains why sporting goods stores that bought too many skis in October put them on sale in March (demand has fallen relative to supply). It also explains why the price of oranges rises after a cold winter in Florida (supply has fallen relative to demand). Supply and demand can even explain the way a whole market behaves: the stock market, for instance. Suppose Mobil Oil discovers a new offshore strike. More people now want to buy Mobil shares than wanted to yesterday, and fewer people want to sell them. So the price of a share rises. Now suppose that the Justice Department hauls Mobil into court on serious price-fixing charges. The stock suddenly doesn't look so good, and the price falls.

The market as a whole responds to supply and demand just the way an individual stock does. Favorable economic news persuades a few more investors to buy stocks, and the Dow-Jones goes up. Unfavorable economic news—the election of a Democrat to the presidency, traditionally—causes the market to fall. Supply and demand vary as investors' perceptions, expectations, and strategies change.* Stock prices respond to these changes with astonishing sensitivity and quickness. They do so, of course, because of competition. A dim-witted broker trying to peddle a stock for more than the going price wouldn't find any takers. Buyers would simply take their business to the next broker in line.

Elsewhere in the economy, however, things aren't so simple. To be sure, economists frequently use the same word: a "market" is simply all the ways by which buyers and sellers of anything get in touch with one another and conduct their business. But the market for toothpaste, for psychoanalysis, or for the services of a computer programmer doesn't look much like the New York Stock Exchange. In these markets, supply and demand are but dim shadows of their former selves. They are limited, interfered with, regulated, propped up, constrained, or controlled. Competition is muted, restricted, or banished entirely. Prices, as a result, do not glide effortlessly up and down the way they do on the stock market. They move jerkily, and they depend more on what the seller decides than on what the marketplace determines.

Most markets, to put it succinctly, are rigged. Since they are rigged to favor the seller rather than the buyer, prices will go up more easily than they go down. That is the First —maybe the Only—Law of Inflation. The next few chapters will explain how it works. In the meantime, note only that rigging a market is neither as difficult nor as reprehensible as it might seem. The mechanisms by which various companies, industries, professions, and workers accomplish it

---

* The long-run supply of stock—that is, the total number of shares issued by companies listed on a stock exchange—is huge, and changes only by small increments. "Supply" in this context means existing shares that are offered for sale on the market.

will not, once they are pointed out, sound either strange or evil.

Managing the marketplace

In 1882, an oatmeal producer named Henry P. Crowell built a fancy new mill—"the first in the world," as one historian describes it, that could "grade, clean, hull, cut, package, and ship oatmeal to interstate markets in a continuous process." The only trouble with the mill was that there weren't enough buyers for all the oatmeal it could turn out.

Then Crowell hit upon an idea. He packaged his brand—it was called Quaker Oats—and called it a breakfast cereal, a commodity that was virtually unknown in America at the time. He advertised it heavily, employing box-top premiums, prizes, testimonials, scientific endorsements, and other gimmicks. He set up sales offices to market the product and hired field agents to buy oats directly from midwestern farmers. In 1888 Crowell joined with two other big producers of oatmeal to form the American Cereal Company, and thirteen years later the firm became the Quaker Oats Company. It shortly added new products—wheat cereals, farina, hominy, cornmeal, specialized baby foods, and animal feeds—and by 1917 was the fifteenth largest food products concern in the country.

Today Quaker Oats is, so to speak, a medium-sized giant corporation. It does about two billion dollars' worth of business a year, and ranks twenty-fourth in size among food-processing companies. In breakfast cereals Quaker is now fourth, behind Kellogg's, General Mills, and General Foods. Together these four firms sell nearly all of the breakfast cereal sold in America. Among their brand names are Puffed Rice, Puffed Wheat, Life, Corn Bran, Cap'n Crunch, Crunch Berries, Quips, Total, Body Buddies, Count Chocula, Boo Berry, Cocoa Puffs, Kix, and Trix, as well as the familiar Wheaties, Cheerios, Corn Flakes, and the like.

With appropriate variations, the story of Quaker Oats and its colleagues in the cereal business is the story of the several hundred other giant industrial firms that dominate the $2.5 trillion American economy. In the late nineteenth century, the rapid spread of railroad lines opened up huge markets, and made it possible for manufacturers to obtain large supplies of raw materials relatively cheaply. The abundance of coal for steam engines meant that factories no longer had to rely on water power to run their machinery; it also made possible the development of new industrial processes requiring intense heat, such as the Bessemer process of steel production. Other technological development, on the order of Henry Crowell's continuous-process mill, vastly increased the speed at which plants could turn out finished products. Companies that first took advantage of the new techniques and new markets grew very large very quickly. Typically a few of the biggest then combined into one even larger behemoth, just as Crowell joined with his erstwhile competitors to form American Cereal.

At present, the 500 largest industrial firms—Quaker Oats ranks 176th on *Fortune* magazine's famous list—do an average of nearly $3 billion worth of business a year. Together they account for more than three quarters of everything manufactured in America. They employ approximately one worker out of every six—an average of 32,400 per firm. They own more than a trillion dollars' worth of assets, and in 1979 made more than $78 billion in profits.

Typically, a few of these giant firms dominate an industry, often with several other good-sized companies doing most of the remaining business. All manufacture and market a variety of individual products. Most of these are sold on a brand-name basis: they are differentiated from others in the industry and advertised for their special advantages. These advantages may be real, as with an unusually dependable television set. Or they may be imaginary, as with the gusto that characterizes the life of Schlitz drinkers.

The companies are for the most part highly integrated. They own outright some of the farms, mines, and manufacturers that supply them with materials, parts, and equip-

OTHER BIG COMPANIES

Large size is not limited to industrial concerns.

• In *retailing*, Sears, Roebuck & Company did some $17 billion worth of business in 1979, about 2 percent of total retail sales in that year. Safeway and K mart, two other giant retailers, each did more than $12 billion worth.

• In the *food and lodging* industry, McDonald's, Marriott, and Holiday Inns are all billion-dollar corporations. In *communications*, the giants are Time, Inc. ($2.5 billion in sales for 1979), the Times-Mirror Company ($1.6 billion), the Gannett chain ($1 billion), and of course the broadcasting networks.

• The largest *banks* in America are BankAmerica (based in California) and Citicorp (based in New York). The biggest insurance company is Aetna Life & Casualty. And the biggest company of all, measured by profits and by number of employees, is the American Telephone & Telegraph Company.

SOURCE: *"Business Week*'s Corporate Scoreboard: How 1,200 Companies Performed in 1979," *Business Week*, March 17, 1980, pp. 81–116.

ment. U.S. Steel, for instance, gets two thirds of the coal it uses from its own mines. In other cases they establish long-term contracts with their suppliers, often on terms they themselves dictate. They assure markets for their products not only through sophisticated selling techniques (of which conventional advertising is only a part) but through an extensive sales force, network of distributors, or both. The reason for their long reach is not obscure. No billion-dollar corporation can afford to depend on uncontrolled sources of supply. Nor can it produce a million boxes of oatmeal or a hundred thousand steel ingots and hope that somebody somewhere will buy them at a reasonable price. Supply and demand are thus managed, not by the invisible hand of the marketplace but by the visible hand (in historian Alfred D. Chandler's phrase) of corporate management.

No industry is exactly typical. One, though, can be seen as prototypical: it illustrates in virtually pure form how the big companies conduct their business. Art students learn technique by studying the masters. Students of the economy can learn much from those who have cultivated the art of managing the marketplace.

In 1880, a man named James Bonsack filed for a patent on a machine capable of manufacturing cigarettes. As William Bennett describes it, the machine "poured a uniform flow of tobacco through a device resembling the wool feeder of a carding machine into a thin strip of paper. The paper was rolled into a single continuous tube. As it emerged from the machine, the tobacco-filled tube was cut into equal lengths." At the time, the most highly skilled worker could turn out several thousand handmade cigarettes a day. Bonsack's machine produced over 70,000 a day while still in its experimental stages; by the late 1880s it could make over 120,000 a day. "Fifteen such machines," writes Alfred D. Chandler, "could fill the total demand for cigarettes in the United States in 1880, and thirty could have saturated the 1885 market."

James B. Duke, a North Carolina tobacco entrepreneur, signed a contract with Bonsack in 1885. In 1890 Duke and four other firms joined to form the American Tobacco Company. By 1900, after pioneering in some of the advertising and marketing techniques that Quaker Oats's Crowell and others would later imitate, Duke controlled more than three fifths of the smoking and chewing tobacco industry. In 1911 the American Tobacco Company was broken up by the Supreme Court in an antitrust decision. The three new companies that were created after the decision—R.J. Reynolds, Liggett & Myers, and P. Lorillard—accounted, along with American Tobacco, for over 90 percent of the cigarette market by 1925.

Today, some of the companies have new names. American Brands has replaced American Tobacco (no more "tobacco is our middle name" ads), and the Liggett Group has replaced Liggett & Myers. Lorillard is a division of Loew's Corporation. R.J. Reynolds ranks thirty-ninth on *Fortune*'s list of the 500 largest industrial companies; Philip Morris ranks forty-ninth. These five companies, along with the Brown & Williamson Tobacco Corp. (a subsidiary of a British concern), produce virtually all of the roughly 700 billion cigarettes manufactured in America. Reynolds and Philip Morris alone account for over 60 percent of the market.

Production is even more highly mechanized than it used to be. At Philip Morris's modern Richmond, Virginia, plant, reports *The Boston Globe,* machines do virtually all the work: "From the time workers peel the wooden sides from the 1000-pound hogsheads of tobacco there is not another hand operation until workers stack cases of packaged cigarettes in the packing room." The cigarettes themselves have undergone refinement as well. "Much of the tobacco in modern cigarettes," says the *Globe,* "has been pulverized to a paste, homogenized, sterilized, reconstituted, freeze-dried, chemically altered . . . and then sprayed with flavors that sound more like the recipe for chicken curry or candy than cigarettes." These flavors include "cardamom, pepper, clove, nutmeg, cascarilla, vanilla, rum, honey, raisin, prune, dates, and the old standbys cocoa and licorice. And these are just the natural flavors."

Nowhere, however, have the improvements been as dramatic as in marketing. The companies have a lot at stake in this area. According to industry analysts, 1 percent of the cigarette market amounts to about $100 million worth of sales, or about $20 million in pre-tax profits. To increase their market share, the companies have hit upon an unusual but effective strategy: "dividing the smoking population into relatively tiny sociological groups," as *The Wall Street Journal* describes it, "and then aiming one or more brands at each group." Once most smokers "chose from among three brands: Camel, Chesterfield, and Lucky Strike. Today, more than 160 brands adorn the retail shelves."

Brands are differentiated from each other, and directed at the target population, partly by the content and style of their advertising: "Vantage and Merit, for example, are aimed at young women, and Camel and Winston are aimed mostly at rural smokers." They are also differentiated by paper color, package color, location and style of filter, length, and package design. Long cigarettes and recessed filters appeal to women. The brown paper of More cigarettes "is supposed to convey a 'riverboat gambler look.' " Red packs suggest flavor, green packs coolness, white packs safety. Philip Morris "heightened the appeal to the stylish of its Benson & Hedges brand by printing the company's Park Avenue address on the front and back of each pack." The same company's Merit brand—in a package with big yellow, brown, and orange racing stripes—"is intended to connote a 'flamboyant, young-in-spirit image.' " One company market-tested thirty-three different packages before deciding on a blue, gold, and red design (Viceroy Rich Lights).

All this costs money. The industry spent nearly half a billion dollars on newspaper and magazine advertising alone in 1978, and the investment necessary to bring out a new cigarette has recently been estimated as high as $50 million. But it has paid off. Despite a ban on television advertising and despite increasingly stringent health warnings printed at the government's behest on all advertisements and cigarette packages, per capita consumption of cigarettes has stayed roughly constant at about 4,000 per year, or an average of half a pack a day for smokers and nonsmokers alike. Industry profits, meanwhile, went up 32 percent in 1979 over 1978, a gain in real terms of nearly one fifth.

Managing prices

Even if you don't smoke, one fact about cigarettes is unlikely to have escaped you. You do not see signs on the window of the grocery store down the street saying "Camels—special this week. Only 50¢ the pack." Nor do you see magazine ads contending that Winstons cost less than Marlboros. As every smoker knows, cigarettes all cost the same. If this were the stock market, we would be forced to conclude that the ratio of supply to demand was the same for every brand. Moreover, since cigarette prices all go up at the same time, the ratio would always have to be changing at the same rate. Since it is the cigarette market, we may entertain more plausible hypotheses as to why cigarettes all cost the same. These hypotheses, however, will have to apply to a lot of different industries, for cigarettes are more nearly typical of the way things are priced than are stocks. Ordinarily, big companies sell their wares at prices very similar to those of their competitors. Ordinarily, too, these prices change by similar amounts at roughly the same time. To understand why prices behave this way is to understand one important element of inflation.

Sometimes prices are similar because companies have conspired to fix them. In a single week in 1980, for example, *The Wall Street Journal* reported that four big gypsum firms had settled a fifteen-year-old price-fixing suit brought by the Justice Department; that five companies had been indicted on charges of fixing the prices for glassine and greaseproof paper; and that two school-supply companies were close to settling a Federal Trade Commission and grand-jury investigation charging them with fixing the price of wax crayons. Indictments and settlements, of course, do not constitute guilt. But the number of cases suggests that price-fixing is not yet a thing of the past.

More often, price-fixing is unnecessary. One firm simply

acts as "price leader," with the others following suit. For many years U.S. Steel played this role in its industry. "About 20 years ago," writes economist Robert R. Nathan, "when Estes Kefauver was chairman of the Senate Subcommittee on Monopoly, he had some steel executives testifying before him. He said to one steel executive, 'When U.S. Steel raised its price 5.738 percent, why did you raise your price 5.738 percent?' The fellow answered, 'To be competitive.'" The usage has grown common. The phrase "competitive prices," in the lexicon of the business world, usually means prices that are the same as everybody else's, not prices designed to undercut the competition.

Recently, U.S. Steel has come on hard times. This has not changed the practice of price leadership, only the roles. "U.S. Steel Corp.," reported *The Wall Street Journal* in March of 1980, "joined several other major steelmakers in a 5% average price increase on sheet and strip products." Around the same time, the Aluminum Company of America (Alcoa) raised that metal's price from 66¢ to 72¢ a pound. "Other major producers," commented the *Journal* drily, "are expected to follow." A day later, the *Journal* reported that General Motors was raising new-car prices 2.2 percent. Within seven days Ford, American Motors, Chrysler, and Volkswagen announced increases in the same range. Ford's and Chrysler's were exactly 2.2 percent.

At times the prices charged by big companies for their consumer goods seem unnecessarily high. Bristol-Myers' Bufferin, for example, was retailing for $2.35 per 100-tablet bottle as this book went to press. The price was roughly comparable to that of other nationally advertised pain relievers: Anacin ($2.66), and Excedrin ($2.39). It did not compare so well with a bottle of generic buffered aspirin manufactured by the Republic Drug Corporation of Buffalo, New York, and located on the pharmacist's shelf right next to the Bufferin. That product—essentially identical to Bufferin—was going for $1.85, or about 80 percent of what Bufferin cost.

Other times the prices of manufactured goods seem reason-

CIGARETTES AND STOCKS

How Two Sets of Prices Rose and Fell in the 1970s

* "Tobacco Products" price index, Bureau of Labor Statistics

* Standard & Poor's common index (500 stocks)

SOURCES: The "tobacco products" price index is found in the *Handbook of Labor Statistics*, and is updated in the *Monthly Labor Review*. Standard & Poor's common index appears in the *Statistical Abstract*, p. 543, and is updated in the Commerce Department's monthly magazine *Survey of Current Business*.

able; certainly they are low in comparison with what they would be if the goods were manufactured by hand or with less advanced equipment. Ordinarily, the prices of manufactured goods fall dramatically as a young industry develops its technology, costs drop, and competition pushes prices down: processed oats or cigarettes in the nineteenth century, automobiles in the 1920s, electronic equipment today. A moderately sophisticated pocket calculator that cost $150 only a few years ago retails for perhaps $22.95 now. Then prices level off as the industry matures.

How are these prices determined? By most accounts, the big firm calculates its costs, figures a "target" profit rate, and sets prices high enough to meet that target. Since most large companies in the same industry face similar costs and seek similar rates of return, prices are very much alike. Target profit rates in most circumstances are not to be monkeyed with. A *Business Week* article on the appliance industry, for instance, noted that manufacturers were considering raising prices in spite of possible consumer resistance. The alternative of lower profit margins, the magazine concluded, was "untenable." In all cases, cost increases must be passed on as quickly as possible.

With costs covered and profit rates assured, however, a company will not necessarily raise its prices simply because consumers want more of what it has to sell. Doing so can be inconvenient and risky, in that it involves publishing new price schedules and possibly antagonizing a firm's distributors or customers. Price hikes, particularly price hikes that are not matched by one's competitors, also may damage a company's market share and chances for growth. Management teams that pursue such courses may find themselves unpopular with shareholders and boards of directors.

In principle, almost any big company could cut its prices dramatically for a while and spend a lot of money advertising the fact. It might thereby attract a lot of new customers, grow bigger, and maybe even drive its competitors out of business.

In practice, cutthroat competition of this sort is rare. One reason is that the antitrust laws frown on successful attempts to put one's competitors out of business; R. J. Reynolds needs Philip Morris and Liggett just as General Motors needs Ford and Chrysler. A second reason is that the logic of mass marketing may not allow for significant variation in price. Procter & Gamble presumably makes a lot of money on Tide because it sells so much of the stuff (it considers the exact amount a trade secret), not because it turns a large profit on each box that is sold. Yet Tide would have to be substantially cheaper than, say, Fab to induce the habitual user of the latter to switch over. A price cut of a dime, which may be a large fraction of P&G's profit on a box of Tide, won't do the trick; consumers looking for bargains in detergents can already find discount brands going for 70 or 80 percent of the nationally advertised brands (and not doing as well). Unless P&G could put Colgate-Palmolive and the others out of business quickly —an event hard to imagine—it would find itself in the proverbial unhappy position of trying to sell at a loss and make it up in volume.*

A third reason is that price cutting by one firm would doubtless engender immediate retribution. Businesses learned about the possibilities for mutual destruction by this means in the nineteenth century. The railroads, which were the first giant enterprises to operate on a national scale, competed so strenuously by slashing their prices that, in Alfred D. Chandler's words, "the logic of such competition appeared to be bankruptcy for all." Railroad men therefore devoted enormous energies to setting up associa-

---

* "Cents off" coupons—a form of temporary discounting that is about as close as most companies get to lowering their prices—has more in common with box-top premiums and other advertising gimmicks than with true price competition. Consider the difference between a coupon entitling the bearer to 22¢ off his or her next box of Tide, and an announcement by Procter & Gamble that henceforth it would sell Tide for 10 percent less than the detergents made by any competitor. The latter is unimaginable—and not because P&G couldn't afford to do it.

tions, pools, and cartels to set rates for all.* Other businesses
followed suit. In the 1870s, writes Chandler, virtually every
industry in America had established trade associations "for
the purpose of controlling price and production"; by the
1880s these federations "had become part of the normal
way of doing business" and frequently "allocated specific
markets to different firms." The associations were fragile
creatures, however, for they had no legal authority over
their members. Much more effective, from the businessman's
point of view, was to combine with your competitors into
one big company (American Tobacco, U.S. Steel); to set up
an overarching trust that owned many hitherto competing
firms (Standard Oil); or simply to buy out the competition.†
"Most businessmen believed in competition—theoretically,"
says the writer Frederick Lewis Allen about turn-of-the-
century capitalism. "But in practice there was a ceaseless
search for ways in which to prevent it." Thanks to that
search—and despite the Sherman Antitrust Act, passed in
1890—the industrial economy by the time of World War I
looked very much as it does today: a few big firms dominating most industries, and little if any price competition.

To be sure, price cutting has not disappeared. But it
crops up mainly in unusual circumstances, and it may run
counter to the laws of supply and demand as often as it

---

* The passage of the Interstate Commerce Act in 1887 in effect accomplished for the railroads what they had been unable to accomplish
for themselves. The act called for "just and reasonable rates" and "pro-
hibited temporary short-lived rate changes."

† Until 1888 it was in most cases illegal for one corporation to own
stock in another. "Buying out" another company therefore meant that
the owners of Company A had to buy up Company B's stock: a costly
and risky procedure for the individuals involved. In its 1888–89 session,
however, the New Jersey legislature passed a law permitting corporations registered in that state to buy stock in other corporations. To no
one's surprise, this move touched off a rush of companies wanting to
register (for a small fee) in New Jersey. The state's revenues rose considerably, and "New Jersey holding companies" became a familiar
feature of the economic landscape.

obeys them. In 1980, for instance, several major airlines were waging a price war on their profitable East Coast and transcontinental flights. Phased deregulation of the air had begun, ending decades of rate setting by the Civil Aeronautics Board, and the airlines were experimenting with ways to increase their market. Not one, however, was happy with the situation; industry earnings dropped substantially in the first year of deregulation, thanks largely to the rising cost of jet fuel and the new competitive pressures.

It wasn't long before the airlines were inventing new ways to compete without slashing fares. United, American, and TWA began to offer lottery tickets by which passengers (and others who requested them) could win extra trips and other prizes. The hope, explained *New York Times* writer Winston Williams, was that games of chance would "provide the competitive outlet that is needed to minimize costly fare wars such as those now being waged. . . ." At the same time the airlines were quietly raising fares, despite the fact that passenger traffic was down 3 percent in the first three months of 1980.

Automobile companies too were engaged in a little price competition, and they weren't any happier than the airlines. Chrysler's unprecedented program of rebates in 1979 and 1980, which included, at one point, a $50 bonus paid to anyone who so much as test-drove a Chrysler car and then went on to buy it or any other car, was a response to a drastic drop in sales following the company's announcement of possible bankruptcy. Ford was offering rebates too, though for a while its logic was the opposite of Chrysler's. Ford was "rebating its popular Fairmonts and Thunderbirds," one report noted, "but offering no rebates on the sluggish LTD." The logic? " 'We fish where the fish are biting,' says Ford VP and division manager Phillip E. Benton Jr. Ford figures it can get 'more bang for the buck' rebating the better sellers." All these rebates, of course, were coming at a time when sticker prices were rising that 2.2 percent mentioned above (2.2 percent of a $7,000 list price is $154). And the sticker price hikes, which were still there when the rebating programs were over, occurred in spite of the fact that sales of American cars were plummeting.

Sticky prices and inflation

This sketch of the industrial system and the way it sets its prices has dramatic implications for the economy as a whole and for inflation in particular. MIT economist Robert M. Solow, in a memorably curious turn of phrase, has termed this effect "the upward bias of sticky down."

Some price, somewhere, is rising in real terms all the time. A bad harvest raises the price of grain by restricting supply. Speculation in the silver futures market raises the price of the metal and thereby the cost of manufacturing photographic film. Strong demand for small, fuel-efficient cars persuades General Motors to hike the price of its compact X-body line. A new wage settlement raises the cost of doing business in the aluminum industry, and aluminum firms raise the price of ingots.

These price increases reverberate through the economy. More expensive grain means more expensive flour, not only for the consumer buying five pounds of Gold Medal, but also for ITT Continental Baking Company and for Dunkin' Donuts. The price of wheat-based breakfast cereals may go up a little, and the price of cereals based on other grains (oats, rice) may rise too "to stay competitive." Higher aluminum prices lead not only to higher costs for aluminum products like soft drink cans, they may also persuade the steel industry that it can get away with hiking its prices a little. Or, to turn the example around, a generous wage settlement for aluminum workers may encourage the steelworkers to demand a higher wage settlement than otherwise, in turn leading to higher steel prices.

Economists call this process "leapfrogging." Companies and unions come to expect a certain pattern of relative prices, not only within an industry but among different industries. Price hikes in an industry facing higher costs encourage discretionary price hikes by other industries seeking to redress the balance or simply to enlarge profit margins a little.

Theoretically, prices should be dropping here and there too, thanks to abundant harvests, cheap silver, slackening demand for cars, or lower wages (more likely, wage settlements that are more than compensated for by gains in output per worker). Some prices actually do fall. Agricultural prices drop when harvests are good, though not too far, as we shall see in the next chapter. Raw materials prices sometimes go down too, as do the prices of industrial bulk materials (processed metals, chemicals, and the like). These price changes should also reverberate throughout the economy.

They don't. Cost savings—unless they are dramatic, as with changes in technology—are rarely passed on to consumers. When business falls off (when demand declines, in the economist's terminology) prices don't: as the British economist Joan Robinson puts it, "It is considered very bad form to start cutting prices, and sometimes they are even raised 'in order to cover costs.'" During the recessionary period from May 1974 to March 1975, the late Brookings economist Arthur Okun pointed out, the prices of industrial raw materials fell an average of 15 percent. "During that same 10-month interval," wrote Okun, "producers' prices of finished goods other than food and fuel rose by 10 percent." At around the same time, the world price of sugar jumped to a record 66¢ a pound, and the prices of processed foods requiring a lot of sugar soared. Later sugar dropped to 6¢ a pound. "Soft drinks and other products containing sugar or corn sweeteners declined somewhat," an analysis in *The New York Times* observed, "but not in proportion to the drop in price of the commodity."

No conspiracy is necessary to effect this result. Cost savings from lower raw materials prices may not amount to much for most companies, and wages and overhead expenses probably aren't decreasing. "Don't expect these lower input prices to be reflected in consumer prices," a Labor Department official cautioned a reporter in 1980 when a few raw materials had begun to drop. "There are energy and labor costs which easily take up the slack of these lower input prices." Most important, the same factors that militate against price competition militate against price cuts in general. Companies may not have much leeway to cut prices, and they certainly do not want to get involved in a price war with their competitors if it can be avoided. A responsible management will not look askance at an unusually good profit now and then, particularly if it thinks raw materials costs are likely to go up again before too long. And the competitive pressure that would drive prices down is virtually nonexistent.

Kodak offers a textbook example of sticky prices. The Rochester, New York, giant—30th on the *Fortune* 500, with more than $8 billion in sales—accounts for about 90 percent of the photographic film sold in the United States. In late 1979 and early 1980, the Hunt brothers from Dallas were speculating heavily in the silver futures market, driving prices up to nearly $50 a troy ounce. Silver is a prime component of photographic film, and Kodak raised its prices accordingly—nearly 100 percent on X-ray film, according to *Business Week*, and an average of 27 percent on other products.

By April 1980 the price of silver had dropped to around $14 an ounce, not far from where it had been the previous fall. Kodak, faced with modest competitive pressures in specialty-film areas, reduced the price of X-ray film about 20 percent in two months and trimmed the price of professional 35-millimeter motion-picture film. It also cut some other prices—though not, the *Times* noted, the "10 to 20 percent increases in instant, 110 and 35-millimeter film" announced earlier. "Even when prices decline," said the *Times*, "they seldom make it all the way back to their previous levels." The movie film on which Kodak cut its prices went from

$70.20 a roll to $61.70 after the cuts. The same film "sold for $42.50 a roll until last October 26."

In general, *Business Week* noted, the company was "likely to maintain most of the other price increases announced in December." As a result it "stood to improve margins and earnings substantially." On May 1, 1980, Kodak announced first-quarter earnings 10 percent higher than the previous year's.

Companies faced with declining sales—the time when economic theory says they should cut prices—usually have a variety of options to choose from. If investors decide they want fewer shares of Coca-Cola stock, the price falls. If consumers decide they want to drink less Coke, the price stays the same but the company mounts a new advertising campaign ("Have a Coke and a Smile"). If things really get desperate—as they have in recent years for the likes of Lockheed, U.S. Steel, and Chrysler—the government can be called in to bail the company out (or at least protect it from imports).

Most typically, however, a firm's response to declining sales is simply to cut back production rather than adjust its prices. When Firestone realized in 1980 that its bias-ply tires were not selling well, it didn't cut the price; it closed six plants, throwing more than 7,000 people out of work. The economist Gardiner C. Means, in a famous 1934 memorandum to the Secretary of Agriculture, found that the idle plants of the Depression were in large measure attributable to production cutbacks of this sort. In markets that were largely competitive, such as agriculture, producers kept on producing but prices fell. In large industrial markets, production dropped and prices stayed largely where they were.

To return to the stock market for a moment, the price of a stock varies because "supply" and "demand" are moving autonomously, in response to the decisions of many different investors. In product markets, however, a big company can control how much of something it supplies (Firestone tires,

Winstons, Quaker Oats). It can also influence consumers' decisions about how much to buy, through advertising and other marketing techniques. Supply and demand are still there, but they are subject to manipulation. And the price at which goods are sold need not move at all.

This is one example—probably the most important one—of a system of markets that is rigged to favor the seller rather than the buyer. The market for most of the brand-name industrial products we buy is rigged in the sense that each manufacturer is big enough to exercise considerable control over the supply of its products, the demand for its products, and thereby its products' prices. Prices rise easily; they fall with difficulty.

All this does not mean that big corporations face no competition. General Motors must compete not only with Ford and Chrysler but with Volkswagen and Toyota—even, in a sense, with trains and buses. But the competition seldom turns primarily on price. Nor does it mean that the big corporations somehow "cause" inflation. They are by no means inconsequential; their price and wage patterns, for example, frequently serve as guidelines for smaller companies and even for government agencies. But they have as much incentive to keep prices low, thereby expanding their market shares and enhancing their prospects for growth, as they have to keep them high.

What is important about the big companies is not that they systematically jack their prices up higher than they should, by whatever standard, but that they have a significant amount of discretion over what their prices will be. If costs go up, prices will too—quickly. If costs drop, prices might go down a little—slowly—or they may not move at all. If business is good, companies won't necessarily raise their prices. But if it's bad, they are highly unlikely to cut them, and may even raise them to maintain profit margins. The "upward bias of sticky down" means only that prices tend to adjust upwards. In that sense the industrial system builds a predisposition to inflation into our economy.

The industrial system, in any event, has been around since the early decades of this century. Yet the years from 1890 to 1940 witnessed some of the more pronounced deflations the industrial world had ever seen Evidently we need more pieces to the puzzle. One of the more important ones, the subject of the next chapter, is the fact that the secret has gotten out. Big companies can protect themselves from falling prices by manipulating supply, demand, and often the price itself. So, as it turns out, can a large fraction of the other firms and individuals who make up the American economy.

3. The Inflationary System:
Not-So-Big Business

The giant corporations that dominate America's industrial economy are hard to ignore. So is the fact that these companies exercise considerable influence over the various markets in which they operate. They determine, in large measure, how much of their products they will sell and at what price. When business turns down or competition intensifies, they develop new product mixes or new marketing strategies rather than accept lower prices and consequently lower earnings. Nor is this behavior thought peculiar. There are few who believe that large corporations can, should, or are likely to act otherwise.

Once in a while, of course, even a ranking member of the *Fortune* 500 discovers that the marketplace is out of control. Thus General Motors, Ford, and Chrysler awoke one morning in 1980 to find that no amount of advertising was persuading consumers to buy their gas guzzlers, and all three firms began to report record losses. Companies as big and as diverse as U.S. Steel and A&P have come upon hard times in recent years. And the competition, as with the airline rate war described earlier, can sometimes get cutthroat. Throughout the business world, profits fluctuate and corporate managers worry.

It is tempting, when the news of a giant in trouble hits the headlines, to assume that big corporations aren't so powerful after all. The occasional price war or business setback is taken as evidence that the marketplace works: that the consumer is sovereign and competition effective. This belief is comforting, for it fits the image of a free-enterprise, free-market economy that most of us carry around in our heads—it's the way capitalism ought to work. If big companies really could dominate the marketplace, why would business executives get ulcers?

What happens occasionally, however, should not blind us to what happens regularly. The Lockheed 1011 Tri-Star widebody jet is sometimes grounded by storms, just like a Piper Cub. But if you believe that the Tri-Star is as dependent upon low winds and good visibility as a smaller plane, you'll be left with a serious misconception about its ability to fly a regular schedule. Similarly, the worries of corporate managers usually focus on matters like whether this year's profits will outpace last year's. This can be a topic of some concern to the manager: if profits don't pick up, his or her career may not go far either. But only in unusual circumstances do such fluctuations affect the fundamental economic health of the large corporation. The market rules only in extreme situations.

A more persuasive view of America as a predominantly market-dominated free-enterprise system focuses on the parts of the economy not populated by giant firms. A walk through the streets of a big city reveals dozens of grocery stores, pharmacies, restaurants, and apparel shops. A glance through the *Yellow Pages* turns up hundreds of small manufacturers, tradespeople, dentists, and construction firms. The countryside nearly everywhere in America is dotted with farms. None of these enterprises wields anything like the economic clout of a Quaker Oats or a Kodak. For them, it seems, the market must reign supreme, and capitalism must work the way it is supposed to.

Where prices are concerned, though, the distinction between the giants and everybody else is not always clear. Like the big firms, small companies frequently find ways to compete without cutting prices. Some trades manage to keep prices up by limiting the number of people licensed to do business. Others are the beneficiaries of extensive government intervention in the marketplace. In all these instances supply and demand are manipulated, and prices are influenced either directly or indirectly by the seller. These rigged markets lead to sticky prices, hence inflation, as surely as the control exercised by the *Fortune* 500.

Small businesses

In any sizable metropolitan area in the northern part of this country, a family with an oil-burning furnace can find dozens of companies willing and eager to supply it with oil. All will deliver anywhere in the metropolitan area with reasonable reliability. All offer essentially the same product: Exxon's home heating oil No. 2 is no different from Texaco's. And all provide the same convenience of doing business. A phone call does the trick.*

No supplier of oil, therefore, can afford to charge his customers more than a fraction of a cent more per gallon than his competitors do. If he tried to do so, he would soon find himself out of business. If the price of oil at wholesale should drop (which it still does once in a very great while), the savings would probably be passed on quickly to consumers. Kellogg's may know that its two or three main competitors are not going to get involved in cutting prices, but the Ajax Oil Company knows no such thing about its thirty-seven competitors.

A consumer looking for a hair stylist is entering a marketplace quite different from that faced by the oil-burning homeowner. The chances are that there are only a few hair stylists within easy walking distance of home or job, and why look any farther? Experimentation will reveal that some are more

---

* "Discount" oil dealers, which can be found in some cities, fall into a separate category. They do charge less for their oil, but they typically offer no free maintenance and repair service. Nor do they send out bills: the rule is cash on delivery. Thus their "product" is different from that sold by most dealers.

competent, friendly, and efficient than others; that some play loud rock music while others are as quiet as the public library; and that some are more expensive than others. All of these considerations will enter a customer's decision about which establishment to patronize. Price may be decidedly secondary. Its effect may even be opposite from the expected. A more expensive establishment may confer a sense of prestige and self-worth on the customer that cut-rate stylists can't match.

The oil dealer facing a loss of business cannot usually do much about it. Advertising won't help: it just costs money, and he doesn't have much to advertise that is different from any other dealer. Very likely the drop in business reflects declining demand for the whole industry. Consumers may be keeping their homes cooler or switching to natural gas. If the situation keeps up, companies that can afford to do so will cut prices a little to compete more effectively. Those that cannot afford to do so will be forced out of business.

The hair stylist faced with declining business has other choices short of shutting up shop. She can advertise, maybe just by passing out flyers in the neighborhood. She can install a new carpet or get rid of a surly employee. She can lower her prices, or raise them. (The latter, in the euphemistic terminology of business, is called repositioning oneself in the market.) No such choice is open to the oil dealer.

Oil dealers and hair stylists, in short, face two different kinds of markets. One kind, the oil dealer's, is very much like the stock market. There are many sellers, and what they offer for sale is essentially identical. Since everyone has to charge the going rate, the price automatically falls to its "market" level—the level determined by supply and demand. The other kind, the hair stylist's, is more like the world of the large corporation. The goods and services being offered are particular combinations of quality, convenience, service, aesthetic appeal, advertised virtues, and so forth. Price is of course a part of the package. But the seller has a good deal of discretion over what it will be, and frequently can choose to compete on other turf entirely.

Most smaller companies operate in a marketplace some-where between these two extremes. The supermarket business in most cities, for instance, exhibits a considerable amount of price competition. The printing business, though also highly competitive, exhibits a good deal less; press capacities, quality controls, and ancillary services are usually as important as price in determining who gets the customers. In many businesses each company sells to a small geographic market. In others each company sells a highly differentiated or unique product—Cantonese meals, for example, prepared by a well-known chef. In both cases firms can end up as relatively big fish in relatively small ponds. Prices then behave the way they do in the world of giant corporations. If companies don't have too much competition in their particular market niche, and if they can offer customers the right combination of quality, variety, and service, they automatically have some discretion over the prices they charge. When this is the case, prices won't fall as easily as they do in markets that resemble the stock market.

Licensing

Frequently there is no way by which an entrepreneur or company can grow large or easily distinguish itself from the competition. Except in the smallest of cities, general-practice lawyers will find several other attorneys happy to take their business away. So will plumbers and liquor-store owners. In this circumstance, it is advantageous to be able to limit by law the number of people in your line of work.

A surprising number of industries and trades have been successful in obtaining such a limitation. You can't set up a radio or television station without approval from the Federal Communications Commission. You can't run an airline without an OK from the Civil Aeronautics Board. A proposal for a new bank requires approval by the state banking commission or some other governmental agency. If you want to do business in interstate trucking, you need a go-ahead from the Interstate Commerce Commission. Doctors, lawyers, architects, accountants, pharmacists, stockbrokers, dentists, plumbers, and electricians are some of the more common tradespeople who ordinarily require a license to operate. Some of the less common occupations in this category were listed not long ago by a writer named Peter Meyer. "A study being conducted by the Labor Department," Meyer wrote, "finds that some 350 different occupations are now licensed by state authorities and another 500 occupations require state certification or registration. A cross section of jobs that now need licenses includes falconry, hairdressing, well-pump sales, weather modifying, social work (fifteen different categories), hunting and trapping guide, shampooing (hair), television-antenna installation, phrenology, prophylactic sales, tattooing, lightning-rod installation, and cesspool cleaning."

Obviously there are good reasons for licensing many of these professions, notably those related to medicine. But the rationale (or lack of it) in any given case should not obscure the economic effects of licensing. Most licenses are contingent upon successful completion of extensive, often costly, educational or apprenticeship programs. The time and expense required by such programs work wonders in keeping down the number of applications for licenses. The difficulties of obtaining a license may help create a sense of fellowship and common interest among those who succeed. Frequently the licensing board itself is run by members of the profession in question, thus ensuring that the licensees' interests will be looked after.

Sometimes a license to operate carries a fee schedule along with it. Thus interstate trucking rates are set by the ICC; and taxi fares (though not tips) are usually set by the city agency that dispenses taxi licenses. These fee schedules are seldom painful. Trucking companies, according to *Business Week,* have been making profits as high as 20 percent; the recent deregulation bill may or may not cut these profits.*

---

* The bill, passed in mid-1980, does not remove the ICC's jurisdiction over truck routes and freight rates, as deregulation proponents had originally hoped. It does make entry into the business easier by shift-

There are about 12,000 taxicabs licensed to operate in New York City. The licenses, called medallions, can be bought and sold on the open market, and in 1980 were going for as much as $68,000. This fact led some observers to conclude that things couldn't be as bad as the industry had claimed when it asked for a rate hike that year. If the situation really was so dismal, *The New York Times* asked editorially, "why then are prospective taxi owners willing to pay between $53,000 and $68,000 for the right to run a cab in the city?" Fares were evidently higher than they would have been if anyone was free to operate a cab.

In most regulated industries, rates are not set by public agencies. Restrictions on who can sell something become all the more important. Keeping down the number of competitors not only reduces the chance of direct price competition—remember Kellogg's versus the Ajax Oil Company—it also facilitates informal measures aimed at rigging markets or manipulating prices. It is hard to imagine, for example, that a plumber could charge $25 (sometimes twice that in big cities) just for walking in a customer's front door if plumbing were a profession open to all comers. It is also hard to imagine that other trades could have gotten away with price-fixing as long as they did. Lawyers, until recently, were provided with "minimum fee schedules" by state bar associations, which, though not legally binding, helped establish a price floor for legal services. The American Society of Anesthesiology, until recently, required hospitals to hire its members on a fee-for-service basis rather than at a salary, a device that turned out to raise the cost of anesthesiology and the incomes of anesthesiologists. Only recently have opticians in many states been allowed to advertise the price of eyeglasses or pharmacists the price of drugs. For a long time, professional associa-

---

ing the burden of proof from those who propose new service to those who oppose it. It requires truckers, beginning in 1984, to apply individually to the ICC for certain rate changes, rather than agreeing on rates beforehand and applying jointly. And it allows firms to raise or lower rates 10 percent without an OK from the ICC.

tions and regulatory boards were able to shield many such trades from the rigors of the marketplace.

Laws, court cases, and Federal Trade Commission decisions during the last few years have limited the variety and scope of practices like these, and of similar anticompetitive measures in unregulated industries. Congress, in the Consumer Goods Pricing Act of 1975, outlawed state "fair trade" laws and its own Miller-Tydings Act, both of which were designed to protect small retailers from "unfair" price competition. The Supreme Court in 1977 ruled that lawyers have a constitutional right to advertise—a decision, according to reports, that has led to lower legal fees in some areas. Both the Federal Trade Commission and the Justice Department began in 1980 to investigate "industry practices" aimed at fixing prices; among such practices, said one report, "are the specific assignment of dealerships by territory; the policy of an industry or area leader to set prices and smaller companies to base theirs on those levels; producers selling only to wholesalers or retailers gearing their prices to those suggested, and use of credit . . . [to] keep prices at set levels." So the tide may be turning. How far it will flow out remains to be seen.

"No business," writes management consultant Rolf H. Wild, "particularly welcomes competition, because real competition is expensive and detrimental to the competitors." Measures designed to increase competition will therefore provoke howls of pain—much like the howls that the 1980 trucking deregulation bill elicited from the American Trucking Associations. Without competition, however, there is little downward pressure on prices. Regulated rates and rules about who can supply a particular good or service both lead to prices that are sticky. From the affected business's point of view, that's a pleasant situation.

Housing and health care

Not all industries lend themselves to supply restrictions. Rather than let themselves be buffeted by the ill winds of the marketplace, though, some have found ways to prop up consumer demand for what they sell. This too has a salutary effect on price from the seller's point of view. The usual means by which demand is kept high is government subsidy. The usual rationale, often unexceptionable, is that the items being sold are critical to the nation's well-being. The best examples are housing and health care. Together they account for about a quarter of the average household's expenses.

Median prices of existing homes rose about 65 percent more than the Consumer Price Index during the 1970s. New-home prices went up about twice as much as the index. The average price of a new house in 1980 was $72,000. The increase, as noted earlier, is due to many factors, the baby boom and inflation among them. Without the government, however, housing would not be where it is today.

Consider the homeowner's tax break all by itself. The Johnsons—a hypothetical family of four with an income of $20,000—would have paid $2,271 to Washington in 1979 if they took the standard deduction on Form 1040. But suppose the Johnsons own a $60,000 house, with a 5-year-old mortgage of $40,000 at 9 percent. Interest on the mortgage loan comes to perhaps $3,000 a year. Property taxes are probably another $1,200. Both are tax-deductible. So they fill out Schedule A and find that housing expenses alone reduce their tax liability by about $250. And now that they're filling out Schedule A anyway, they can take deductions for medical expenses, charitable contributions, credit-card and other interest costs, and so on. All might be worth another $100 or so off the tax bill. As long as the Johnsons own their own home (and keep it well mortgaged) the government might as well send them a check for $350 every year. If the Johnsons get richer, even if they get richer only in nominal terms because of inflation, the size of the check increases. If they buy a more expensive house or get a more expensive mortgage, the check gets bigger too. Overall, these tax breaks cost the government an estimated $14 billion in uncollected revenue in fiscal 1979.

That isn't all the government does. Since 1968 it has subsidized construction of housing for low- and moderate-income families on a substantial scale. For much longer than that, the Veterans Administration and the Federal Housing Administration (FHA) have been guaranteeing mortgage loans. Families taking advantage of these programs can borrow at low interest rates with smaller down payments than banks would otherwise require. And the programs are frequently expanded. In 1977, for instance, Congress lowered the down payment required on FHA-insured mortgages. Other measures reduced the taxes most homeowners must pay when they sell their house and buy a new one, and changed mortgage-repayment rules to permit lower payments in the first years of a mortgage.

As interest rates rose during 1980, buyers were forced out of the market and home prices fell a small amount. Realtors tried to postpone the fall as long as they could; in lieu of reducing prices, *The Wall Street Journal* reported, some were pursuing gimmicks like giving away a compact car with the purchase of a sufficiently expensive home.* Meanwhile, the *Journal* also noted, the declining housing market "was provoking anguished cries from builders and unions for a multi-billion-dollar infusion of federal mortgage subsidies." Insofar as the government rescues the industry—and it is always under considerable pressure to do so from prospective buyers and sellers as well as from trade groups—prices do not easily go down.

In health care, which has risen in cost about 10 percent more than the Consumer Price Index as a whole during the 1970s, inflation is built into the financing system. As Harvard

---

* A $5,000 car is better than a $5,000 price cut from the broker's point of view because he or she can't collect a commission on the price cut. Also, many brokers are themselves real estate owners or developers and have an interest in keeping nominal prices up.

Brokers' commissions, which represent the price of brokers' services, seem to stay constant regardless of trends in home prices. One midwestern broker who attempted to reduce his commission when faced with a sagging market was immediately accused by his colleagues of "unethical" behavior.

sociologists Paul Starr and Gosta Esping-Andersen explain it, three factors affect the price of health care. First is the fact that "payment for most medical care today is made by a 'third party' "—Blue Cross, Medicare, or a conventional insurance company. So neither the patient nor the hospital nor the doctor providing the care has to pay out of pocket for what is "sold." Second, doctors and hospitals get paid on a fee-for-service basis: the more treatment that is prescribed, the more money the provider makes. Third, "reimbursements to hospitals and other institutions under Medicare and Blue Cross are determined on the basis of costs." The result is that "the hospital that spends wantonly today will reap its rewards in higher rates of reimbursement tomorrow." Medicare, which was passed in 1965, was particularly profligate. Hospitals could compute their costs in two different ways and use whichever method proved most favorable; and they got an extra 2 percent on top to cover "whatever costs might have been omitted."

The direct effect of Medicare and Medicaid was to make fully paid hospital coverage available to a poor and elderly population that hitherto had been unable to afford it. Their indirect effect was to increase hospital spending dramatically. "In the year before Medicare," write Starr and Esping-Andersen, "hospital costs were rising at about 6 percent annually; in the year afterward, they rose 16 percent. Between 1965 and 1977, hospital expenditures quintupled from $13.1 billion to $65.6 billion—an average increase of 14 percent a year, more than double the rise in the consumer price index and higher than medical costs overall." Spending on Medicare, meanwhile, has been doubling every four years. In 1980, according to *The New York Times*, it was expected to reach $34 billion.

The world of health care—particularly hospital care, which now accounts for over 40 percent of all medical expenditures —is not one of price competition: quite the opposite. It is a world of approved fee schedules and reimbursements. Nor is it sensitive (as the housing industry is) to declining demand due to bad business conditions. People who are sick do not put off getting treated. Some have already paid the bill anyway, through payroll deductions for Blue Cross or another insurance plan. For others the government will pick up the tab. As a result the health care system exhibits, in the Harvard experts' words, "a continuously high rate of inflation that is apparently impervious to changes in the economy."

Farming

The scope of free, unrestricted, competitive markets, as the reader will notice, is getting smaller. Most manufacturing is excluded. So are the regulated utilities, the big retailers like Sears and service companies like Marriott, many smaller retailing and service concerns, a lot of the trades and professions, now housing and health care. In most cases competition has not vanished. Companies still have to take into account what their customers want and can afford, and how much their competitors are charging. But most have found ways to tame the competitive jungle—to keep down the number of competitors, for instance, or to make sure that there are plenty of customers for all.

Once that's done, prices are no longer as flexible as they once were. They still can move up. But they don't fall so easily. If the housing market is bad, you rarely find builders and lumber companies slashing their prices, or homeowners selling out at a loss. Instead you find most people waiting until things get better, and in the meantime asking for government help.

The one part of the economy where free markets really do seem to work is agriculture. You can see the evidence in the supermarket every week. The prices of unprocessed foods— meat, dairy products, eggs, coffee, and so on—really do go up and down, just as they are supposed to. The newspapers correctly remind us that these fluctuations reflect changes in supply or demand, usually supply, since consumer demand for food items remains essentially constant. Between 1976 and 1977, as coffee drinkers will remember, bad harvests in

Brazil led to an 85 percent increase in the price of coffee, $1.87 a pound to $3.47 a pound on the average. By mid-1979, however, the price had dropped nearly 25 percent, back down to $2.67. Yet the average price level was rising 20 percent in the same period.

From the farmer's point of view, the market is pretty effective too: he sells his produce for whatever it will bring (although large midwestern grain farmers sometimes stockpile it in hopes of getting a better price). Considered as businesses, most farmers are small. Yet the market for farm produce is regional or national in scope. Even the producer of a highly perishable commodity, the Vermont dairy farmer, say, rarely sells his wares to his neighbors. Instead, his milk is marketed by big dairy enterprises and cooperatives throughout New England.

For nearly fifty years, however, the government has propped up or manipulated the market for farm produce in a variety of ways. The Agricultural Adjustment Act of 1933, signed by Roosevelt on May 12 of that year, provided for benefit payments to farmers who agreed to limit production; it also allowed for "marketing agreements" to fix prices for agricultural commodities. Later the government established support prices at which it would, if necessary, buy farm output. And in 1973 it instituted the so-called target price system, which allowed market prices to fluctuate more than before (and thus keep U.S. grain competitive on the world market) while still maintaining farmers' incomes. If the market price for wheat, say, falls 25¢ a bushel below the target, the government mails the farmer a check for 25¢ times every bushel he sells. Target prices are supposed to reflect a combination of farm costs, expected demand, and world market prices. They are issued annually, and can be increased (but not decreased) at any time by the Secretary of Agriculture. The temptation to increase them in an election year can prove irresistible: Jimmy Carter, for example, announced higher targets for some crops not long before the 1980 election.

The system varies from crop to crop. Dairy farmers, for

example, sell their milk to bottlers and processors at prices that are not allowed to fall below government-established minimums. If more milk is produced than processors can eventually sell, the processors take it anyway and turn it into butter, cheese, and powdered milk. An agency called the Commodity Credit Corporation then buys the surplus products and stores them in government warehouses. They can be sold only at prices at least 5 percent higher than the support level. Meanwhile, the government limits imports of dairy products to protect domestic farmers and processors from foreign competition.

Under a 1979 law, minimum dairy prices must be adjusted twice (rather than once) a year to keep up with inflation. Because of the way the Department of Agriculture calculates these adjustments, support prices have been rising faster than milk producers' costs. The semiannual adjustment in April 1980, according to *The New York Times*, would mean an extra $7,500 in gross income over a six-month period for a dairy farm with fifty cows. It would raise the price of milk to the consumer an estimated 8¢ per gallon, and the price of butter and cheese about 9¢ a pound. The whole program was expected to cost the government nearly a billion dollars in 1980.

Tobacco farmers grow their crop on "allotments" determined by the federal government; it is the only crop whose production is still strictly limited. In the 1930s, when the price of tobacco had dropped to 6¢ a pound, the government began assigning tobacco-growing rights to farmers on the basis of how much they had traditionally raised. These allotments, which have changed little over the years, limit both the number of tobacco farmers and the amount of tobacco that can be grown. "A farmer who doesn't have an allotment," as one writer explains it, "can't grow tobacco today unless he finds someone willing to lease him growing rights or else sell him land with an allotment." Land with an allotment, not surprisingly, is considerably more expensive than comparable land without one.

The Department of Agriculture also supports tobacco prices; any tobacco not sold at the government-determined minimum price is purchased by a company operating with federal money. The company stores it in warehouses until prices go up, then sells it for a profit, and pays back the loan. The plan makes tobacco more expensive than it otherwise would be and helps those who grow it considerably. "A 'bacca farmer just can't operate and not make money," one North Carolina grower told a reporter.

More fruit and vegetable farmers live in California than in any other state; California is the leading producer of artichokes, asparagus, lima beans, broccoli, Brussels sprouts, cantaloupes, carrots, cauliflower, celery, garlic, honeydew, lettuce, onions, spinach, strawberries, peaches, pears, grapes, plums, lemons, and tomatoes. Fruits and vegetables are not covered by federal price support programs. Often, however, producers will band together and issue "marketing orders" that set standards for the produce, thus insuring themselves against unanticipated excess supply. And a few of the vegetables—tomatoes, for example—are grown in ways that resemble industrial production. California grows 85 percent of U.S. tomatoes. The 600 or so big farm operations that raise them plant an average of over 350 acres apiece. The fruit they plant is genetically selected for a variety of characteristics: "thick-walledness, less acidity, more uniform ripening, oblongness, leafiness, and high yield," as the writer Mark Kramer describes them. It is harvested by huge machines a week or two after airplanes have sprayed the entire crop with ethylene, an agent that hastens ripening. Six of the machines can harvest a 766-acre field bearing 100 million tomatoes in about a month.

Seven out of every eight tomatoes are bought for processing rather than fresh consumption. Four canners—Del Monte, Heinz, Campbell, and Libby, McNeill, & Libby—sell 72 percent of the nation's tomato sauce and a substantial fraction of most other tomato products. In recent years, large growers and canning companies have set up a system called "joint contracting" for producing tomatoes. Under this system, both parties share the expense (and responsibility) of "investing" in the crop: seeds, herbicides and pesticides, machinery, water, labor, and management. The tomatoes are "sold" by farmer to canner at a price agreed upon in an advance contract.

"Under this sort of business condition," observes Kramer, "the marketplace is fully occupied by giants. It is no place for the little guy with a truckload or two of tomatoes—even if his price is right. Farmers who once planted twenty or thirty acres of cannery tomatoes as a speculative complement to other farming endeavors are for the most part out of the picture, with no place to market their crops and no place to finance their operating expenses."

In all these cases, the normal fluctuations of the market are softened, and prices are prevented from falling too far. It is worth remembering too that most of the food we eat does not exactly go straight from the farm to the supermarket. Instead, like tomatoes, it is canned, frozen, processed, packaged, and marketed like an industrial product. Pringles, Sugar Smacks, even Dannon Yogurt are produced and sold by some of the biggest companies in America. (Dannon's parent is the giant Beatrice conglomerate, which also owns Canada Dry, Schweppes, RC Cola, Sunbeam Bread, and dozens of other companies.) They are extensively processed, heavily advertised, and sold at a premium. Their price responds to farm-price fluctuations the way Kodak film prices respond to silver fluctuations: easy up, sticky down.

Back to the marketplace?

Since by now the devout inflation-fighter will be appropriately indignant about corporate and governmental meddling with the market, it is worth a moment to consider the alternative. Again, agriculture is a useful example. Before the Agricultural Adjustment Act of 1933, farmers really did operate in what was essentially a free market. As we should expect in such a market, food prices rose and fell with ease, reflecting supply and demand with considerable accuracy.

The best years for the farmer under this system came during and right after World War I: as the historian Lester V. Chandler describes it, "cotton rose from about 12 cents to 35 cents a pound, wheat from about 90 cents to $2.16 a bushel, and corn from about 65 cents to $1.52 a bushel." The parity ratio—a measure of farm-product prices in relation to farm costs—rose from 100 in the base period of 1910–1914 to a high of 120 in 1917. Farmers bought more land and brought new land under cultivation. They bought new equipment. To finance it all they went deeper in debt.

Between May 1920 and the end of 1921, farm prices dropped more than 40 percent. Net farm income, thanks to the larger debt load, decreased nearly 60 percent. For most of the 1920s, parity hovered around 90. In retrospect, the cause of this decline is clear: farm output had increased substantially and demand, thanks to a rapidly shrinking export market, had not kept pace. During the Depression things got worse. The prices paid farmers for their produce dropped by more than half between 1929 and 1932; parity bottomed out at 58. Net farm income decreased almost 70 percent in the same period.

By the time of the Agricultural Adjustment Act in 1933, roughly half of all the farms mortgaged in the United States were reported delinquent.* Farm output, however, did not drop; in fact it was slightly higher in 1932 than in 1929. The reason was that no individual farmer had much to gain by restricting his own output, and there was no effective way by which farmers could work together to restrain output.

---

* By no means were all of these mortgages foreclosed. In many cases creditors were tolerant of farmers' difficulties; in others they simply despaired of being able to do anything with a foreclosed farm. In some places, farmers joined together to prevent foreclosure, occasionally throwing the foreclosers off the place bodily, occasionally through more subtle means. In Shelby, Nebraska, says Lester Chandler, "A farm mortgaged to a bank for $4,100 was bid in by friendly neighbors for $49.50 and turned back to the owner." The practice was not unknown elsewhere too.

Farming might be a bad business, but there were no jobs available anywhere else anyway.

Until 1933, in other words, farmers were at the mercy of supply and demand conditions over which they had no control. Their incomes boomed in good times, plummeted in bad times. Though agriculture is in some ways a special case, much the same will be true of any unregulated, uncontrolled free market. New England fishermen, for example, are in much the same situation now that farmers were in before 1933. Unlike Canada, which regulates the size of its fishing fleet, the United States leaves its fishermen largely unregulated. When prices are good more boats go out and bring back more fish. The resulting oversupply depresses prices and hurts everyone's incomes. Some fishing boats go bankrupt, and supply eventually decreases. Ironically, the low prices received by the fishermen in times of oversupply do not show up in the retail price of fish. Drops in fresh fish prices, say economists at the University of Rhode Island, "fail to show up at the retail level because the retail market for fish is relatively uncompetitive." "We don't like to fluctuate our prices too much," one fish store owner told a reporter.

In a competitive marketplace like fishing, those who sell a particular good or service are under the thumb of impersonal forces. In the world of Adam Smith, that works out to everybody's benefit. In the real world, it means that a business's income may change dramatically: riches one minute, poverty the next, and you never know what's around the corner. Few sane people can be happy with such a situation indefinitely.

Some businesses control the marketplace by growing large enough to manipulate their own supply, demand, and prices. Those who cannot grow so big must rely on governmental action for the same end. Over the years, a large number of groups have convinced legislators in Washington and elsewhere that what they do is important enough to merit governmental protection or support. As a result, a substantial fraction of our economy is protected against the drop in incomes that would result from free competition and freely falling prices. Prices are sticky down. So, as the next chapter will explain, are wages.

There is much to be said for an economy in which those who provide goods and services are protected in these ways. Life is more secure. Planning is easier. Maybe more gets produced. Such an economy, however, cannot easily avoid inflation. Unless prices can fall as easily as they rise, the long-term trend can only be upward.

4. The Inflationary System:
Labor

Unfettered competition is a little like corporal punishment in the schools. It is esteemed by the traditionally minded, except those old enough to remember its use. It has fallen into disrepute in the modern age. Some would bring it back, though usually for their neighbors rather than for themselves. Others are glad to see it gone.

Even people in the latter category, however, should not blind themselves to the effects of its disappearance. School children arguably have a right not to be rapped on the knuckles with a rattan cane. But a major incentive to good behavior has been lost. Similarly, businesses may fare better in a world where government bailouts, subsidies, and other forms of protection have replaced competition and the threat of bankruptcy. But a major incentive to flexible pricing policies has vanished as well.

To be sure, vestiges of the marketplace remain. And if *costs* were dropping, prices might too. More competition and less protection would doubtless hasten the process. But even monopolistic Kodak cut its prices a little when silver fell. If other costs fell too, it would probably have cut them even more. "Other costs," of course, are the rub. Most of them are labor costs, the wages and salaries paid those who do the work. For reasons this chapter will explain, these costs seldom fall. Because wages are "sticky down," prices are too.

Like prices, wages were once flexible: they went down as

well as up. A mason working on the Erie Canal in New York State made an average of $2.50 a day in 1876 and only $2.00 a day two years later; the "common labor" wage on the canal dropped from $1.50 to $1.00 over the same period. Blacksmiths earning $2.66 a day in 1871 were getting only $2.31 by the end of the decade. A worker in a textile plant saw her wages drop more than 10 percent between 1893 and 1898. Average hourly wages for all manufacturing workers went down in 1894, 1898, 1908, and again in the early 1920s. The long-run trend, of course, was up, as the economy grew and production increased. But whenever business dropped off both prices and wages were likely to decline.

The labor market that brought about this flexibility in wages, however, was not particularly pleasant to behold. One writer observed the Chicago factories around 1900:

> On cold, rainy mornings, at the dusk of dawn, I have been awakened, two hours before my rising time, by the monotonous clatter of hobnailed boots on the plank sidewalks, as the procession to the factory passed under my window. Heavy, brooding men; tired, anxious women; thinly dressed, unkempt little girls and frail, joyless lads passed along, half awake, not one uttering a word, as they hurried to the great factory. . . . Hundreds of others, obviously a hungrier, poorer lot . . . waited in front of a closed gate until finally a great red-bearded man came out and selected twenty-three of the strongest, best-looking men. For these the gates were opened, and the others, with downcast eyes, marched off to seek employment elsewhere or to sit at home, or in a saloon, or in a lodging house. . . .

Nor is this description overdrawn, despite the lugubrious prose. With unions representing only about 3 percent of the labor force and enjoying no governmental protection, employers could essentially hire and fire at will. The hours of work were long (typically 60 a week in 1900), accidents frequent, and safety precautions few. Minimum-wage laws and workers' compensation were unknown. Even child labor was not yet illegal: the first law regulating the employment of people between the ages of fourteen and eighteen wasn't passed until 1916, and it was declared unconstitutional shortly thereafter.* In 1900, about a quarter of the boys and a tenth of the girls between age ten and age fifteen were working. In a sense, wages were the least of a worker's problems. When wages went down prices usually did too, so real wages didn't change much. Still, knowing that the employer can and will cut your pay if things look bad does not increase one's peace of mind, especially if the wages aren't much above the poverty level to begin with.

The Depression of the 1930s underscored the effects of this kind of labor market. Nearly a quarter of the labor force was out of work. Production workers' hourly wages fell more than 20 percent between 1929 and 1933. Unions were still small and weak in the early thirties, and government had not yet begun to regulate conditions of work. Workers were still on their own, and doing worse than ever.

A decade of Depression and five years of war, however, essentially transformed the relationship between employer and employee. The changes were rooted in the new politics of the thirties, and in the new economics of postwar America. Today we take most of them for granted, and even complain now and then that unions and government interfere too

---

* That law banned the employment of children under fourteen in factories and those under sixteen in mines. It was declared unconstitutional in 1918. A milder law passed in 1919 was held unconstitutional in 1920. An attempt by the American Federation of Labor to amend the Constitution so that Congress could pass a child-labor law was never successful. "When ratification came before the voters of Massachusetts," writes one historian, "Daniel Cardinal O'Connell and other high-ranking prelates of the Roman Catholic Church attacked the proposal and urged its defeat." One may suppose that the interests of employers coincided with the interests of at least some Catholic workers, whose incomes depended on everyone in the family working.

Child labor was not finally regulated on a national scale until the Fair Labor Standards Act of 1938.

much with companies' ability to run their own affairs. Those who manage companies (or would like to) also complain about the fact that wages, like prices, are sticky down. Probably the grousing is inevitable. But it's a measure, in a sense, of how far we have come from the "free" labor markets of the past. A review of how we got where we are today shows not only how but why the labor market contributes to inflation.

Unions before the Depression

At the Carnegie Company's Homestead Steel Works near Pittsburgh, the contract between management and its 3,800 employees was due to expire in July 1892. In those days a union called the Amalgamated Association of Iron, Steel, and Tin Workers represented about a quarter of the nation's steelworkers. Its strongest local was at Homestead. In fact the local essentially controlled the way the plant operated. The skilled workers who dominated the union worked much like independent contractors. They produced steel with company equipment but largely according to union rules, and they hired and paid their own unskilled help. By agreement, the company's payments to the skilled workers rose and fell with the market price of steel.

Homestead at the time was run by an accomplished union-buster named Henry Clay Frick, who was second in command only to Andrew Carnegie himself. Frick didn't like the way the plant was working. The burgeoning market for steel in the 1880s had brought intense competition to the industry, and the union-dominated production system made it virtually impossible for management to cut costs by figuring out ways for the workers to produce more. Shortly before the contract ended Frick built a fence topped with barbed wire around the plant. He also, writes Katherine Stone, "had platforms for sentinels constructed and holes for rifles put in along the fence; and he had barracks built inside it to house strike-breakers." On June 25 the corporation secretary announced that henceforth the company would make its own decision about wage scales and about the terms of the new contract. The issue, said Frick, was "whether the Carnegie Company or the Amalgamated Association shall have absolute control of our plant and business at Homestead."

Four days later the plant's employees voted to go out on strike. Frick had already requested Robert Pinkerton to assemble, in secret, 300 of his guards to help break the strike. On the night of July 4 the Pinkertons were put on barges at a point below Pittsburgh and towed up the Ohio River and then the Monongahela by a tugboat named *Little Bill*. A union lookout in Pittsburgh noticed the barges and wired the strikers. When the Pinkertons arrived, a crowd of thousands, some armed, was waiting on the riverbank to meet them.

"The Pinkertons," writes the historian Philip Taft, "pushed a gangplank ashore, and one of the crowd threw himself before them to prevent their passage. During the argument a shot was fired, followed by a volley from the crowd and general firing from the barges. Two strikers and two Pinkertons were killed.

"Two hours later, another attempt at landing was made, and it was met by a fusillade from the strikers who were now partially protected by embankments of steel and iron. The Pinkertons again retreated to their boats and answered the strikers' fire through the windows and port holes. The tugboat *Little Bill*, which had carried the barges to their destination, now sought to bring them back. It was met by a volley of shot and finally escaped up the river to Pittsburgh, leaving the barges exposed. Oil was spread on the river in the hope of burning the barges, and dynamite was thrown at them, but these maneuvers failed. Finally, the Pinkertons raised a white flag as a token of surrender, but for a time it was ignored. By five o'clock in the evening, Hugh O'Donnell, the chairman of the strikers' advisory committee, agreed to the surrender of the Pinkertons and assured them safe passage. The crowd was of another mind; it swept over the barges and carried off the movable goods, and the Pinkertons fared badly as they ran through a gauntlet of men, women, and children who had seen some of their friends and relatives felled or killed."

The Amalgamated's victory was short-lived. The following week Governor Robert E. Pattison of Pennsylvania ordered 7,000 troops to Homestead, where they forced the strikers out of the plant. By July 15 the furnaces were lit again, and on July 22 a new work force of nonunion men entered the plant. On November 14 the strikers voted to return to work, their demands wholly unmet. Within two years the Amalgamated, its morale broken, had lost almost half of its membership.

Thus was inaugurated—in steel, at least—the Golden Age of Union-Busting. In 1901 the Amalgamated greeted the new century by losing a series of strikes against several of the companies that made up the new United States Steel Corporation. In 1909 the American Sheet and Tin Plate Company (part of U.S. Steel) announced that henceforth its plants would all be operated as nonunion shops and that wages would be cut. The Amalgamated walked out, requesting help from the rest of the labor movement. Thirty-six unions responded by launching an organizing drive, but to no avail. After fourteen months the Amalgamated gave up the strike. By 1911 its membership numbered just over 4,000.

In 1918 the American Federation of Labor launched another organizing drive, this one under the aegis of the National Committee for Organizing the Iron and Steel Workers. In September of 1919, shortly after the end of World War I, some 367,000 steelworkers went out on strike. By modern standards they weren't asking much: an eight-hour day with one day off in every seven; abolition of the twenty-four-hour shift; and a guarantee of collective bargaining rights. Nevertheless they met fierce opposition. The governor of Indiana sent first the National Guard and then federal troops to Gary to maintain order. The companies began reopening their plants with nonunion workers. On January 5, 1920, after eighteen strikers and two others had been killed, the executive board of the Amalgamated requested an end to the strike. The other unions quickly complied, and the strike was over, a failure.

In 1936 the weak Amalgamated, under strong pressure from the new Committee for Industrial Organization led by United Mine Workers president John L. Lewis, agreed to go along with yet another organizing campaign. This one was to be engineered and funded (to the tune of half a million dollars) by the CIO. The Steel Workers Organizing Committee (SWOC) was set up to launch the drive. As its first move, the historian William E. Leuchtenburg observes, it "brazenly rented offices in downtown Pittsburgh on the thirty-sixth floor of the Grant Building, an edifice which housed more steel barons than any other in the nation." More than 200 organizers spread out over the steel regions, and again workers signed up in droves.

This time the opposition came from what was quaintly known as Little Steel—the giant corporations of Republic Steel, Youngstown Sheet and Tube, Inland, and Bethlehem Steel, "little" only by comparison with U.S. Steel. A strike began on May 25, 1937. Again there was bloodshed. On Memorial Day in Chicago, a protest meeting called by the union ended with ten strikers dead at the hands of police. A Republic Steel plant in Monroe, Michigan, was opened by 200 special police. In Johnstown, Pennsylvania, a "citizens committee" formed to fight the strike encouraged violence against picketing workers, and the Bethlehem Steel plant there supplied itself with tear gas and munitions. Governor George H. Earle declared martial law and sent in troops. Later that month Ohio governor Martin L. Davey sent troops to Youngstown after a picket was killed at the Sheet and Tube plant. Slowly the mills reopened. Eighteen had been killed and 168 injured.

In the meantime, however, the Golden Age had ended. Within a few years all the Little Steel companies had been compelled to recognize and to sign contracts with the Steel

Workers Organizing Committee. U.S. Steel, meanwhile, had "folded without a fight" and signed a contract with the union granting a wage boost and a forty-hour week. Jones & Laughlin, Wheeling Steel, and Caterpillar Tractor signed contracts too. The SWOC, which already boasted 325,000 members by early 1937, continued to grow. In 1942 the Committee, together with the aging remains of the old Amalgamated Association, formed the United Steel Workers of America. The steel industry, after half a century of union-busting, had been organized in about five years.

The turning point

What made the difference, of course, was the New Deal. Not so much Franklin D. Roosevelt himself: FDR, says Leuchtenburg, was "somewhat perturbed at being cast in the role of midwife of industrial unionism." But the Democratic landslide of 1932 and the new political climate it reflected were making possible initiatives that would have sunk in a well of apoplexy and disbelief only a few years before.

In December 1932, for example, Alabama Senator Hugo Black introduced a bill aimed at creating more employment by cutting the work week to an unheard-of 30 hours; AFL president William Green "startled the country, and perhaps himself" by threatening a general strike in support. The Senate passed the bill shortly after Roosevelt's inauguration. FDR in turn set in motion the hearings and studies that would soon lead to the National Industrial Recovery Act. The NIRA set up procedures allowing businesses to establish industrial practices and to fix prices without fear of the antitrust laws; its Blue Eagle and the slogan "We Do Our Part" quickly became familiar features on store windows, factory walls, and newspaper mastheads. At Senator Robert Wagner's insistence it contained a famous provision—Section 7A—stipulating that the new industrial codes set minimum wages and maximum hours for labor and guaranteeing the right to collective bargaining.

The effect was dramatic. "In the grimy alleys of Birmingham, in the drab bars of Akron, on Seattle's wharves, workers were saying what for so long they had not dared to say: 'Organize!' " John L. Lewis's United Mine Workers added 350,000 new members in 1933 and 1934. The American Federation of Labor took on 800,000 new members in 1933 alone. The NIRA was declared unconstitutional by the Supreme Court in 1935, in the so-called sick chicken decision.* But shortly thereafter Roosevelt signed an even more far-reaching piece of legislation. The Wagner Act, as it was known, created the National Labor Relations Board and established the procedure for unionizing a plant that is still in effect today. Under the act, workers in a plant can petition the board for a "certification" election establishing a particular union as their bargaining agent. If a majority of workers votes yes in the election, the employer must recognize the union as bargaining agent for all the employees in a unit.

The law's provisions have never stopped employers from appealing election results and finding other ways to stall. The thirties were no exception to this rule, particularly since most employers were in doubt as to the law's constitutionality. U.S. Steel capitulated, but it was several years before government pressure forced the Little Steel companies to accept unionization. The auto companies recognized the United Auto Workers only after a wave of sit-down strikes, beginning in 1936 at General Motors Fisher Body No. 1 plant in Flint, Michigan. But the tide nevertheless was flowing. "As steel and auto went," writes Leuchtenburg, "so went much of the nation."

After an eight-week strike in March and April, 1937, Firestone Tire & Rubber capitulated to the United

---

* So called because the plaintiff was a Brooklyn poultry firm convicted of violating the National Recovery Administration's codes on several counts, including selling diseased chickens. With the law behind the codes declared unconstitutional, the firm's conviction had to be reversed.

Rubber Workers. By the end of 1937, General Electric, RCA-Victor, and Philco had recognized the United Electrical and Radio Workers. The Textile Workers Organizing Committee, run by Sidney Hillman, brought into line industry titans like American Woolen in Lawrence; by early October, it boasted 450,000 members.

Meanwhile, starting in 1934, John L. Lewis and his allies had begun pressuring the American Federation of Labor to begin organizing "industrial unions"—unions that included everyone working in an industry rather than, as with most of the AFL unions, the members of a specific trade or craft. The AFL wasn't buying the idea. At its 1935 convention Lewis punched Big Bill Hutcheson of the Carpenters Union in the face, and the AFL voted down a report favoring industrial unionism by a three-to-two margin. Shortly thereafter Lewis and eight other union leaders established the Committee for Industrial Organization, and in October 1938 the Congress of Industrial Organizations was born. The CIO was responsible for most of the large-scale organizing drives that swelled the ranks of American labor.

Swell them they did. In 1930 about 3.4 million workers, not quite 7 percent of the total labor force, belonged to a union. By 1940, the figures were 8.7 million and 15 percent; by 1950, 14.3 million and 22 percent. They haven't varied much since. In 1976 about 20 million workers—one out of every five, and one of every four nonfarm workers—belonged to a union. The Teamsters alone have nearly 2 million members. Five other unions include an average of more than a million members each.

The gross statistics of union representation and the widely touted fact that union membership has been dropping off as a percentage of the total labor force don't do justice to unions' impact on the economy. For one thing, unions are concentrated in key economic sectors. More than half the workers in most manufacturing industries belong to a union.

THE TEN BIGGEST UNIONS IN AMERICA

Union	Membership (1978)
Intl'l Brotherhood of Teamsters	1,973,272
United Auto Workers	1,544,859
National Education Association *	1,470,212
United Steel Workers of America	1,300,000
Int'l Brotherhood of Electrical Workers	991,228
Int'l Association of Machinists	943,280
United Brotherhood of Carpenters	820,000
Retail Clerks International Union	650,876
Laborers' International Union	650,000
American Federation of State, County, and Municipal Employees	648,160

* The NEA, though not a traditional union, has in recent years begun to function much like a union, partly because of competition with the American Federation of Teachers, AFL-CIO.

Except for the Teamsters, Auto Workers, and NEA, all unions listed belong to the AFL-CIO.

SOURCE: *The World Almanac and Book of Facts*, 1980 (New York: Newspaper Enterprise Association, 1979), p. 111.

In transportation and construction the figure is over 75 percent. Some unions regulate the supply of labor: the building trades, for example, where union membership is often a precondition to getting a job. All engage in collective bargaining and thereby help determine wage rates and working conditions for their members.

Unions' indirect influence extends even farther. Many nonunion employers peg their wages to the scale established by some union. Some do this by custom, others because they are afraid their own plants will be organized if they don't. The same fear of unionization effectively precludes wage cutting in many industries. Under the Davis-Bacon Act (another product of the Depression) and subsequent legislation, firms working on government contracts or on federally assisted projects must usually pay union-scale wages. And union wage gains often drive up the salaries of white-collar and managerial employees who are thought entitled to earn more than blue-collar workers.

Unions, in short, are an enormous monkey wrench in the works of a flexible labor market. Once in a while you read of a union that has agreed to accept a wage cut—"Union Accord on Pay Cuts Averts Closing," read one headline about a 1980 agreement between Uniroyal and the United Rubber Workers. This is a news story on the order of man bites dog. For the most part, unions effectively prevent wages from falling. Unless union leaders can win wage gains, they don't get reelected. Unless a contract contains an increase, the membership will reject it. Employers who would like to cut wages nearly always cannot.

Instead, of course, they raise prices. If wages cannot fall, prices seldom can either. And one more piece of the inflationary puzzle is in place.

Income security

Unions aren't the only interference with the labor market. The government meddles too. Once again the roots of this meddling lie in the Great Depression.

If the labor market is to work the way it used to, people who are not working should not eat. If they have some other means of support, they may choose not to work at all, or they may choose to work only when wages are high enough and other conditions of employment are fair. Nor will they be disposed to accept wage cuts. Faced with one, they're likely to quit instead.

Before the 1930s, people who were out of work had little to fall back on. It didn't make much difference whether they had been fired or laid off, had quit, had taken sick or grown old, or were needed at home to care for children. If they had some savings (or a pension plan, in the case of the elderly, which only a few had), they might get by for a while. If not, they were dependent upon relatives, friends, and whatever provisions their state, county, municipality, or church made for relief. "Welfare" of this sort was not ordinarily generous. Nor did it need to be as long as most of the population lived and worked on farms. With the growth of cities and industry, though, living off the land was not so easy. When times were hard people were in trouble. And never were times harder than in the thirties. In 1932, total spending for relief by states, counties, and municipalities (there was no federal relief at the time) came to about $366 million. That averaged out to about $30 a year for each of the 12 million unemployed.

Shortly after Roosevelt's election, an agency called the Federal Emergency Relief Administration began dishing out money. In 1934 relief spending came to about a billion dollars, with more than half the total coming from Washington. The government also began putting the unemployed to work. The Civil Works Administration set up by Harry Hopkins in 1933 was employing more than four million people by mid-January of the following year. The Public Works Administration directed by Harold Ickes moved more slowly, but it was soon building everything from rural post offices to New York's Triborough Bridge. The Civilian Conservation Corps sent unemployed men off to work camps in the country, and the National Youth Administration in seven years "gave part-time employment to more than six hundred thousand college students and to over one and a half million high school students." The Works Progress Administration created in 1935 employed some three million jobless workers.

In 1935, Roosevelt signed into law the Social Security Act. The act created not only the familiar system of payments to the retired but a host of other programs as well: the first national unemployment insurance system, federal aid to families with dependent children (precursor of the best-known "welfare" program today), aid to the blind and the elderly poor. The funding was not large, and a lot of workers were excluded from coverage. But the principle the act embodied helped transform the labor market almost as much as unions did.

Today, Old Age, Survivors, Disability and Health Insurance (OASDHI)—the full name of the social security program —covers most of the working population. In 1980 more than 35 million people were receiving benefits. Those not covered and those without other sources of income are eligible for the Supplemental Security Income program, begun in 1974 and now covering more than four million people. Mothers with young children and no other means of support are eligible for Aid to Families with Dependent Children (AFDC). Most workers who are laid off can get unemployment benefits of roughly half their previous wages for between six and nine months (sometimes up to a year). Some workers get supplemental benefits paid for by their employer or union, often adding up to 90 percent of their average wage. People who lose their jobs because of competition from imports are eligible for additional government aid under the Trade Adjustment Assistance Program.

Medicare pays doctors' fees and hospital bills for the elderly (it's the "health" part of OASDHI). Medicaid, though variable from state to state, does essentially the same for the poor. Everybody with incomes under a certain figure (the cutoff in 1980 was between $800 and $1,000 a month, depending on individual circumstances) can get food stamps from the U.S. Department of Agriculture. All told, "transfer payments" like these add up to more than one eighth of all personal income in the United States. They account for roughly two fifths of the federal government's spending and nearly a third of all government spending (state and local as well as federal).

Theoretically, most of the programs are fully available only to those who are not working. Even social security recipients lose a dollar of benefits for every two dollars they earn (over a certain minimum) up to age 72. "Not working," however, is partly a matter of what else is available. In 1890, nearly seven out of every ten men over sixty-five were either working or looking for work. The proportion now is about two out of ten. If social security did not exist, the figure still might not be as high now as it was in 1890, since Americans are richer now on the average than they used to be. But it would surely be higher than it is.

A similar point can be made about welfare, unemployment insurance, and the like. Those who oppose such programs claim they encourage sloth and degeneracy by making it possible for people to avoid working. The claim is usually overstated: very few people deliberately rely on welfare or unemployment for extended periods of time. But there is a grain of truth in it. Welfare, unemployment insurance, and other transfer payments do make it possible for people to get along for a while without jobs. They also make it possible for employers to lay off workers without consigning them to living out of garbage cans. In the old days this option wasn't available. Hard-pressed employers more frequently cut their workers' wages, and hard-pressed workers more frequently accepted those cuts.

One other modern development keeps wages from falling, at least at the bottom end of the scale: the minimum wage. Again we take it for granted; and again it was a long time coming. The codes of the National Recovery Administration were the first attempt to establish national minimums, but they weren't very effective. Not until the Fair Labor Standards Act of 1938 was a minimum wage enacted. Even that didn't have easy sailing. Southerners in Congress feared, with some justification, that the bill was a conspiracy dreamed up by northern businessmen to undermine the South's cheap-labor factories. The American Federation of Labor, which at first gave the bill a lukewarm endorsement, shortly came out against it. The minimum wage, AFL president William Green noted sagely, "tends to become the maximum."

On May 3, 1938, though, Florida senator Claude Pepper won handily in a well-publicized primary; he owed his victory, by all accounts, to his support for the bill. Within two months the act was law. There were many exemptions. Representative Martin Dies at one point filed a satirical amendment calling for the administration to determine "whether anyone is subject to this bill." Nevertheless, the act covered about 11 million workers, and immediately raised the wages or lowered the hours of more than a million. The initial minimum wage was 25¢ an hour and the maximum work week 44 hours. A year later the minimum rose to 30¢ and the week decreased to 42; an additional 3 million workers benefited.

On January 1, 1981, the minimum wage rose to $3.35 an hour. About 75 million workers are covered by its provisions, including half a million agricultural workers and more than a million household employees; both groups had no coverage at all prior to 1966. The minimum is not inordinately high, at least by historical standards. In 1950, for example, it was more than half of the average hourly earnings of production workers in manufacturing. By 1979 it had dropped to 45 percent of that average.

How the labor market works

If wages were set by supply and demand interacting in something approaching a free labor market, we might expect workers to be paid less in bad times, when unemployment was high and a lot of people were looking for work, and more in good times. In the past that's pretty much how things worked. Now, wages still tend to rise when the economy is booming. But they very rarely fall. Part of the reason, as we have seen, is unions and the fear of unions. Another part is the many government programs that put a "floor" under wages and that make unemployment or retirement more tolerable alternatives than they used to be. A third factor is the peculiar nature of the labor market itself. Some economists, in fact, believe that the labor market's characteristics are as important as unions and government transfers in persuading employers not to cut wages. These economists point out that, though wages used to fall, they usually didn't fall far enough to get rid of unemployment. In this view wages have always been "sticky down," and are just more so today. Three peculiarities of the labor market help keep them so.

1. There is no single labor market. Employers looking for workers do not automatically take the first warm body that walks in the front door. Some want particular skills, experience, or credentials. Others want a particular skin color, sex, or personal manner. Most workers, by the same token, are not looking for the first job that comes along. If they were, our current unemployment rate would ensure that no want ad in the newspaper ran for more than a day. Rather, workers are looking for jobs that match their skills or interests, that are in areas where they have experience, that are easy to get to, that have good fringe benefits or a good future. Some want temporary or part-time work; others are seeking full-time, year-round employment. Some are looking in San Diego, others in Hoboken. If you are unemployed and there are a thousand jobs available in your city, you might consider applying for ten.

2. The wage goes with the job. Jim Rice may be considerably more valuable to the Boston Red Sox than a lesser outfielder and hence commands more money than most. But the difference between one welder, typist, or salesclerk and another is harder to measure; nor are their skills as scarce as Jim Rice's. So employers typically offer the same wage to all applicants: "The job pays $285 a week." What the actual wage is depends more on the region and industry than on an individual's skills or qualifications. The same unskilled laborer who makes the minimum wage packing shrimp in Louisiana will make maybe twice as much working in a northern manufacturing plant. A truck driver's wage may vary by nearly 100 percent depending on the size of the company he works for and what he is hauling. Yet there is no evidence a driver's skills have anything to do with these variables.

3. Labor is the only commodity that has an opinion about what it is worth. It has to be "purchased" over and over again: the employee makes an implicit decision every day about whether to show up for work or quit. Workers who feel they aren't being paid fairly will quit sooner, and in the meantime will be less cooperative and productive. Employers thus have an interest in paying a wage their workers consider fair, not so much for reasons of altruism as for reasons of practicality. A stable, contented work force is worth money. Some employers, in fact, raise their workers' wages whenever they can for precisely this reason. Nearly all refuse to cut wages for the same reason.

All these features of the labor market mean that conventional rules of supply and demand don't necessarily apply in determining labor's "price." Unemployment among West Virginia coal miners—an excess supply of labor, in economic terms—does not lead to lower wages among California aerospace workers. An abundance of competent truck drivers working for small, low-wage firms does not induce big firms to cut the wages of their truckers. A company just starting up will normally pay prevailing wages for its industry or region regardless of the number of applicants for work; anything less would be unfair.

The fairness of a given wage, by and large, seems to be determined not by any absolute standard but by what other people are making. City police compare their wages to those of fire fighters. Auto workers compare theirs to the wages earned by unionized steelworkers. College professors in

Philadelphia look at what college professors in Arizona are making. Government accountants look at what accountants working for banks are getting. Everyone compares their wages to those of their friends, relatives, and neighbors who are similarly situated.

The result is what the labor economist John T. Dunlop long ago christened "wage contours"—patterns of wages that prevail throughout an industry, a profession, a region, or an occupational group. These contours may rise together but usually bear a constant relationship to each other. They may change slowly over time, reflecting shifts in the supply of, and demand for, different kinds of workers. In the short run, though, the contours are a much stronger influence on wages than fluctuations in supply and demand. In 1980, for example, there was a nationwide shortage of nurses, to the point where some hospitals tried offering a "bounty" of $500 to any employee who brought in a registered nurse for employment. Despite the shortage, average nurses' wages were only $6.78 an hour, about the same as a secretary's in many parts of the country.

Raising nurses' pay to, say, $12 an hour (about $25,000 a year, still less than a graduate of the Harvard Business School can expect to make in his or her first job) would undoubtedly work wonders to alleviate this shortage. Older nurses would return to work. Nurses staying home with the children would discover the benefits of day care. Eager students would flock to nursing schools. Hospitals wouldn't necessarily be any worse off in the short run, since they are usually reimbursed for whatever they spend anyway. But the wage contour of the medical profession would be turned inside out. Doctors, medical technicians, lab workers, and orderlies would demand immediate pay hikes. So would dental hygienists, licensed practical nurses, physical therapists, school health officers, and members of a dozen other professions. Employers who responded to these demands with a lesson in the economics of supply and demand would not find themselves winning many arguments. Knowing this, they are unlikely to monkey with nurses' wages in the first place.

Wages, in sum, are determined by employers, but without much leeway. Companies with unionized shops (or shops that are in danger of being unionized) must worry about what the union wants. Companies with low-wage workers have to comply with the minimum-wage laws. All are more likely to lay off workers when business is bad than they are to cut wages. Most employers have to take into account what their employees think of as fair, and what their employees could be making elsewhere or receiving from the government. Most, obviously, do not want to pay more for labor than they have to. But they often have to pay more (and sometimes get to pay less, as with nurses) than simple rules of supply and demand say they "should."

Wages go up, over time, partly because workers expect to get raises, which seems fair, and partly because unions have the power to force them up. They also go up because of the comparison effect of wage contours. All these factors work in only one direction, like a ratchet. Because wages tend to move only one way, prices do too. Both are easy up, sticky down.

The story, however, is not yet complete. In particular, "sticky" does not mean "stuck." It is easier for prices and wages to rise than it is for them to fall. That does not mean that no prices and wages ever fall; nor does it mean they will be equally sticky in all situations. A truly impressive depression, for example, might make both prices and wages come unstuck. In the 1930s, prices of even the goods offered by giant companies dropped some, and wages even in unionized firms fell. Maybe, despite all that has changed since then, another depression of that magnitude would have the same effect. Yet no depression that bad has occurred for forty years, and none is likely to occur in the foreseeable future. To understand why this is so is to understand the last piece of the inflationary puzzle.

5. The Inflationary System:
Government

Inflation, people once thought, was an ailment of the business cycle. When times were good and business was booming, prices rose. When the economy turned down, prices fell.

The logic behind this view is simple enough. In good times, everyone is working. Businesses are investing and consumers are buying. When workers demand higher wages they are likely to get them; employers are feeling optimistic, maybe even generous, and don't want to risk a dissatisfied work force. Prices that are responsive to supply and demand go up because demand is high. Prices that are determined on a cost-plus basis go up too, as wage hikes and other cost increases are passed on to the consumer.

In bad times, the opposite occurs. Demand drops and inventories pile up. Business executives get nervous and don't invest. Workers, fearful for their jobs, don't demand higher wages. Many get laid off anyway as their employers cut back production. Unemployment rises, and consumer spending falls off even more. Business gets worse. With demand down, prices fall.

For a good part of our country's history, the economy boomed and crashed in just this way. Its movements were at times dramatic and painful, but they were largely without long-term effects since in a year or two the tide would turn the other way. Prices rose and fell with the economy as a whole.

Back then, inflation was a boon. It signaled good times: booming production, high wages, cheaper dollars with which to pay off debts. Deflation—falling prices—was the enemy. As prices fell wages were likely to fall too. And debt, figured in real terms, mounted. Paying off a large mortgage with a dollar that takes more time to earn than it used to take is not a happy prospect. Bankers and other lenders, of course, saw things from the opposite perspective, so there were always plenty of loud voices warning against the dangers of inflation. For most, though, a period of rising prices meant prosperity. Economic life may have resembled a roller coaster, but at least it had its ups as well as its downs.

In the 1930s, the roller-coaster ride ended. The economy coasted down the track and just stayed there, instead of going up the next loop. No one, least of all the economists and politicians of the time, had foreseen such a breakdown, and few indeed were more than dimly aware that it had occurred. Most just kept studying the tracks they had already traveled over and predicting that pretty soon the car would get moving again. Happily, one economist saw a little more clearly than most. His name was John Maynard Keynes (rhymes with rains), and he both analyzed the difficulty and prescribed a cure. Over time, most of his prescriptions were adopted, though not always deliberately and not always as Keynes would have wanted.

In the process, the economic roller coaster has been banked, leveled, graded, straightened, and smoothed out to the point where it is almost unrecognizable. The modern Keynesian economy still has its business cycles. If the old cycles were Demolition Derbies, though, the modern ones are amusement-park-style Kiddie Bumper Cars: tame, and not capable of doing too much damage. Almost incidentally, they have lost their capacity to control rising prices.

The story of this change is the story of the growth of government. It begins in the 1930s.

Out of the Depression

Not everyone remembers the Great Depression. Most Americans—about 70 percent, at last count—were born after 1935, when it was half over. Still, it has been widely written up, and nearly everyone knows an anecdote or two from their parents or grandparents. So a few reminders can substitute for a complete description.

Production—gross national product—began to fall even before the famous stock market crash of October 1929. Total GNP dropped 30 percent in the four years after the crash. Investment levels fell nearly 90 percent. In 1932 the steel industry was operating at about 12 percent of capacity. Automobile production was off 65 percent, residential construction 95 percent. Eighty-five thousand businesses failed, notes the economist Robert L. Heilbroner, and by 1933 "the average standard of living was back where it had been twenty years before."

Unemployment was highest in the industrial cities and regions. About two fifths of Chicago's workers were out of a job by October 1931. In Detroit roughly a third were jobless, in Cincinnati about a quarter. There was no unemployment insurance and little welfare. Needy families in Cincinnati got $7 or $8 a week, the equivalent of maybe $35 or $40 today. In rural Pennsylvania families got $8 to $12 a month. In Chicago, writes the historian Lester V. Chandler, the unemployed "had lost $2 million of wages a day, but only $100,000 a day was available for relief. Help was being given only to the totally destitute."

Somewhere between one million and two million people, mostly men, took to the road. Many "threw together makeshift shacks of boxes and scrap metal" that were known as Hoovervilles. The largest was in St. Louis. Others could be found below Riverside Drive in New York City, under the Pulaski Skyway in New Jersey, "along the banks of the Tennessee in Knoxville," and "in the huge dumps off Blue Island Avenue in Chicago." There was "scarcely a city that did not harbor at least one" such settlement.

Wage cuts began in earnest in 1931 and continued in 1932. A National Industrial Conference Board study of a number of businesses found that 90 percent had lowered wages and salaries by about a fifth. Farm workers' wages fell by half. Counting both the employed and the unemployed, American workers as a group were earning only 60 percent (80 percent in real terms) of what they had earned before the Depression.

Two questions about the Depression plague those who have grown up after World War II. One is how people survived. Some of course didn't; they died from starvation or lack of medical care. Some others, writes Lester V. Chandler, "would have met the same end if they had been too proud to paw through garbage for scraps of food." But most managed to get by one way or another. The twenties had been relatively prosperous, and many people had some savings or assets (a house, for instance) to borrow against. For those without resources, grocers sometimes extended credit, at least until they too went broke. Landlords often refused to evict tenants who couldn't pay the rent; some were kind, others simply realized they couldn't rent the apartments to anyone else anyway. People pulled together. The "invisible relief" of help from family, neighbors, and friends probably kept a lot of people from starving.

The other question is why people put up with it for so long—why, in short, the government didn't do something. The answer is apparent from the history sketched above, but it is still surprising to the modern ear. Depressions were a part of life. Government wasn't expected to do anything about them, and wouldn't have known what to do in any case.

Just ten years before the crash of 1929, for example, America experienced a sharp postwar slowdown. Output fell over 15 percent between 1918 and 1921. Unemployment rose to nearly 12 percent in 1921. Yet by 1922 the economy was on the mend: in that year GNP rose 16 percent. Nor were the early twenties unique. The nation had experienced panics, crashes, and crises throughout the nineteenth century (including a five-year slump in the 1870s) and again in 1907. "We have been passing," said Herbert Hoover in May 1930, "through one of those great economic storms which periodically bring hardship and suffering upon our people.

A RECESSION BY ANY OTHER NAME

During the last century and until 1907, the United States had panics, and that, unabashedly, was what they were called. But, by 1907, language was becoming, like so much else, the servant of economic interest. To minimize the shock to confidence, businessmen and bankers had started to explain that any current economic setback was not really a panic, only a crisis. They were undeterred by the use of this term in a much more ominous context—that of the ultimate capitalist crisis—by Marx. By the 1920s, however, the word crisis had also acquired the fearsome connotation of the event it described. Accordingly, men offered reassurance by explaining that it was not a crisis, only a depression. A very soft word. Then the Great Depression associated the most frightful of economic misfortunes with that term, and economic semanticists now explained that no depression was in prospect, at most only a recession. In the 1950s, when there was a modest setback, economists and public officials were united in denying that it was a recession—only a sidewise movement or a rolling readjustment. Mr. Herbert Stein, the amiable man whose difficult honor it was to serve as the economic voice of Richard Nixon, would have referred to the panic of 1893 as a growth correction.

—JOHN KENNETH GALBRAITH,
Money, p. 103.

While the crash only took place six months ago, I am convinced that we have now passed the worst and with continued unity of effort we shall rapidly recover." In the light of history, Hoover's statement is both less Panglossian and less disingenuous than it sounds today. Like most other Americans, he had little reason to believe that this was the storm that would very nearly capsize the ship.

By the economic theory of the day, depressions were self-correcting. As production fell, wages and prices would too. So would the rate of interest, since with nobody doing much borrowing the supply of money would be greater than the demand for it. Eventually labor, money, and everything else would get so cheap that businesses would find it profitable to invest. A few would do so, putting some people back to work and putting more money in circulation. Then a few more would do so, and the economy would gradually get moving.

In the thirties, however, the theory didn't work. Economists and historians disagree about the reasons, but at least three factors seem important. For one thing, the economy was no longer a collection of farms and small businesses. Investing in a steel mill or an automobile plant is a little different from plowing an extra field or putting a new wing on your shoemaking shop; it requires both more money and more optimism about the prospects. So investment lagged and kept on lagging.

Second, wages and prices fell, but not as far or as fast as they once had. Only agriculture behaved the way economists expected it to. There, wages and prices both fell by half. In industry, however, wage cuts were not so dramatic, and the real wages of those who kept their jobs fell scarcely at all. Industrial prices dropped, but not as much as other prices.

Third, interest rates were not allowed to move freely, and wouldn't have made much difference anyway. Since its inception in 1914, the Federal Reserve Board had lent money to banks belonging to the Federal Reserve System at what is termed the discount rate. When the board thought the economy should be slowed, it would raise the discount rate. Banks would then find it more expensive to borrow money and would raise their own loan rates. When the Fed thought the economy should be stimulated, it would lower the discount rate, with the opposite effect. The Fed's thinking, however, was not always clear. In 1921, with the economy in recession, it raised the discount rate to an unprecedented level of 6 percent, thus making the recession worse. In 1929 and 1930 it let the interest rate fall, but slowly.

Nevertheless, the rate reached 1.5 percent in 1931. If cheap money were enough to make business pick up, business should have picked up. It didn't. The reason—this was one of Keynes's main insights—was that business executives may not think they can make a profit on investment no matter how little it costs to borrow money. If things look bleak enough—and they did, with so many people out of work and factories lying idle—only a fool would think about building a new plant.

The only thing that would get the economy going again, Keynes saw, was for someone to spend money. Consumers couldn't; most of them were just barely getting by as it was. Businesses wouldn't, since the prospects for making money looked so gloomy. The only part of the economy that could be made to spend money was the government. So the government, Keynes argued, should borrow and spend as much as it possibly could. All that spending would create jobs, put money in people's pockets, lead to higher consumer spending and better business conditions. It would "prime the pump," and pretty soon the water would begin to flow of its own accord.

Roosevelt's administration, for the most part, never understood this theory. The federal government's spending did go up, from $4.6 billion in 1933 to $8.8 billion in 1939. But the increase was due more to pragmatic problem-solving than to conscious economic policy. If the administration had known what it was doing, it wouldn't have made so many mistakes. In 1937, for example, another downturn was threatening the still-shaky recovery from the depths of 1933. Yet Roosevelt reduced government spending. Partly as a result, says William Leuchtenburg, the economy in 1938 "plunged downhill" and Roosevelt "did not know how to stop it."

What pulled the country out of the Depression was precisely what Keynes had advocated: massive government spending. The reason for all the spending, though, was not the New Deal's war against poverty and unemployment, such as it was; it was the Allies' war against the Germans and the Japanese. By 1942 the federal government's outlays had risen to almost four times their 1939 level and over seven times what they had been in 1932. Unemployment virtually disappeared and production skyrocketed. America was back at work, the Depression over.

Stabilizing the economy

Depression never came back. Despite fears of a postwar slump, the economy rapidly converted to peacetime operation. Production kept rising, and unemployment stayed low. To be sure, we still get recessions, seven since the end of World War II, counting the most recent (which started in 1980). But by historical standards these are pretty puny affairs. The longest and worst postwar slump to date took place in 1974 and 1975. Real output fell an average of 1.3 percent a year for two years, and unemployment among nonfarm workers peaked at just under 10 percent. The recession of 1919–21 by contrast, never mind the Great Depression itself, saw output fall an average of more than 5 percent a year for three years and nonfarm unemployment rise to almost 20 percent.

Not coincidentally prices fell by a fair measure in 1920 and 1921. In 1974 and 1975 the rate of inflation eventually slowed, but prices kept going up. Whipping inflation, evidently, requires a good old-fashioned slump, not one of the delicate modern variety. Unhappily for inflation-whippers the modern economy does not easily lend itself to old-fashioned slumps. The reason can be summed up in a word: government. Five major developments since 1932—some attributable to Keynes's ideas, others to the exigencies of modern life and politics—have reshaped government's economic role. As a result we now have an economy that is largely protected against depressions of the 1930s variety. We also have one that is inordinately vulnerable to inflation.

The five changes are of course interrelated. All, in different ways, mark a tremendous increase in the importance of what transpires in Washington.

1. Government employment

In 1929, the federal government employed 579,559 civilians. Just over half worked for the Post Office. Not quite 20 percent were attached to the War and Navy departments. Only about 30 percent of the total—180,000 people—worked for every other branch of the federal government. Counting both these civilian employees and the military (roughly 255,000 soldiers, sailors, and marines), the federal government in 1929 employed slightly less than 2 percent of the labor force. State and local governments employed another 2.5 million, or about 5 percent of the labor force. All told, one American worker in fifteen worked for government at some level.

Today the Defense Department alone employs more civilians (almost a million) than the whole federal government did back then. The federal government as a whole employs nearly 3 million civilians and more than 2 million military personnel on active duty. State and local employment has burgeoned to almost 13 million. Counting the armed forces, government at some level now employs about 17 percent of the labor force. Indirect government employment—people working for firms with government contracts, for example—has been estimated to include another 11 percent of the labor force. So more than a quarter of U.S. workers depend directly or indirectly on government expenditure.

From the employee's point of view, working for the government is pleasant because you seldom get laid off. The well-publicized cutbacks of city workers during the past few years don't contradict this statement, they're just the exception that proves the rule. When twenty police officers lose their jobs it's a scandal; when two thousand rubber workers lose theirs it's a fact of life. Unemployment rates for people who have worked in government are lower than for any other major occupational group: they're usually less than half the national average. The reason, of course, is that businesses lay off some workers any time sales drop, or whenever the future looks bleak. Governments don't face the same constraints. Only when a particular jurisdiction finds it hard to raise taxes—New York City, for instance, or Cleveland—will it even begin to think about layoffs. And even then the federal government (which always has plenty of money, for reasons we'll get to shortly) can often be called in to help.

From the economist's point of view, all these government workers are an immense stabilizing force on the economy. When business is slow, industries begin laying off workers. Production falls; so does purchasing power. Immediately things look worse than they did before. So more businesses lay off workers, and the downturn gets more severe. Not so with the government. Business may be bad, but children still have to be taught, the roads maintained, and criminals put in jail. Moreover, Congress may decide to fund a new missile system or build a new dam—thereby increasing government employment—precisely *because* business looks bad. Thus the business cycle is stabilized or even counteracted by a large government sector.

2. Transfer payments

State and local employment has grown considerably in recent years. It doubled, for example, between 1960 and 1978. Civilian and military federal employment, however, has increased only a little since the late forties and has actually fallen off in the last ten years. What has accounted for the recent growth in federal spending is transfer payments.

As the last chapter observed, transfer payments are essentially an invention of the last fifty years. In 1929 about the only money the federal government paid out to individuals other than its employees went to veterans and bondholders. In 1979 transfer payments (*excluding* interest on bonds) came to more than $200 billion, or roughly 40 percent of total federal outlays. In the 1970s alone transfer payments increased 76 percent in real terms.

When numbers like these appear in the newspaper, irate citizens frequently conclude that welfare recipients are gobbling up more and more of their tax dollars. In fact most of the transfer payments represent programs that we don't usually think of as "welfare." A hypothetical tax dollar going to transfer payments—hypothetical only because the taxes that actually pay for these programs come from many different sources—would be divided up this way: About 75¢ goes to cash benefits—45¢ to social security, 10¢ to retired federal employees, 5¢ apiece to veterans, welfare recipients, the unemployed, and miscellaneous other beneficiaries. The other 25¢ goes to in-kind benefits: food stamps, public housing, and (the largest) Medicare.

From the recipient's point of view, these transfers make retirement or lack of work a lot more tolerable than they otherwise might be. They also provide something of an alternative to jobs that pay too little, or jobs where the employer tries to cut wages. From the point of view of the whole economy, transfers are a tremendously important way of stabilizing purchasing power. The poor and the elderly have considerably more income to spend than they otherwise might. Workers who lose their jobs get unemployment benefits, giving them some money to spend too. In the past, even the threat of a slump led people to cut their spending; the slump itself might reduce their incomes to zero. Today recessions can be painful, but our incomes fall nowhere near as far or as fast as they once did. So the downturn is apt to be less severe, and recovery that much quicker.*

3. Fiscal policy

Government spending of all kinds adds up to about a third of gross national product. Washington's disbursements alone account for more than a fifth of GNP. (Though state and local governments employ more people, the federal government's enormous transfer payments give it a much bigger budget.) All this spending helps anchor the economy through the business cycle, maintaining people's purchasing power during bad times and good. The federal budget plays another role too: it can counteract the business cycle by running in deficit when the economy is slow and running in surplus when the economy is booming. This "countercyclical" effect, as economists term it, reflects the government's "fiscal" or tax-and-spending policies.

A budget surplus is simple enough to understand. Washington, in effect, is taking more money out of the economy than it is putting back in. So purchasing power is less than it otherwise would be. Less gets bought, less is produced, and the economy slows down. Insofar as that eases pressure on prices and wages, inflation should slow down too.

---

* Readers with a logical turn of mind or a little training in economics will realize that where the money for transfer payments comes from is just as important as where it goes. Other things being equal, after all, a transfer payment that gives Mr. Jones $100 to spend may reduce Mr. Smith's income by the same amount, and purchasing power won't change a bit.

In general, people with lower incomes spend a higher proportion of their money than people with higher incomes. (The latter are more apt to save some instead of spending it.) So if you take $100 from a rich man and give it to a poor one, chances are that more of it will be spent. By and large, transfer payments like social security, unemployment, and welfare take money from those who are working and give it to those who would otherwise have little or no money. So more money is spent and total purchasing power rises.

Deficits are a little harder to comprehend but not much. The key to understanding federal deficits is to remember that the government is simply borrowing the extra money that it's spending. The factory worker who buys saving bonds on a payroll deduction plan and the New York bank that buys a million dollars' worth of Treasury bills are both lending the government money to cover its deficit. As the government borrows, the national debt increases. But this is not, in most cases, a cause for alarm. Just as a company can borrow more and more every year as long as business is good and the firm is growing, the government can borrow more and more as long as the economy is growing. The national debt has increased in dollar terms every year since 1950. But debt as a proportion of GNP has grown smaller almost every year. The debt "burden" on the taxpayers is thus decreasing, despite the fact that government deficits in the 1970s hit record levels.*

More worrisome than the national debt is what might happen if the government does *not* run a deficit. Without a defi-

---

* "Burden" is the wrong word in any case. To understand why, imagine what would happen if the debt were suddenly paid off. A company that is in debt owes money to "outsiders"—banks, bondholders, and so forth. A government that is in debt owes money for the most part to its own taxpaying citizens. Suppose Congress votes tomorrow to pay off the national debt this year. The move requires a stiff new tax—nearly $800 billion worth—but Congress passes it, the taxpayers pay it, and everyone holding a U.S. government security is paid off.

The immediate effect is an enormous redistribution of income. Those who own no government bonds are a lot poorer, those who own many are a lot richer, in cash terms. But the bondholders no longer have the assets they once had. No savings bonds for their old age; no Treasury bonds to pass on to their grandchildren. Doubtless they will be looking for something to do with all their newfound cash. Doubtless too the federal government will want to borrow some money to finance all the food stamps, unemployment benefits, and the like made necessary by the tax-induced impoverishment of everybody else. Maybe the people who have just been paid off would like to lend their money again—U.S. government bonds, after all, are probably the safest investment in the world. So the debt, in a short time, is re-created.

cit there's a good chance that purchasing power (economists call it aggregate demand) won't be sufficient to keep the economy going at full speed. Why this should be so is no mystery. Suppose, for example, that you make $20,000 a year. According to the way these things are figured, you have produced $20,000 worth of goods or services that somebody now has to buy. But you may not want to spend your whole $20,000. You may want to put a little in the bank, or maybe buy some stocks or bonds. In good times, businesses are looking for ways to expand: building a new plant, say, or replacing old machinery with the latest model. To do so they need to borrow money. So they sell you a bond, or they go to the same bank you put your savings in, borrow your savings, and spend it. In that case every dollar that has been earned gets spent, and the economy keeps humming.

But suppose business looks bad, and companies aren't doing much investing. Your savings, and everybody else's, start to pile up in the banks. Now you have "produced" more dollars than you're spending. Everybody else who's doing any saving has done the same thing. Unsold goods begin to pile up on the shelves. Companies notice this and begin to cut back production. A recession threatens.

Here's where the government steps in. If it borrows your money (either directly or from the bank) and spends it, the money you saved will stay in circulation. Everything that is produced will be bought. No unsold goods on the shelves, no cutbacks. In fact business will look good: companies too will want to borrow so they can expand, and the economy will grow. But note that the government must run a deficit in order to assure this happy result. It must spend all it takes in in taxes, borrow some more, and spend that too. It has to spend your savings as well as its "own" money. It can run a surplus only when it's willing to risk recession (to fight inflation, say), or when it believes that business will invest enough on its own to keep the economy hopping.

The government budget's countercyclical effect varies automatically with what the rest of the economy is doing. When unemployment rises, spending for jobless benefits and other relief programs goes up too. Yet tax revenues fall, since people who aren't working don't pay taxes. So the federal balance sheet tilts toward a deficit. When the economy is booming, on the other hand, tax revenues rise and spending falls, thereby tending to create a surplus.

In principle, whatever administration is in power sets its fiscal policy by adjusting tax and spending levels to achieve the desired effect. If recession threatens, the government should cut taxes or increase spending, thereby boosting purchasing power. If inflation is thought to be the greater danger, the supposed cure is to increase taxes or reduce spending. In real life, of course, the choice is seldom so simple. The trade-off between inflation and recession (as we shall see in Chapter Eight) is not always clear. And political considerations always impart a certain asymmetry to fiscal policy changes. Any politician will find it easier to cut taxes than to raise them. Politicians will also find it easier to increase spending, thereby keeping various interest groups and federal agencies happy, than to cut it.

Fiscal policy therefore more often focuses on stimulating the economy than on slowing it down. In the past twenty years the budget has been in significant surplus exactly twice. The result is higher levels of employment and fewer (or milder) recessions than we otherwise might have had. Another result, probably, is more inflation.

4. Monetary policy

Like an engine that runs on gasoline, the economy runs on money. If there isn't enough, the economy won't run very fast, and will be prone to fits and starts. Plenty of money will not, all by itself, ensure a fast-growing, smoothly working economy; you still need people, businesses, and governments willing and able to spend that money. But if you don't have the money you can't have the spending.

The word "money" in ordinary parlance usually refers to currency: bills and coins. Those who accuse the government of cheapening the dollar frequently accuse it of "printing too much money," as if the presses that turn out $5 bills were working overtime. In reality, of course, most of what we use as money isn't currency at all; it's the "money" that is in our checking accounts.

This money is neither more nor less than a bookkeeping account on the bank's ledgers. It is created, in part, by the banking system itself.

Suppose, for example, you take $1,000 in cash to a bank and open an account. You now have a brand-new checkbook, and you know you can write checks up to a total of $1,000. Suppose at the same time your neighbor applies to the same bank for a loan of $1,000. When she gets the loan, the bank doesn't necessarily give her your $1,000 in cash; more likely it gives her a checkbook too and credits her account with $1,000. Now you and she have a total of $2,000 to draw on, but the bank, let us assume, only has your original $1,000 in currency. As long as neither of you wants $1,000 in cash at the same time, the bank is sitting pretty. By this process the supply of money—that is, the total deposits the banking system carries on its books—grows well beyond the volume of cash that is in circulation at any given time.

Obviously, however, there has to be some limit on the amount of money so created. If banks lend mony to all comers, they'll soon find themselves in trouble. And if the banking system creates too much money in relation to what there is to buy, the excess purchasing power will drive prices up. The dollar will be worth less, then, simply because there are too many dollars in circulation.

The growth of the money supply can be limited in two ways. One is the way of "hard" money, fiscal responsibility, reliance on the market. The other is the way of "soft" money and political interference with the market. By all the standards of good conservatism, the first sounds preferable. When it was tried, however, it had two rather severe drawbacks. Coping with these drawbacks led to the inflationary monetary system we have today.

Under the traditional system of managing the money supply (in effect in this country throughout much of the nineteenth century and changed only gradually in the twentieth) every paper dollar is theoretically redeemable in gold. The government can issue only as much currency as it can safely cover with the gold in its vaults. Banks have to have access to enough currency or gold to satisfy any of their depositors who want it. The gold standard thus imposes rather severe limits on how fast the money supply can grow.

A country's gold supply depends on how much of the metal is being mined, and on how much is coming in from abroad to purchase goods and services. Its need for money, however, depends on how much real economic activity there is—how much people want to borrow and spend. If people want to borrow and spend more money than is easily available with the existing gold supply, interest rates shoot up. Banks make fewer loans, and businesses don't invest. The supply of money can thus limit economic growth. It may even provoke a recession. That's why the Populists—William Jennings Bryan and his followers, for instance—fought so hard against the gold standard. If more money were available (if, for example, all the currency could be backed by silver as well as gold), then booms would be longer, panics fewer. The price to be paid—inflation—was one the Populists were willing to pay.

In a series of steps beginning with Roosevelt's 1933 ban on gold transactions and ending with Nixon's renunciation of the international gold standard in 1971, the United States went "off gold." The particular reasons for each step were different. Ultimately, however, gold is too inflexible a standard for a rapidly growing economy. If we were still on the gold standard, we would either be limiting ourselves to a very slow rate of growth (essentially the rate at which gold could be obtained) or else we would constantly be making the dollar worth less in terms of the amount of gold it would buy. The former choice would be disastrous for the economy. The latter, though theoretically possible, would appear to undermine ("devalue") the currency repeatedly by deliberate government action. A rapidly expanding economy can't work with a money supply that is fixed either by fiat or by custom, any more than a growing number of automobiles can easily run on the oil produced by a fixed number of wells.

So the dollar today has no "gold backing" at all. If you take a $1 bill to the Treasury and ask for metal you will probably be given a Susan B. Anthony copper-and-nickel coin, worth less than 3¢ melted down. Instead, limits on the money supply are set, through a variety of devices, by the Federal Reserve System. The Fed tells banks how much money they can lend in proportion to their "reserves" (currency and money the banks keep on deposit at the Fed). It sets the discount rate at which it will loan money to banks, thus influencing other interest rates. And it buys and sells government securities on the open market, thus pumping money into the system (when it buys) or taking money out of the system (when it sells).

The details of these procedures are intricate. The only people who really care about them are those who get paid to do so. For the rest of us, the important point is simple enough. The rate at which the money supply is allowed to grow is now determined not by gold or any other impersonal force, but by the Federal Reserve. The Fed officials who determine how fast the money supply will grow are not elected, but they are appointed by the president and are not wholly insensitive either to his wishes or to Congress. If they keep too tight a lid on the money supply, recession is likely to threaten. Recessions are not popular with elected officials, particularly with presidents seeking reelection. In ordinary times, therefore, the Fed has a strong incentive to let the money supply grow. As it does, prices tend to rise.

Fiscal and monetary policy—tax-and-spending policies on the one hand, regulating the money supply on the other—fit together in an important way. In real life, there is no such thing as running a deficit exactly big enough to make sure that "everything that is produced will be bought," as in the simplified explanation above. Instead the government tries to run whatever deficit it thinks is necessary to stimulate the economy. An expanding economy, however, typically re-quires *new* money, which is exactly what the Fed provides when it buys a bond from the Treasury.* The deficit is thus "monetized," in the language of economics, and both total spending and the money supply expand.

On the other side of the ledger, an expansionary fiscal pol-icy ensures that expansionary monetary policy will work. In the 1930s, remember, the money supply didn't grow despite the rock-bottom interest rates: nobody was doing any borrow-ing. A big government deficit, though, means that new money will automatically be spent. Again, total spending and the money supply increase together.

5. The end of "panics"

The old monetary system's second drawback was that it relied largely on prudence (and the marketplace) to enforce its constraints. A prudent banker, in theory, would lend only as much as he could safely "cover" with gold or currency. Despite their carefully cultivated image, however, bankers are seldom more prudent or less greedy than other human beings. So in practice the operating principle was let the de-positor beware. If you put your money in a bank that wasn't run carefully, so much the worse for you.

What happened was this. If a panic was in the air, or if some depositors began to get nervous about a bank's financial soundness, a lot of them might show up at the teller's window all at once, demanding cash. If the depositors wanted more cash than the bank had or could get, it had to close for a while. Now it was really in trouble. When it reopened, vir-tually every depositor would be waiting in line to take out

---

* The Fed typically pays for its bonds by crediting the Treasury's ac-count on its books. The effect is the same as if it paid for the bonds with newly printed Federal Reserve Notes (currency).

his or her money. In most cases there was no way the bank could get enough cash to satisfy all its depositors. So it simply shut up shop. In the language of the time, a "run" on the bank led to its "failure."

Banks often failed in groups, not only because similar economic circumstances affected them all, but also because a bank failure in the next neighborhood might make depositors in your neighborhood worry about their own bank. Between 1870 and 1900 at least ten banks in the United States failed every single year. In each of four years, more than a hundred banks failed, and in one year (1893), nearly five hundred went under. In the twentieth century things got worse. Between 1900 and 1920 dozens of banks failed every year. From 1920 through 1929 at least 500 banks closed their doors almost every year. When the Depression hit, the number soared to more than 1,000 a year. In 1933, more than 4,000 banks shut down.

When banks failed, their deposits vanished into the depths of bankruptcy proceedings; with luck, depositors might get a little money back when the assets and liabilities of the bank were toted up. But frequently the deposits vanished into thin air. The 4,000 banks that closed in 1933, for example, took with them some $3.6 billion in deposits. The money supply could thus contract violently at any point, causing untold hardship to people's lives and livelihoods and significantly worsening any incipient slump. People whose checking accounts have just disappeared are not likely to win prizes for big spending. And banks that have just gone under aren't likely to be making many loans.

In 1933, Congress passed and Roosevelt signed the Glass-Steagall Act, a law reforming the banking system. A major provision of the act provided for the separation of investment banks from commercial banks. A minor provision, not much noticed at the time, established the Federal Deposit Insurance Corporation. The new FDIC insured bank deposits up to $5,000 per depositor. Over the years that limit has been raised: it now insures bank deposits up to $100,000 per depositor.

In one little-noticed swoop the fear that had led to runs on banks was legislated out of existence. If deposits were insured by the government, there was no need to make sure they were there. Over a period of years, bank failures grew rare. In the 1970s, exactly eleven banks failed. Thanks to the FDIC, little money was lost by depositors. In most cases, the failed banks were simply taken over by healthy ones in the banker's equivalent of a shotgun marriage.

The government has set up other mechanisms as well to prevent the kind of panic that in the past usually preceded a slump. The Federal Reserve sets limits ("margin requirements") on how much stock you can buy with money borrowed from your broker, thus preventing the wild stock speculation that preceded the Crash of 1929. The Securities and Exchange Commission and the Commodity Futures Trading Commission regulate offerings and procedures in the financial markets. The FDIC, however, is probably the most important, because bank failures affect not only public confidence but the actual supply of money. In recent years some have argued that the FDIC is in trouble, because its reserve funds have been steadily shrinking in proportion to the amount of insured deposits. So far it has passed all its tests, including helping to rescue the mammoth First Pennsylvania Corporation in 1980, an endeavor that involved nearly $500 million in assistance to the financially troubled bank. If the FDIC does get in trouble in the future, so will the monetary system that has so far kept economic slumps from worsening as rapidly as they once did.

The inflationary system

With this chapter, most of the pieces that make up the jigsaw puzzle of inflation are now in place.

If prices responded directly to supply and demand—the way they do on the stock market, say—they would rise and fall with equal facility. They don't. Supply, demand, and prices themselves are manipulated in most parts of the economy in a variety of ways. Giant industrial firms control their own markets and strenuously avoid price cutting whenever possible. Smaller firms are sometimes big enough in their own markets to get away with the same behavior. Plumbers, lawyers, and a host of other tradespeople make sure they don't have too many competitors by setting up stringent rules about who is allowed to practice. Some try to work on fixed fee schedules as well. Farmers, doctors, home builders, and electric utility companies sell their goods or services at prices that are determined or propped up by the government. The marketplace, in short, is rigged. People have found ways to protect themselves from the market's invisible hand. Prices can still go up, but they go down only with difficulty.

The same is true of wages. Unions, or an employer's fear of unions, can usually protect workers against wage cuts. Minimum wage laws and income-transfer payments help protect workers at the low end of the scale from wage cuts. Moreover, workers have opinions about what constitutes a fair day's pay. An employer who cuts wages below the standard does so at his peril.

A real depression might shake this whole applecart. It might break the conventions that keep wages from falling. It might make companies desperate enough for sales that they would begin to slash prices. It might make the government so poor that it could no longer afford health care for all, tax breaks for homeowners, price supports for farmers, and bailouts for endangered companies. A depression of this magnitude, however, is unlikely. The government itself employs so many people that the economy isn't as vulnerable to the business cycle as it once was. Government transfer payments help maintain purchasing power when people can't find work. Budget deficits ensure that total spending keeps up with production. A regulated banking system under the Fed's control allows the money supply to expand as required and protect it from violent contractions. Booms are thus fed, busts cushioned. The slumps that we do get seem no longer capable of wringing inflation out of the economy.

All these developments, in short, have created a system where inflation is hard to avoid. If prices are to fall as well as rise, then the economy must contract sharply as well as expand. Workers must be willing to accept wage cuts, and prices must be driven down by competition. As a nation we have learned to protect ourselves from these grim possibilities. But that very protection leads to inflation. Wage hikes and price increases ripple through the economy, driving other prices up. There is no comparable force driving prices down.

There is, however, one more piece of the puzzle still to be laid in place. Most of the institutions, policies, and practices described so far were in operation by the end of World War II. Yet for twenty years from 1945 to 1965 inflation was almost always gentle, with prices going up a percent or two a year. In the mid-1960s someone apparently kicked the throttle up a couple of notches, and in recent years the engines seem to have been running on All Ahead Full. To understand *this* inflation—the double-digit variety, the kind that makes headlines in the newspapers and seems to eat holes in our wallets—we need to look not just at a system but at the peculiar history of the last fifteen years.

6. Why Things Got Worse in the 1970s

Nazi Germany surrendered to the Allies on May 7, 1945. Three months later, on August 6 and 9, the United States dropped atomic bombs on the Japanese cities of Hiroshima and Nagasaki. Japan surrendered on August 14, 1945, and World War II was over.

In 1946 the troops came home. Factories shut down their wartime production lines, and America's gross national product fell nearly 12 percent. Inflation, held in check by price controls during the war, hit 8 percent soon after the controls were lifted. The next year things got worse. Output continued to fall for a while, and prices jumped even more. War, true to form, had been hell. Now peace was starting to look like some kind of economic purgatory, haunted on the one side by the ghost of the Depression and on the other by the specter of runaway inflation.

During the next twenty years, that purgatory would be transformed into Hog Heaven. Homes in the suburbs, Buicks in the garages, chickens in every pot.

Not that the apparitions vanished immediately. But it seemed, just as it had before the war, that the one scared away the other. In 1948 inflation looked bad but production was booming. In 1949 and 1950 the economy slid downhill but inflation disappeared altogether. (Prices actually fell a little between December 1948 and December 1949.) During the 1950s periods of good times and modest inflation alternated with periods of mild recession. But the economy grew more than 3 percent a year in real terms: Americans were getting progressively richer.

In the early 1960s the pace picked up and the specters disappeared. John F. Kennedy, campaigning against Eisenhower's vice president during the last of Eisenhower's recessions, promised to "get this country moving again." A few more people (about 119,000 out of a total vote for both candidates of over 68 million) thought he would do a better job of it than Richard M. Nixon. They may have been right. Production rose 6.6 percent between 1961 and 1962, about double the average annual growth rate of the previous decade. From then on it went up 4, 5, or 6 percent every year: no more recessions. Prices kept inching upward, but even more slowly than they had in the fifties. Up to 1966, inflation under Presidents Kennedy and Johnson was never more than 1.9 percent a year.

A growing economy with plenty for all, low unemployment, steady prices: such was the vision of what Henry Luce had first christened the American Century. There was more to it, of course. America was also to lead the Free World, to fight communism, to instruct the unwashed in the virtues of democracy and free enterprise. And it would have to do something about the poverty and discrimination that were slowly entering the national consciousness at home. But none of this was possible without a strong, growing economy. And it looked as if the Democrats in the early 1960s had somehow found the secret. As GNP rose, America's promise seemed boundless.

Now, fifteen years have passed and the vision has collapsed. What seemed like the Promised Land feels today like a fool's paradise.

The changes came almost unnoticeably. During those fifteen years, American armed forces lost a minor war but no major one. The nation's physical security was no more threatened than it had been in the era of Kennedy, Khrushchev, and the Cuban missile crisis. No depression destroyed the American economy; despite a couple of recessions it continued to grow nearly as fast as it had in the good years. But in the end events teamed up to overwhelm some of the power and most of the promise of the American empire. Vietnam, and the protest it engendered; Watergate; the energy crisis; and finally the Iranian hostages all combined to create and reinforce an image of America as a helpless giant, corrupt and corrupting, an idea whose time was past.

Behind the general disillusion was a real decline in the United States's capacity to control international events. Also behind it were some new economic realities. Productivity, or output per hour, rose less than half as fast in the 1970s as in the two previous decades. Factory workers' real wages rose by half between 1950 and 1969; since then they have increased scarcely at all. Unemployment in the seventies averaged more than a full percentage point higher than unemployment in the fifties and sixties.

Nowhere was the difference so marked or so widely felt as in the rate of inflation. Some of the gloomy contrasts have been mentioned in earlier chapters. For the two decades beginning in 1950, the Consumer Price Index rose an average of just over 2 percent a year. In the 1970s it went up an average of about 7 percent a year. The long-term inflation rate, in other words, more than tripled. Between the Korean War and 1965, the *most* prices rose in any one year was 3 percent in 1957. Since 1970 the *least* they have risen is 3.4 percent (in 1971 and 1972). The average annual price rise for the last decade is more than double the highest annual increase between 1951 and 1968. In 1974 and again in 1979, inflation hit double digits.

As the inflation rate got worse, pundits and politicians began to single out villains. The Vietnam War was a logical candidate until the war ended and prices kept going up. Nixon's inept and contradictory economic policies came in for their share of the blame too, though Nixon's defenders correctly observed that he was not the first president in recent memory to pursue inept and contradictory policies. In the early 1970s a variety of random occurrences—a failure of the anchovy crop off the coast of Peru, a bad harvest in the Soviet Union—seemed to be contributing to rising prices. The Organization of Petroleum Exporting Countries (OPEC) too was a favorite culprit, though those who traced all our difficulties to "the Arabs" weren't always sure why inflation had been so bad before the 1973 oil embargo.

All these villains did play a part in the drama, of course, and the rest of this chapter will explain each one's role. Spotlighting the actors, however, should not blind us to the sets, stages, and theaters where they're performing: without the economic structures described in the preceding chapters, what happened during the seventies might have turned out quite differently. Then too, the important actors weren't always the ones that got star billing. Those who manipulate the murky world of international finance, for example, turned up frequently on center stage, though the audience's attention as often as not was elsewhere. Inflation in the seventies was a curious morality play in which most of us, most of the time, weren't quite sure what was happening. The only certainty was that prices kept on going up.

Wartime deficits, recession, and controls

Beginning in 1966 or so, successive administrations pursued policies that were remarkably effective in stimulating inflation. Policies that might have curbed it were postponed, curtailed, or never even considered.

• On June 29, 1966, American pilots began bombing Hanoi, the capital city of North Vietnam. The signal was unmistakable: henceforth it would be the United States's war, not just the South Vietnamese government's, to win or lose. By the end of 1966, U.S. troop levels in South Vietnam had risen to 385,000—more than double the number of a year earlier—with another 100,000 stationed offshore or in Thailand. In the next two years an additional 160,000 arrived, bringing the total to over half a million before withdrawals began in 1969.

The fighting required hefty increases in the Pentagon's budget. Military spending rose from not quite $50 billion in 1965 to $55 billion in 1966 and almost $70 billion in 1967, finally peaking at nearly $80 billion in 1969. After stalling as long as he could, Johnson asked Congress for a surtax to pay for the war's costs in 1967. As the president expected, Congress was not pleased with the prospect of raising taxes to pay for an unpopular conflict and took months to accede to the request. By the time the new tax was enacted in June 1968, the federal budget deficit had climbed to $25 billion.

By today's standards that deficit looks small, at least until you correct for inflation. At the time it was twice as big as the largest previous deficit for any year since the end of World War II, and it was five times the average budget deficit of the previous seven years. With unemployment at a near-record low of 3.6 percent, meaning that the economy was operating at very nearly full capacity, a deficit that big would bring inflation unless the Fed kept a very tight lid on the money supply. It didn't. In 1968 prices jumped more than 4 percent and in 1969 more than 6 percent.

• In 1968, Robert F. Kennedy and Martin Luther King, Jr., died at the hands of assassins. The Soviet Union invaded Czechoslovakia. A nation of freaks invaded Woodstock, New York, for the granddaddy of all rock festivals. And Richard M. Nixon was elected president of the United States for the first time.

Nixon proceeded, very slowly, to disengage from Vietnam. Peace talks had begun shortly before his election, and some troops were withdrawn beginning in July 1969. The policy of Vietnamization, meaning it was no longer "our" war but "theirs," was announced on November 3. Defense spending leveled off, and thanks to Johnson's surtax the federal budget began to show a small surplus. Worried about inflation,

Federal Reserve chairman William McChesney Martin tightened the screws on the money supply a little. Output fell, and by 1970 the economy was in recession for the first time in a decade.

The recession did not last long. Having lost the 1960 election because of Eisenhower's recession, Nixon was determined that 1972 should be a year of economic expansion. For three years the government proceeded to run big budget deficits, and the money supply expanded. (Martin's term at the Fed had expired in January 1970, and when Arthur Burns was sworn in as its new chairman Nixon is reported to have said, "Dr. Burns, please give us some money.") In 1971 the economy grew 3 percent. In 1972 the growth rate was back up near 6 percent.

Unlike every previous postwar recession, the 1969–70 slump put scarcely a dent in inflation. Prices rose more than 5 percent during 1970 and were going up at about the same rate in early 1971. In retrospect, it seems likely that Nixon administered the wrong medicine. Recessions typically lead to price drops in highly competitive industries like textiles and farming. Prices in industries dominated by a few big firms may not fall at all: managers may instead decide to raise prices to maintain profit margins. In the event, that's just what happened. The wholesale price of farm products fell, and prices in competitive industries rose only slightly. But prices went up 6 or 8 percent in concentrated industries like transportation equipment, machinery, and metal products. For most of the 1960s, the government's chief weapon against price hikes by big firms that dominated their markets was "jawboning"—using a combination of threats and persuasion to dissuade companies from raising their prices. Nixon and his advisers believed that jawboning was an ill-advised form of intervention in the market system. His reward for this belief was an unusual (at the time) combination of recession and inflation.

• In July 1971, Dr. Paul W. McCracken, then chairman

of Nixon's Council of Economic Advisers, wrote an article in *The Washington Post* against wage and price controls. "General wage and price control," he intoned, "would be a serious threat to individual freedom." A few weeks later, Nixon invited McCracken and other top aides to an urgent meeting at Camp David. Right after the meeting—Sunday night, August 15—he announced a ninety-day wage and price freeze.

The freeze was Phase I of what was dubbed the New Economic Policy. Phase II, a system of wage and price controls administered in good bureaucratic fashion by a Price Commission and a Pay Board overseen by a Cost of Living Council, began in November. In 1972 Nixon was reelected by a startling margin: only Massachusetts and Washington D.C. gave their electoral votes to his opponent. It wasn't long before he had terminated Phase II and announced the beginning of Phase III. This phase both reduced the scope of controls and left their "administration" more up to companies and unions themselves. Prices started to take off again. Nixon again froze wages and prices (June 1973), and imposed a new system of controls known as Phase IV.

Phase IV soon petered out. By then Nixon had other things on his mind anyway. In early 1973 the Watergate break-in defendants were found guilty, and in June former Nixon counsel John Dean began singing to the Senate about the cancer growing on the presidency. A year later, after a series of Watergate revelations, resignations, and impeachment hearings, Nixon resigned.

While they were in effect, Nixon's Phase II wage and price controls didn't work so badly. To be sure, a lot of items weren't covered: food prices, for example, rose nearly 5 percent from the end of 1971 to the end of 1972. And there were irrationalities. Chickens for broiling came under price controls: plucked and ready for use they were no longer considered a "raw agricultural product" and hence were not exempt. Since they were a popular consumer item, the Price Commission was not enthusiastic about letting their price go up. Feed grain for chickens, however, was outside the commission's jurisdiction, and its price rose rapidly. In short order poultry farmers found their costs of production outpacing the price they were allowed to get for their broilers.

For all the problems, inflation was held at least partly in check. Prices rose only 3.4 percent overall in 1972, and consumer prices other than food went up only about 2.5 percent. The vaguer guidelines of 1973's Phase III were predictably less effective. "Major corporations," wrote the economist Robert Lekachman, "interpreted Phase III as full of sound and fury, signifying nothing."

The departure from Phase II's strict controls, as John Kenneth Galbraith put it, reflected the novel notion "that if a policy is working, it should be abandoned." Politically, of course, the controls had already worked: they had gotten Nixon reelected in 1972. For more than a year before the election he had managed to stimulate the economy into recovery while avoiding the drastic price hikes everyone feared. He had also placated the growing number of voices in Congress and elsewhere who were demanding measures to control inflation. In political terms it was a well-conceived and well-executed policy. Economically its effects were temporary. When controls were lifted, inflation revived.

International finance: the shrinking dollar

Wage and price controls, though dominating the headlines, made up only half of Nixon's New Economic Policy. In fact, as then Treasury Secretary George P. Shultz and others have suggested, they may have been designed partly to distract attention from the policy's international side.

Ordinarily, nobody's attention has to be distracted from international economic matters: attention is seldom on them in the first place. Ordinarily too, pronouncements on the subject have as much political effect as pronouncements on National Library Week. This time Nixon had reason to feel that the impact might be greater than usual. In 1971 there were funny things going on with the world's money. As the decade progressed the situation got worse. Eventually the international monetary system of the postwar period essentially collapsed, and a new, makeshift system emerged to take its place. In that change lay the roots of more inflation.

For twenty-five years after World War II, the dollar had been the linchpin of international finance. It was the one currency everyone was willing to accept, and it was the yardstick against which everybody else's money was measured. The reasons for its emergence in the postwar years weren't hard to find. It was issued, as the writer Nicholas von Hoffman put it, "by the government of the one society in the world that had a lot to sell." It also seemed safe. America's military might and political stability encouraged people to believe that the dollar would be worth just as much tomorrow as it was today. So did the Treasury's promise to redeem dollars for gold at $35 to the ounce.* It wasn't long before international trade came to be conducted almost exclusively in dollars. And just as a growing economy needs an expanding money supply, so the growing volume of international trade required an ever-expanding supply of dollars.

This need meshed nicely with the dominant economic and political role the United States was playing in the postwar world. With the vast European market temporarily devastated, American companies built plants abroad, and American investors bought the stocks and bonds issued by European firms. The United States government sought to win friends and influence people by maintaining a huge military establishment overseas. American citizens took cheap European vacations and bought cheap Japanese goods. To be sure, the United States was exporting considerably more goods than it imported, meaning that on trade alone we were making money in the international marketplace. But American investments, military spending, tourism, and other expenditures abroad tipped the international ledger

---

* Though Americans had been unable to trade their dollars in for gold since 1933, foreign banks could still do so.

the other way. Our "balance of payments," as economists put it, was recurrently "in deficit."

In the past, accounts between nations were customarily settled in gold. A payments deficit thus usually led to an outflow of gold and was a sign of trouble. Too many deficits and your gold supply would run out, at which point nobody would want your money. For the United States the situation was a little different. Foreign banks and companies wanted dollars to finance international trade, and so were willing to accept them in lieu of gold. It was a little like, in economist Paul M. Sweezy's words, "owning a free gold mine"— or like being the banker in a game of Monopoly, with the right to use the bank's money as your own.

The only trouble was that it probably couldn't last. Once the European and Japanese economies were fully rebuilt, American exports would face stiffer competition on the world market. That would reduce the surplus we were earning on trade and thus enlarge the payments deficit. Yet the dollar, to maintain its value, had to remain both sufficiently stable and sufficiently scarce in the eyes of other nations' businesses and banks. If there were a surplus of dollars—or if people lost confidence in the dollar and wanted to exchange it for gold—the jig was up.

As the 1960s progressed, in fact, the dollar was looking a little shaky. The Vietnam War (and America's war-generated inflation) cast doubts on the dollar's stability. Yet the expenditures required to pay for the war contributed to payments deficits that were bigger than ever. Already by 1965 there were more dollars in the hands of foreign banks than the gold in Fort Knox was worth. By 1970 foreign bankers and others held upwards of $40 billion while America's gold supply (at $35 an ounce) was worth only $10 billion. Now if anyone began to worry about the dollar's stability and ask for gold instead, the resultant run on the bank we were operating would empty Fort Knox quicker than a burglar in a jewelry drawer—except that the United States would lock the gates and call out the cavalry long before any raiders could reach the fort. Seeing this, no big foreign bank pressed its luck.

Presidents had tried various measures to stem the balance of payments deficit and thus bolster confidence in the dollar; President Kennedy, for example, imposed an "interest equalization tax" aimed at discouraging Americans from buying foreign securities. All such measures were like fingers in a crumbling dike. The only answer from one point of view was to devalue the dollar—to make it worth less in terms of gold and in terms of foreign currencies than it had been before. Such a move would make imports more expensive and exports cheaper; a big enough devaluation would automatically reverse the payments deficit as consumers adjusted

THE INCREASE IN THE INFLATION RATE

(Percent change in the Consumer Price Index, December to December)

The 1950s		The 1960s		The 1970s	
1950	5.8%	1960	1.5%	1970	5.5%
1951	5.9	1961	.7	1971	3.4
1952	.9	1962	1.2	1972	3.4
1953	.6	1963	1.6	1973	8.8
1954	—.5	1964	1.2	1974	12.2
1955	.4	1965	1.9	1975	7.0
1956	2.9	1966	3.4	1976	4.8
1957	3.0	1967	3.0	1977	6.8
1958	1.8	1968	4.7	1978	9.0
1959	1.5	1969	6.1	1979	13.3

Ten-year average: 2.2%	Ten-year average: 2.5%	Ten-year average: 7.4%

SOURCE: *Economic Report of the President*, p. 263.

to these new prices and began buying more U.S. goods. It would also make our gold supply worth more in dollars than it had been.

From another point of view, though, devaluation would be a robbery big enough to make the Brink's job look like shoplifting a Hershey bar. No devaluation is ever popular with other countries—what helps Nation A's exports, after all, hurts the exports of Nations B through Z—and competitive devaluations in the early 1930s helped make the Depression as bad as it was. When the currency being devalued is the dollar, other countries pay a double price. For many years they had been accumulating dollars in lieu of gold, secure in the belief they were as good as gold. Now the Monopoly banker, who has been shoveling out money to all who would take it, announces that everybody's money is suddenly worth less than it used to be. The output of the free gold mine turns out to be fool's gold, and those who have been holding it look like suckers. For this reason the United States postponed devaluation again and again.

In the end it could be postponed no longer. By the spring of 1971, Americans were importing more goods than they exported; the dollar surplus on trade, which for so long had made manageable the deficits racked up by the Pentagon, investors, and tourists, had disappeared, and the outflow of dollars grew to a flood. In May, speculators and everybody else began to trade in their dollars for other currencies; the Germans quit buying them on May 5 when they were asked to sell a billion dollars' worth of marks in the first hour of business. In early August, the Bank of England asked the Fed in effect to guarantee the value of $750 million it had purchased during July. That meant the Fed would take the loss if the dollar were devalued, and it meant other countries would soon be asking for the same guarantee. At that point Nixon called his advisers to Camp David—quickly.

On August 15, at the same time he announced the price freeze, Nixon proclaimed that the United States would no longer redeem dollars for gold ("closing the gold window," the move was delicately termed). He also announced a 10 percent surcharge on all U.S. imports—a kind of backhanded, one-way devaluation of the dollar—knowing that other countries would now have to come to the table to negotiate new exchange rates. By the end of the year, an international conference at the Smithsonian in Washington had ratified new rates. Despite Nixon's description of it as "the most significant monetary agreement in the history of the world," it wasn't enough. In early 1973 the dollar was devalued again, and new rates negotiated.

But before long the central banks found it impossible to keep up any semblance of fixed exchange rates, mainly because countries were experiencing different rates of inflation. Most major currencies, including the dollar, began to "float" against each other, rising and falling on the marketplace as banks, governments, businesses, and individuals bought and sold each one. The dollar floated downwards in relation to the currencies of its main industrial competitors. In 1970 it was worth 357 Japanese yen, 3.6 West German marks, and 5.5 French francs. By 1980 the figures were 210 yen, 1.8 marks, and a little over 4 francs. It was quite a fall, and it came about mostly because the United States tried to get away with playing Monopoly a little too long.

The aftermath—plus OPEC

When Phase II's strict controls were removed in early 1973, prices began to take off like a Saturn rocket. Part of the reason was the delayed effects of devaluation. Other changes in the world's finances and politics played a role too.

• In 1972, the world was awash with money. Early in the year—it was an election year, remember—the Fed began to pump money into the U.S. banking system, cutting the discount rate and letting other interest rates fall. The German central bank followed suit, partly to prevent American investors from worsening the U.S. balance of payments situation (and thus the whole shaky system) by buying up higher-interest German bonds. The British, French, and Japanese were pursuing expansionary policies too. Between 1970 and 1972 the world's supply of "international money" (mainly the gold and major currencies held by central banks) grew 70 percent. In 1973 it rose another 18 percent.

Meanwhile, the years 1971 and 1972 brought a series of agricultural disasters. Much of Africa was riddled with drought. Asian rice crops failed. The anchovy crop—anchovies are used in livestock feed—mysteriously failed to turn up off the coast of Peru. With a lot of money chasing scarce goods, world commodity prices went up 65 percent from the end of 1971 to the spring of 1973. "There was pressure from all directions," writes Martin Mayer in his book *The Fate of the Dollar*, "on the world's productive capacities."

Into this tight market stepped Russian grain buyers. The Soviets had bought a considerable amount of grain in 1970 and 1971 though they had bumper crops of their own. In 1972 their harvest failed, and with the dollar devalued U.S. grain looked like a bargain. On July 10 the U.S. government announced that the Soviet Union would be buying $750 million worth of grain over a three-year period.

"Suddenly," says *Washington Post* journalist Dan Morgan in his book *Merchants of Grain*, "the United States was hemorrhaging grain. Monumental tie-ups and traffic jams occurred as thousands of freight trains full of grain converged on the Gulf Coast ports of New Orleans and Houston." The massive exports, which reduced U.S. wheat stocks from 23.5 million tons to under 7 million tons in about a year, were "only partially the doing of the Russians." Other countries too were looking for cheap U.S. produce, and "when grain prices began to rise, customers panicked, and many nations bid up the price."

The next year—1973—high prices rippled through the Farm Belt. High corn prices, as Morgan explains it, led to a beef shortage; feedlot operators couldn't afford to buy cattle at the going rate, so ranchers sold young animals to the slaughterhouses instead. Pig farmers decided to sell their grain rather than feed it to their hogs; pork prices came down as the pigs were slaughtered, but soon went back up as "fewer sows produced fewer new litters." By the end of the year consumer food prices were up 20 percent; the Consumer Price Index had jumped 8.8 percent. And oil had scarcely risen at all.

• The Organization of Petroleum Exporting Countries had been around for a while. It was modeled, the financial writer Adam Smith has pointed out, on the Texas Railroad Commission. "Back when the problem was too much oil," writes Smith, "producers worried about how to keep the price up. The Texas Railroad Commission, which was in charge of oil in that state, would restrict production. If the price started to sag, the commission would reduce the number of days per month that producers could pump.

"In the fifties, a Venezuelan petroleum lawyer called Juan Pablo Pérez Alfonso was in political exile in the United States. He believed that the major oil companies were keeping Venezuela's oil prices down by increasing the production in the Persian Gulf, where it was cheaper, and he studied the activities of the Texans. In 1959, Pérez Alfonso was not only back in Venezuela under a new government, he was Minister of Mines, and he set about creating an international Texas Railroad Commission—without Texans, in fact—to oppose the major oil companies. In 1960, Saudi Arabia, Iran, Iraq, and Kuwait joined Venezuela as charter members of OPEC."

During the 1960s OPEC didn't accomplish much. Back then, the United States was importing only a fifth of the oil Americans used. And it had plenty of spare production capacity: in fact, when the Suez crisis created a temporary shortage in Europe in 1956 we had stepped up production to help meet European needs. As late as 1970 imports amounted to less than a quarter of total U.S. oil use. The world price of oil hit its postwar peak in 1957 at just over $2 a barrel and had been declining ever since.

In the early 1970s the picture began to change. U.S. production was slowly falling, yet demand was on the rise. By 1973 imports had jumped to nearly two fifths of total oil consumption, and a substantial fraction of the imported oil was coming from the Middle East. Then hostilities broke out between the Arabs and the Israelis. Middle Eastern oil producers announced a 70 percent hike in the price of their petroleum, and the Arab nations announced an embargo on oil shipments to the United States. Though the war soon ended, OPEC had gotten the boost it needed. Another price hike, announced in December, brought the wellhead price of Middle Eastern oil to $7.11 a barrel, an increase of nearly fourfold over the October 1 level. That increase showed up almost immediately in the prices Americans paid for gasoline, heating oil, and electric power. The "energy" component of the Consumer Price Index rose nearly 30 percent between 1973 and 1974.

• Oil is not like sardines. If the price of imported sardines rose fourfold, consumers would suddenly discover a taste for the domestic variety, or for herring, or for anchovies, or for salmon. Even if consumer demand did for some reason hold constant, the sardine part of the Consumer Price Index isn't inordinately large. Nor are sardines used for much besides hors d'oeuvres and sandwiches. Oil, by contrast, is hard to replace. Cars may someday run on alcohol or methane, but they don't yet. Home furnaces and electric power plants once burned coal, but most don't anymore. And oil is necessary for a variety of manufactured products, from fertilizer to Baggies.

It is, in short, a particularly powerful example of a general phenomenon. When the price of something goes up, consumer demand is supposed to go down. In the long run, that's probably what will happen, provided the price increases stick. In the short run, though, if the product in question is OPEC oil, South African chromium, or even high-quality Japanese television sets, buyers may decide to keep on buying despite higher prices. When that happens the result is inflation. OPEC had raised the price of oil, and devaluation had raised the price of every other import.

The reverse applies to exports. Shortages and devaluation led to skyrocketing demand for U.S. agricultural products. In the long run, supply might catch up with that demand. In the short run, prices went through the roof. Again, consumers had to pay them. You can get by without steak, but not without foodstuffs made from grain. When you pay those high prices, that too is inflation.

The lessons of inflation

With all these factors at work, the United States and everybody else in the capitalist world lived through a period of hell-for-leather inflation that was entirely new to Americans. Prices rose 9 percent in 1973, 12 percent in 1974, and 7 percent in 1975. At the same time the U.S. economy was plunging like a broken-legged horse into a ravine of recession. The chaos of those years—coped with only lamely by President Gerald Ford, who at one point was passing out buttons marked WIN (for Whip Inflation Now)—set the stage for the chronic inflation of the last five years. For like any good morality play this Western drama taught a number of lessons.

Jimmy Carter's administration learned a lesson it took four years to forget: If Recession Doesn't Stop Inflation, Then Why Have a Recession? To be sure, economists could and did point to the fact that the inflation rate slowed up measurably in the years right after the 1973–75 slump. But that argument came up short when set against the claims of political strategists that the recession had cost Ford the 1976 election. (As with Kennedy against Nixon in 1960, the popular vote was close.) Thanks to the recession, Ford had left a big budget deficit; with the recession over, Carter made it bigger. From 1975 through 1979 the government's deficit never dropped below $27 billion. Usually it was almost double that figure.

Businesses learned a variety of lessons. One was to antici-pate inflation in their pricing policies. A survey by *Business Week* turned up a variety of strategies for keeping up with rising prices: more frequent price reviews, surcharges re-flecting increased costs, escalators reflecting cost-of-living in-creases. "Where we can, we're trying to get complete es-calators included in the contract," a midwestern heavy-goods producer told the magazine. "Where we have to bid a fixed price, we just add 12% a year to offset inflation." Unions learned a similar lesson. They bargained hard, as ever, for wage increases. And they tried more than ever to get cost-of-living adjustments (COLAs) included in the contract.

Businesses and consumers also learned a maxim that would have caused conservative corporate treasurers and family men of the past to throw up their hands in despair. The maxim was simple: Live on Borrowed Money. Real interest rates—interest rates discounted by the inflation rate—were frequently low, sometimes even negative. Business debt es-calated, hitting a record level of 53.9 percent of GNP in 1979. For consumers it was the Decade of the Credit Card. Master Charge (now MasterCard) made its appearance in 1966. BankAmericard became VISA in the mid-1970s. Out-standing "revolving" credit, the kind you get with those two cards as well as with Sears and other charge accounts, rose from $5 billion in 1970 to $52 billion at the end of 1979, a real increase of about fivefold. Total consumer credit went up by about a third (in real terms) in the same inter-val. Mortgage debt, meanwhile, was jumping from $474 bil-lion in 1970 to $1.3 trillion by the end of 1979, a real increase of nearly 40 percent.

There were other lessons too. The Federal Reserve learned it had better provide plenty of money for all this borrowing and spending; the money supply rose an average of 12 per-cent a year between 1975 and 1979. Banks learned several ways to get around whatever restrictions the Fed did try to implement. Thus the largely unregulated "Eurodollar" market (composed of dollar deposits held by banks not located in the United States) mushroomed. So did hitherto obscure financial instruments like certificates of deposit and repurchase agreements, both aimed at circumventing various monetary regulations. On the international front, Carter and others decided not to worry too much about the value of the dollar. It plunged in 1978 but recovered somewhat in 1979.

In the end, though, it all boiled down to one big lesson: inflation is here to stay. For most of the postwar period, people had expected prices to rise, but so slowly as to be almost imperceptible, a percent or two each year. Now they expected prices to rise 5 or 10 percent a year, and that changed their behavior. "It is no longer taken for granted," wrote the economist Robert L. Heilbroner, "that what goes up must come down; on the contrary, what goes up will probably continue to go up indefinitely. With such attitudes, corporations do not feel a need to furl sails rapidly the instant a recession blows up, nor do households feel a need to practice thrift, even if their incomes fall. Unions are emboldened to ask for aggressive wage settlements, because they know their members have the backstop of unemployment compensation behind them. The unemployed do not feel the necessity of taking any kind of work, because the welfare system permits individuals to refuse work they do not like." Wages and prices, always sticky, stopped falling altogether for most of the 1970s. And steep increases one year fed steep increases the next. When people expect rapid inflation, they act accordingly. Those very actions—the borrowing and spending, the cost-of-living allowances, the anticipatory pricing—ensure that inflation will be worse than ever.

Things got worse in the early 1970s because of a series of discrete circumstances. The recession of 1969–70 was brief, and didn't begin to dent price hikes in industries dominated by a few big firms. Price controls served to get Nixon re-elected (though it's doubtful they were really necessary, given his large margin over McGovern), but they only postponed inflation. Devaluation made all imports a little more expensive and OPEC made imported oil a lot more expensive. Food prices skyrocketed as the Russians and others began buying up newly cheap U.S. grain. The inflation grew so virulent that the worst recession since World War II seemed at the time only to make it worse.

By the mid-1970s, inflation had been bad for ten years and the end wasn't in sight. People had already begun to adjust: now they learned to adjust more quickly and in more ways. Unions and corporations anticipated price hikes; businesses and consumers borrowed and spent. Fearful of a recession, the Fed let the money supply grow. Congress and the administration kept government deficits high. The recession at the end of the 1970s was a strong dose of old-fashioned medicine, but whether it would be administered in sufficient quantity, and indeed whether it was still potent at all, was open to question. The prospect, as the 1980s began, was for more of the same—despite the changing of the guard in Washington.

Chapter Eight will take up the question of whether anything can be done about this inflation. First it may help to summarize the overall picture—to reexamine the puzzle from a few different angles, figuring out how much of what people say about inflation is true, and how the history can best be understood. Once that is done, we will be in a position to consider whether there are any effective solutions or whether, like actors in a long-running play, we are compelled to confront the same problems and go through the same motions over and over again.

7. The Causes of Inflation:
A Summing-Up

At one time or another during the last ten years, the following individuals, groups, numbers, policies, institutions, and social or natural phenomena have been blamed for inflation:

—Irresponsible labor leaders, corporation executives, farmers, and consumers;

—Federal budget deficits, resulting from taxes that are too low to cover governmental expenditures; on the other hand, taxes alleged to be so high they discourage work, savings, and investments;

—Interest rates so high that they add noticeably to the cost of homes, cars, and other goods that are bought with borrowed money; also, interest rates not high enough to discourage such borrowing;

—Social-welfare spending (including social security), which accounts for about half of federal outlays; also the Pentagon, which accounts for about a quarter;

—OPEC, also known as "the Arabs," a usage that must surprise the Venezuelans, Nigerians, and Iranians, who together provided the United States with about 30 percent of its imported oil during the 1970s; also the seven major oil companies;

—The Board of Governors of the Federal Reserve System, in particular Arthur Burns and Paul Volcker, the last two chairmen; the banks they regulate; the banks they don't regulate (such as overseas banks and branches); and the money supply itself;

—Jimmy Carter, Gerald Ford, Richard Nixon, and anybody else who had something to say about the way the economy is run; also Lyndon Johnson and his war;

—The Russians, who until recently bought a lot of grain from the United States; the grain dealers who sold it to them; and the U.S. Department of Agriculture, which made it all possible;

—And a potpourri of other factors, including government regulation, the Consumer Price Index (which is thought to overstate inflation—see the Appendix), minimum wage laws, speculation, war, peace, international exchange rates, bad weather, falling productivity, declining moral fiber, and that missing anchovy crop off the coast of Peru.

Once in a while—the last item, for example—an alleged cause of inflation will be reported mainly for the air of knowledge it imparts to the speaker. (Not everyone understands the importance of anchovies in the world economy.) More often, discussions as to who or what is responsible for inflation are simply a way of laying one's preferences and prejudices on the table. When an editorialist or your luncheon companion observes that something is inflationary, it's a safe bet you're going to hear about something he or she doesn't like.

Many of the purported villains listed above have turned up in the preceding chapters. The purpose of this chapter is not to go over old ground, nor is it to scrutinize the case against all the culprits that haven't yet made their appearance. The objectives here are simpler but in the end more useful. One is to illustrate the futility of blaming inflation on some of the more frequently accused miscreants. Another is to look at the whole inflationary system in historical perspective. Both endeavors will reveal much about how inflation should—and should not—be controlled.

Government regulation

In the 1960s and 1970s, the federal government passed a lot of laws that business people weren't particularly fond of: regulations about waste disposal and air pollution, about health and safety at the workplace, even about the racial and sexual makeup of the labor force. In the white businessman's view of the situation, profits were going up in smoke: they were burned up in a furnace stoked by a sixty-eight-year-old Spanish-surnamed gay woman in a wheelchair, who was wearing $1,500 worth of safety equipment. The ashes went up a 50-foot-high stack topped with a scrubbing apparatus costing $2 million. Everyone else working in the plant was back at the office filling out government forms.

Not surprisingly, business executives wanted to fight these regulations. The trouble is, it doesn't sound good to defend your right to pollute the air and water, to let your employees be killed or maimed, or to continue hiring on the basis of sex and skin color. The lobbyists and public relations firms hired to put forth business's point of view had to come up with a better angle. Happily, one was at hand: inflation. Since most regulations add to the cost of doing business, most must therefore add to product prices. When prices go up, as Calvin Coolidge might have said, inflation results. Since nobody likes inflation, it follows that nobody should like the regulations.

There is little doubt that many regulations do add to the cost of doing business. How much they add is less than certain. The conservative economist Murray Weidenbaum, who has studied the subject in detail, estimates that the total cost of government regulation is more than $100 billion: about 4 percent of GNP. Mark Green and Norman Waitzman, associates of Ralph Nader who have also studied the subject, contend that Weidenbaum's estimate is overblown, and cite a Government Accounting Office estimate of regulatory costs only one third as great. Green and Waitzman also note that only 30 percent of Weidenbaum's estimate is attributable to "social" regulation of the sort mentioned above; the rest is due to "cartel" agencies like the Interstate Commerce Commission that regulate competition and rate setting, and to paperwork. Cartel regulation, of course, does not come in for the same kind of opprobrium from business as do the regulations of agencies like the Occupational Safety and Health Administration (OSHA) and the Equal Employment Opportunity Commission.

In any event, adding to the cost of doing business is not the same thing as causing inflation. For one thing, any given regulation increases costs only once. It may make a product more expensive—once. It does not lead to continuing price increases. For another, effective regulations lead to products that are qualitatively different from what was being produced before. If Sony brings out a cassette recorder that works and sounds better than last year's model but costs more, few would describe that price hike as inflationary. If General Motors produces a car that pollutes less air and that injured fewer workers while it was in production, that car too may cost more. Like the Sony recorder, it's worth more.*

---

* The benefits of regulation, though hard to measure, are also usually overlooked in the debate about regulation's costs. Nicholas A. Ashford of MIT's Center for Policy Alternatives has listed some examples of such benefits:

Water pollution control, in a breakdown, produces a reduction in water-borne disease valued at $100 million to $1 billion a year, provides recreational potential valued at up to $9.4 billion a year and substantially increases property values. And these evaluations do not take into account programs directed at such long-term or large-scale problems as carcinogens in water supplies, stratospheric ozone depletion, atmospheric sulfate transport or acid rain.

Inspections by the Occupational Safety and Health Administration are estimated to have prevented between 40,000 and 60,000 accidents in which workdays would have been lost and up to 350 deaths in both 1974 and 1975. . . .

As a result of consumer product safety regulations, child-resistant drug packaging has prevented an estimated 34,000 injuries from accidental drug ingestion between 1973 and 1976. Crib safety standards

Minimum wage laws

Those who believe that people should have the right to work for less than $3.35 an hour—not quite $7,000 a year, assuming full-time year-round employment—are quick to criticize minimum-wage laws as inflationary. Minimum wages do undoubtedly make a few things more expensive than they otherwise would be: laundry service, McDonald's hamburgers, and car washes come to mind. But they are seldom inflationary. Between 1970 and 1980 the minimum wage rose 94 percent. Average manufacturing wages and the Consumer Price Index both rose more. Thus people working for the minimum wage have not even kept up with inflation, let alone caused it. Moreover, only a small fraction of the U.S. work force earns no more than the minimum wage. Blaming inflation in general on a rising minimum wage is like saying that New York Yankee ticket prices are so high because the bat boy makes so much money.

There are two specific situations in which a small amount of inflation can plausibly be attributed to the minimum wage. First, in a year when the minimum goes up faster than other wages or prices it tends to lift the average rate of inflation. Thus in 1978 it rose 15 percent, and, according to economists Robert Gough and Robin Siegel, it thereby added a tenth of a percentage point to the inflation rate. Second, when increases in the minimum wage are mandated in advance (as was the January 1981 increase to $3.35 an hour), other low-wage workers may demand similar increases to maintain traditional wage differentials. How significant

---

have reduced crib-related injuries to infants by 44 percent since 1974. . . .

There are other kinds of benefits too. Without government fuel economy standards, for example, Detroit would probably have made fewer small cars in the last few years, and would have taken an even worse beating than it did in 1979 and 1980 when consumers began buying more small automobiles.

this effect may be, particularly with other wages and prices rising rapidly anyway, is hard to judge.*

OPEC

Blaming OPEC for inflation—in fact, hating OPEC in general—is for an American about as hard as denouncing the Russians for invading Afghanistan. Xenophobes dislike the ominous Arab character of many OPEC nations. Conservative free-marketeers oppose OPEC because it is a cartel. Liberals and radicals object to the traditional, almost feudal nature of some of the more important OPEC states, and note that a lot of the new oil wealth does not get widely distributed. Everybody dislikes paying more for gas and heating oil. About the only Americans who may, in their most private moments, thank the Lord for OPEC are those who own large shares in the oil companies. Between 1972 and 1978 the petroleum industry's net income increased (in real terms) 47 percent.

Between 1973 and mid-1980, the energy component of the Consumer Price Index essentially tripled. Everything else rose only 80 percent. So oil price hikes really do account for a good part of our inflation. Energy costs by most estimates account for about a tenth of our economy's output. A 20 percent hike in energy costs, therefore, generates two points of inflation all by itself. The worst price boosts came

---

* There are two other arguments against the minimum wage. One is that it discourages employers from hiring low-wage workers and thus hurts the very people it is trying to help. This effect may be counterbalanced by the fact that low-wage workers *with* jobs earn more under a minimum-wage law than they otherwise would; the evidence is mixed. The second argument is that the minimum wage actually has a perverse effect on the distribution of income. Since many of the workers in minimum-wage jobs are teenagers, and since teenagers from more affluent families are more likely to get jobs than poor teenagers, the minimum wage seems to help the middle class more than the poor. On both points see Christopher Jencks, "The Minimum Wage Controversy," *Working Papers for a New Society*, March/April 1978, pp. 12–14.

in 1973–74 and in 1979. The rest of the time, oil went up no faster than other items.

OPEC, however, did not act alone. The oil companies, though opposing the increases, were able to pass them on to consumers; company profits thus increased substantially, as did the value of the reserves they hold in non-OPEC countries like the United States and Canada. Consumers, for their part, kept on buying oil and gasoline for a long time regardless of the price: while the wellhead cost was rising from less than $2 to nearly $30 a barrel, U.S. imports were rising from 2.2 million to 6.2 million barrels a day. Most important, the West's central banks and international monetary institutions made sure there was plenty of money around to buy the oil.

To understand the importance of this last phenomenon, imagine, as Robert L. Heilbroner has suggested, that all the coal producers in the nineteenth century got together and formed a domestic version of OPEC aimed at regulating the price of coal. Imagine too that they, like OPEC, started off by jacking the price up to four times what it had been. No one, says Heilbroner, would come to the conclusion that such a move would be inflationary:

> Instead, a coal OPEC would have resulted in the whole-sale shutting down of coal mines unable to sell their product; in the drastic curtailment of steel output as plant managers cut back their unprofitable operations; in a decline of purchasing from the businesses and households affected by this turn of events; and there-after in a fall in "carloadings," the index of general economic activity we used before GNP was invented.

Some such decline actually resulted from the modern OPEC's moves. The initial price jump of late 1973 and early 1974 worsened, if it did not actually cause, the recession that extended to 1975. The price hikes of 1979 probably contributed to the recession of 1980.

OPEC's measures did not touch off worldwide depression,

however, because the money supply was large enough to accommodate the new prices. Remember all those dollars that were floating around? When OPEC nations were paid, they deposited the dollars in American or European banks. The banks in turn "recycled" the "petrodollars," as the new language had it, by lending out the money to poorer nations so they could pay their oil bills. It's exactly as if Americans, faced with the hypothetical coal OPEC of the nineteenth century, had simply borrowed all the money they needed to pay their coal bills and kept right on buying as much as before. Back then, this couldn't have happened—gold and prudence, as explained above, combined to limit the supply of money available for borrowing. In 1973 the limits were off: gold was irrelevant, and the United States kept churning out dollars. Inflation, not depression, was the result.

Government spending (liberal version)

Among the charges leveled against the Defense Department by liberals and other foreign-policy doves is the assertion that fat Pentagon budgets cause inflation. Since the accusation comes from people who oppose much arms spending anyway, it is somewhat suspect, like business charges that government regulation is inflationary. Still, the argument is not entirely specious. Even a conservative writer like Alfred L. Malabre, Jr., of *The Wall Street Journal* has asserted that "military spending tends to exert a particularly inflationary impact."

How can this be? At the simplest level, the belief that defense spending is inflationary hinges on the notion that people are being paid to produce something they can't buy. Thus the income in people's pockets adds up to more than the supply of consumer goods available for purchase, and prices rise accordingly. The flaw in this argument is that it could be applied to nearly everything the government buys for us—parks, dams, state universities, and so forth. From the viewpoint of the economy as a whole, military preparedness is just as much a "purchase" as the nine million cars Americans bought last year, and the Pentagon in this respect is no more responsible for inflation than the automobile industry. Only to the extent that military forces are a total waste of money, and maintaining them therefore akin to digging holes and filling them up again, does the argument make sense. But then the issue should be wasted resources, not higher prices.

Fat Pentagon budgets probably do feed inflation indirectly. They help keep government spending high, stabilizing the economy and preventing a depression. And the Defense Department, despite recent efforts to control costs, is not known for parsimony. As a result most contracts work on a cost-plus basis. A Columbia University engineering professor, Lloyd J. Dumas, describes the effects this way:

> No firm that knows its customers will cover all of its costs—including guaranteed profits—will hold back on spending. The inevitable freewheeling attitude bids up the prices of the various productive resources the various firms buy—resources also needed by civilian firms. In this way the defense budget fuels "cost push" inflation.

Then too, U.S. military spending abroad—the costs of empire, as some commentators have put it—is a prime component of the American payments deficit. As Dumas notes, the United States gained $49 billion on trade alone between the mid-1950s and the mid-1970s. During the same period we spent more than $54 billion abroad for military purposes. "Military spending," Dumas concludes, "thus turned a positive trade situation into a negative overall flow, and caused dollars to pile up overseas." Eventually all those dollars made devaluation necessary, with inflationary effects as described in the last chapter.

Finally, the defense budget represents an enormous diversion of skilled manpower—scientists, mathematicians, engineers—to military endeavors. In principle, these same professionals might otherwise have been working on technological improvements in the civilian economy, which in turn would have led to faster growth rates, higher productivity, and, conceivably, less inflation. The professionals might also have been unemployed. It depends, as with so much else in political debate, on what you assume the government would have done if it hadn't spent so much money on defense. Is defense spending inflationary? Like the old woman who was asked "How's your husband?" a reasonable answer is, Compared to what?

Government spending (conservative version)

Where liberals like to blame the generals for inflation, conservatives like to blame welfare mothers and other less influential recipients of governmental largesse. Government, say the conservatives, dishes out too much money to people who aren't working, and pays too many bureaucrats to provide unwanted or unneeded social services to the poor. Cutbacks in this area would reduce the size of the federal budget, lower the chance of a deficit, and in general encourage more people to work more than they do now. The result would be greater output and less inflation.

Circumstantially, the conservatives have a better case than the liberals. In the late 1960s, rising defense expenditures contributed to Vietnam-era inflation. Since then, however—and during the years when inflation has been at its worst—defense spending has been falling, both as a proportion of GNP and as a share of the federal budget. Governmental transfer payments, in contrast, have been rising steeply. "Income security" passed "national defense" on the budget ledger in fiscal 1974 and has been going up ever since. Logically too the conservatives have a prima facie case. A sharp reduction in social security, welfare benefits, and other transfer programs might lead more people to seek work, might make low-wage workers more willing to accept wage cuts, and almost certainly would make total purchasing power decline, thus precipitating a recession. The recession in turn might be sharp and steep enough to dampen inflation considerably.

In the long run the effects of such moves are harder to predict. Most West European countries spend considerably more on social welfare than the United States, yet inflation rates in Europe vary widely. Then too, the desirability, morality, and political feasibility of the conservative prescription are open to some question. At last count, approximately fifty-five million Americans were receiving a sizable fraction of their income in the form of a government check, with the largest chunk coming from social security payments. A small amount of extra inflation may be a reasonable price to pay for the modest degree of income security enjoyed by Americans who are retired or unemployed.

In general, using inflation as a political club does not make for particularly persuasive arguments. Business executives would be better off pointing out the waste engendered by foolish government regulations than they are in charging that all regulation is inflationary. Liberals are better off attacking the fat in the Pentagon's budget, or even the whole concept of a spiraling arms race in a thermonuclear world, than in laying inflation at its doorstep. After all, those who believe that what OSHA or the Navy does is important are probably willing to put up with whatever inflation they may cause. The same is true of transfer payments.

Deficit spending

Liberals and conservatives alike often agree that federal budget deficits are inflationary. In early 1980, for example—before the recession was recognized for what it was—Democrats and Republicans in Congress competed to see who could come up with a balanced-budget proposal first. There is no doubt that big budget deficits can, at times, generate inflation, as long as the Fed is willing to expand the money supply accordingly. Lyndon Johnson's Vietnam deficits are a prime example. But the matter is not as simple as it sometimes seems.

In principle, you want to run a deficit whenever the economy is running well below capacity and there is widespread unemployment. The only question is how big the deficit should be. Economists try to estimate it by figuring what the budget would look like if everyone were working and paying taxes; that high-employment budget, as it is known, should be roughly in balance. For most of the 1970s, the high-employment budget was in deficit, though not by large amounts. Ironically, one year in which the high-employment budget was in surplus was 1974—the year, until 1979, of the worst inflation ever. So the connection between deficits and price increases is not always clear.

Other comparisons also undermine the apparent link between deficits and inflation. "We had inflation in 1920," notes the historian Arthur Schlesinger Jr. in an article in *The Wall Street Journal*, "when the federal budget ran a surplus. We had appalling deflation in 1930–33—when the federal budget was running unprecedented peacetime deficits. In 1975–76 inflation declined from 12% to 4.8%—while the budget ran deficits of $112 billion. . . . Or take a look abroad. West Germany today has a budget deficit at least two and a half times as large as ours in relation to gross national product—and an inflation rate one fourth of ours."

Finally, looking at Washington's role in the whole government sector of the economy may put the matter in the perspective it needs. In 1979, the federal government ran a $10.5 billion deficit. State and local governments, meanwhile, were running a surplus of over $24 billion. Yet Washington was transferring about $80 billion to states and localities through various aid programs. If that figure had been cut by $10 billion the federal budget would have been in balance; state and local governments would have had less of a surplus; and the inflation rate would not have budged.

Too much money

One source of inflation that nearly everyone agrees on is that you can't have inflation without a lot of money. The

WHAT HAPPENS WHEN THE FEDERAL GOVERNMENT TRIES TO BALANCE THE BUDGET

In March of 1980, shortly before the recession stuck its nose under the tent, President Carter announced some new anti-inflation measures, including a balanced budget. As budget cuts were being discussed in Congress, Democratic Senator Thomas B. Eagleton traveled to his home state of Missouri. There, according to a report in *The Wall Street Journal*, he encountered any number of good reasons to oppose a balanced budget:

• A black minister pleaded with him, "Please don't let them cut the youth program for this summer."

• A building-industry group applauded him for bringing hundreds of millions of dollars in federal construction projects to Missouri; the group's president also told the *Journal* it would "do its best to see that the budgetary axe falls somewhere else."

• In St. Louis, a Job Corps director urged him to defend federal employment programs.

• At a pig farmers' convention, a top official urged him not to let Washington cut the pork research budget.

• An International Association of Machinists official wanted to make sure Labor Department programs didn't get cut.

usual way of explaining this fact is to liken the economy to an auction. Imagine an auction where food, clothing, and other necessities of life are being sold. If there are 100 people with $100 apiece in their pockets, it's a safe bet that $10,000 will be spent. Suppose now that someone comes along and gives everybody an extra $100. People's desires for what's being sold have not changed, nor has the total supply of goods being offered. Yet now, in all likelihood, $20,000

• A leader of the Missouri State Nurses Association said she would refuse to support the senator if he "persists in cutting the nursing-aid budget."

• A man rushed up to him at an airport and announced he was counting on Eagleton to help "increase federal support for diabetes research," and at another airport the board of directors of a Kansas City anti-poverty program waylaid Eagleton to demand more money for their projects.

• In Hannibal, a Laborers Union official announced bluntly that Senator Eagleton was "going to have to reconsider his thoughts" about budget cutting.

Back at the White House, meanwhile, officials counting the mail reported that nearly everyone supported Carter's goal of a balanced budget. Letters about specific budget cuts, however, were running 96 percent against the reductions. Maybe President Reagan will have better luck.

Sources: David Ignatius, "Democrats' Distress: In This Election Year, Balancing of the Budget is a Real Juggling Act," *The Wall Street Journal*, March 14, 1980. Also, Judith Miller, "Congress Under Siege by Lobbyists Pleading Against Budget Slash," *The New York Times*, March 20, 1980.

will be spent: the buyers will bid prices up to double their previous level. Take away half the money, similarly, and you cut prices in half.

Historically, as Milton Friedman and others have demonstrated, changes in the stock of money correlate pretty well with changes in the price level. During the 1970s, for example, the money supply rose considerably faster than it had in the 1950s and 1960s. Moreover, it rose a lot faster than real output. If the two had gone up at the same rate, the average price level might have stayed constant—a little more money would have been chasing a few more goods. As it was, a lot more money was chasing a few more goods. The result was inflation.

Though there is little disagreement that inflation requires more money in circulation, there is much disagreement about whether it makes sense to say that too much money is the cause of inflation. Money, remember, is all the devices people use to store their purchasing power—currency, checking accounts, savings accounts, and (depending on which measure you're using) any of half a dozen other social inventions. Every time you use your VISA card or a corporation borrows on its line of credit at the bank, the "money supply" expands.

Now suppose we're back at the auction—only this time, instead of $100 in cash in our pockets, we have our checkbooks, complete with a reserve-credit provision that allows us to borrow another $500 each from the bank. Suppose too that the auctioneer, being no fool, has suddenly realized that his commissions will go up if he can double the price he gets for his wares. So he takes what he hoped to get for each item, doubles it, and announces that the bids will start there. People need the goods: they grumble, but they write checks for whatever it takes. They then leave the auction, go to work, and demand a raise from the boss. He has heard that prices in the region are doubling—doubling!—and he doesn't want to jeopardize his business by risking a strike. So he gives his workers a 75 percent raise and hikes his prices 90 percent. And he borrows from the bank to finance the higher wage bill until he can begin selling his products at the new prices.

The community, without a doubt, is experiencing inflation. The money supply is expanding too. But did the increase in money cause the inflation? Only in a limited sense. Other causes of the inflation were the auctioneer's raising prices, the workers' demands on the boss, the boss's decision to raise his prices, and so on. Blaming inflation on too much money is like saying the bathtub overflowed because there was too much water. You also need to know why the spigot was left on, what's wrong with the drainpipe, and who was trying to take a bath.

In the real world, of course, the Federal Reserve System is supposed to control both the spigot and the drain. It buys and sells government bonds, thus pumping money into the economy or taking money out. It tells banks how much they can lend out, and it manipulates interest rates, thus encouraging or discouraging borrowing.* None of these tools, it should be pointed out, is exactly like working a bathtub faucet and stopper. It is more like directing a huge crowd through a museum exhibit: you can set up all the signs and ropes you want to, but you can't always be sure people will do what they're supposed to. Rising interest rates, for example, may dissuade some people from borrowing. They may persuade others that interest rates are shooting up and they had better borrow now before things get any worse. Similarly, falling demand due to tight money may persuade some businesses to lower prices. It may persuade others just to cut production.

Monetary policy is thus a clumsy tool. It is also a tool whose use can be hazardous. These are subjects we shall consider in more detail in the next chapter, when we examine possible cures for inflation. For the moment a simple trade-off should be kept in mind. Rising prices—remember the coal OPEC—can lead consumers to purchase less, businesses to cut back, and economic activity to drop.

---

* For most of the recent past, the Fed "watched" interest rates, and intervened in the economy whenever it thought interest rates were too high or too low. Most recently, under Paul Volcker, it has taken to "watching" the money supply and intervening only when the supply seems to be growing too fast or too slow. As a result, interest rates seem to fluctuate more widely and rapidly in the short term than they used to; whether the new policy will be different in other ways is yet to be seen.

But buyers are also likely to look around for more money by demanding higher wages, raising their own prices, asking for government help, maybe borrowing a little in the meantime. If the central bank provides the money that lets all this take place, it is causing inflation in the limited sense noted above. If it doesn't, prices might come down, as companies and unions find they can't make them stick. But production too will drop. And the administration that is in office when all this occurs may not stay in office long.

The causes of inflation

Examining the money supply brings us back to seeing the economy for what it is: a system. Most of the culprits accused of causing inflation are not wholly innocent—even government regulations and minimum wage laws have something to do with rising prices—but most get blamed way out of proportion to the damage they actually do. Alone, none could cause more than a little inflation. Put together, and inserted into a system where the potential for inflation is built in, they can cause a lot. Social scientists, when examining the causes of a complex phenomenon, frequently speak of predisposing and precipitating factors. That's probably the best way to look at the causes of inflation. A predisposition to inflation is built into the fundamental structures of our economy. With those structures in place, many different factors can touch off or worsen an inflationary spiral. The last five chapters have spelled out both the basic structures and the precipitating events of the last decade, shaping the whole picture one piece at a time. Now it's time to look at what we've got and consider the implications.

The first essential element is this. *Most of the important participants in our economy—companies, industries, professions, workers, interest groups—are able to exercise some influence over how the economic pie gets divvied up.* We have seen lots of examples.

• Big firms have the economic muscle to persuade consumers to buy (and suppliers to sell) at prices determined, within broad limits, by the firms themselves. Small firms in particular markets can often get away with the same behavior. All seek to "maintain profit margins," meaning to make sure they get their share.

• Farmers, doctors, home builders, defense-industry workers, the elderly, welfare mothers, and dozens of other groups draw part or all of their incomes from a variety of government programs. So too, of course, do teachers, tax collectors, and everyone else on government payrolls. All can lobby, bargain, support candidates, and otherwise seek to increase the share of the pot going to them.

• Funeral directors, plumbers, doctors, lawyers, social workers, beauticians, electricians, architects, and many other professionals and tradespeople exercise considerable influence, usually through state licensing authorities, over who may set up shop in their field. They are also sometimes able to establish formal or informal fee schedules, preventing too much price competition.

• Workers who belong to a union can vote for leaders who win (or promise to win) big wage gains. Workers who don't belong to a union can threaten to form or join one. Other workers can quit, threaten to leave, slow down, smoke dope, perform acts of sabotage, and generally not cooperate if the conditions of employment (including wage levels) are unacceptable.

Seen as a competition for real resources, some of this jostling for a piece of the pie cancels itself out. Food stamp recipients and aerospace workers have to compete for a share of the federal budget; General Motors and the United Auto Workers must compete for whatever consumers wind up spending on automobiles. In terms of prices and wages, though, all the jostling has the same effect. Anyone faced with an apparent drop in income—lower wages, higher production costs, less government support, whatever—screams bloody murder. Everyone, given half a chance, asks for more. As a result both prices and wages tend to ratchet upward. It is often easier for employers, particularly if they are big enough, to grant higher wages and then raise prices rather than risk a strike. It is easier for Congress to approve a new program or increase subsidy levels, thus making at least one group of constituents very happy, than to take the opposite measures. To be sure, every price increase, wage hike, or new federal program is likely to provoke cries of irresponsibility from editorial writers and other sidewalk superintendents of the economy. What the hand-wringers forget is that the capitalist system is built on the notion that everybody will—indeed, should—try to make as much money as they can, and that our political system is built on the notion that legislators should try to get reelected. "Responsible" union leaders, corporation executives, and politicians, like nice guys, finish last. In that fact lies one prime source of our economy's predisposition to inflation.

The other essential element is the *enormous importance of government spending in the economy.* Thanks to its huge size, the government can stimulate economic activity and expand the money supply almost at will, thereby smoothing out the business cycle and preventing depressions.

This, more than anything else, is what separates the modern era from the past: it is the fundamental reason why prices have never fallen more than a trivial amount since 1940. People have always tried to control the prices they received for their wares or the wages they were paid for their labor: guilds, industry associations, and other conspiracies in restraint of trade crop up regularly in economic history. People have also tried to increase their incomes by currying favor with the authorities, getting special concessions or tariff protections. But in the past most such attempts at monkeying with the marketplace soon failed. Until the twentieth century few companies were big enough. Until the 1930s few unions were strong enough. Before World War II, governments were too small to make much difference.

Most important, the various structures weren't able to survive hard times. Panic and depression led businesses to forget about their agreements not to cut prices. Workers facing lay-off (with no unemployment benefits) readily deserted the union and accepted a wage cut. With tax revenues down statesmen suddenly became penurious. Bank failures and the resultant shrinkage of the money supply forced reductions all around anyway. Prices had nowhere to go but down.

Today—so far anyway—we have no more depressions of the old-fashioned variety. There are recessions, sometimes touched off by factors beyond the government's control, other times deliberately encouraged in hopes of bringing prices down. But when the economy turns down, a number of stabilizers come into action. Tax revenues fall, government spending rises, and the federal deficit swells. The Fed is likely to ease its restraints on the money supply, letting interest rates drop and pumping money into the economy by buying the bonds that the government issues to finance its deficits. Politicians soon begin talking about tax cuts, and, when a cut finally passes, consumers have more spending money. With all these factors working together the economy soon picks up.

In principle, the government could devote as much attention to preventing inflation as it does to preventing depression. It could raise taxes and tighten up the money supply at the first hint of a jump in the Consumer Price Index. It could lay off its employees, cut transfer payments, allow banks to fail and workers to be laid off without compensation. No political genius is required to see why such measures might be unpopular. Policies aimed at fighting recession have the enormous virtue, from a politician's viewpoint, of putting more money into voters' pockets. Policies aimed at fighting inflation necessarily take money out of voters' pockets.* Thus the asymmetry. The system is predisposed

---

* The West Germans and Swiss have been more successful than some in controlling inflation partly because a large part of the cost has been borne by southern European "guest workers," who mostly do not vote. Lester C. Thurow argues that the number of workers expelled by the Germans and Swiss in one year is roughly equivalent to an employ-

toward inflation on what economists call the macro level as well as on the "micro" level of firms, professions, and industries.

Precipitating factors

Despite this structure, inflation can for a while be held in check. But peculiar conditions are required. You need frequent recessions, and probably the memory of a Great Depression too, just so people don't get too confident in the future. You need a populace that's too disorganized or too powerless to win too many benefits from the government. You need to dominate the international economy, just to make sure that nothing from abroad upsets the applecart. And you need to have productivity rising quickly so that workers' wages and corporate profits can both rise without price increases. This was the recipe for the relative price stability of the 1950s and early 1960s.

With the structure in place, though, any one of four factors can touch off inflation or make it worse. And once it gets going, one big factor—expectations—will be enough to keep it going.

1. Demand-pull inflation. This is the Vietnam-era variety. Government runs a big budget deficit on top of an economy operating near capacity, the Fed accommodates, and too much money winds up chasing too few goods. In principle, booming private investment can create the same situation.

2. Administrative inflation.* This kind can take a variety

---

ment rate approaching 30 percent in this country. He adds that both the West Germans and the Swiss enjoyed the benefits of an appreciating currency in the mid-1970s because their currencies had been undervalued in the old system.

* The term was coined by the economist Gardiner C. Means. It includes some of what economists usually call cost-push inflation (caused by union wage increases) and some of what Means calls profit-push inflation (caused by companies trying to maintain profit margins). "Administrative," in his view, was an appropriately neutral term.

of forms. Unions can negotiate catch-up wage increases even when productivity hasn't improved. Companies, if they're big enough, can raise prices even when the demand for their product has dropped off. A government policy—price supports, for example—can fix prices at steadily increasing levels.

3. "Price shock" inflation. Bad harvests, shortages, wars, external cartels like OPEC, and temporary imbalances in the economy can lead to sharply rising prices for particular goods. These price hikes can reverberate through the economy, lifting the prices both of derivative goods (like petrochemicals and fertilizer) and competitive goods (like coal and natural gas).

4. International inflation. This is brought on by a drop in the value of a nation's currency. When the dollar was devalued, the price of imports rose. So did the price of goods like wheat that could be exported, since increased exports meant a smaller supply for the domestic market.

In the 1970s we got it all. Prices rose and rose, with no end in sight. And that generated the worst inflation of all, the inflation of expectations. When people expect prices to go up, they spend money as if it were going out of style, borrowing as much as they can. So overall demand stays high. Unions bargain for generous settlements and companies jack up prices as much as they can. Farmers and other commodity producers sometimes hold their wares off the market, thus creating a temporary shortage, in hopes of getting a better price later. The dollar looks less attractive to international investors and speculators, so its value falls and prices rise.

Everybody who's not keeping up, meanwhile, looks to the government for help. Fearful that the whole overheated structure will collapse, as it started to in 1973–74, the government runs up big deficits and pumps up the money supply, making sure that all the rising prices can be accommodated. Only in late 1979 and early 1980 did Washington begin to apply the brakes, tightening up the money supply and talking about balanced budgets. By then the recession was under way, and in November Jimmy Carter paid the price.

To return for a moment to that list of villains at the beginning of this chapter, each one's place should now be a little clearer. Anything that drives some prices up (OPEC, the Russians, the anchovies) can be a cause of inflation simply because prices of other goods are unlikely to fall. Everyone who manages the economy (presidents, Federal Reserve chairmen, and so on) has a strong incentive to allow inflation because the alternative might be deep depression. When people charge that something they don't like is inflationary—defense spending, say—they usually have unspoken assumptions (often wrong) about what would happen if the object of their dislike were done away with. When people disagree about a cause of inflation (whether taxes and interest rates are too high or too low, for instance), it's usually because they have different ideas about what would happen if the phenomenon in question were changed. There are still, in economics, a lot of things we don't know.

From the viewpoint of history, the cause of inflation on the broadest level can readily be summed up. A free-market, competitive, dog-eat-dog uncontrolled capitalist economy is nobody's paradise. Businesses, facing prices they can't predict and markets they can't control, fear for their economic health. Workers, without control over their wages or their terms of employment, fear for their physical health. Those who can't work fear for their lives. The evidence of this fear is written in the history of the twentieth century. Companies have grown large enough to ensure their survival and profitability in all but the direst straits. Workers, farmers, the elderly, and dozens of other groups have struggled to make the government responsive to their needs and have won huge gains. Economists and political leaders learned that the business cycle can, within broad limits, be controlled; from that time on no administration could afford to risk more than a short recession. In the meantime the government grew large enough not only to meet at least some of the needs of those who were putting forth claims, but also to manage the economy, make sure that there was plenty of money (and to spend it if necessary), and thereby to stabilize the cycle.

The cause of inflation, in a word, has been the long, tortuous, and largely successful escape from the terrible insecurity of the marketplace—from the chilling fingers of the invisible hand.

8. Can Inflation Be Controlled?

There is a simple means of getting rid of the never-ending inflation we have experienced for the last few decades. It works quickly, and it's guaranteed effective.

The first step is to eliminate all the ways the government interferes with the free operation of the marketplace. Abolish social security, welfare, unemployment compensation, minimum-wage and child-labor laws. Declare the National Labor Relations Act null and void. Do away with farm price supports, the Civil Aeronautics Board, the Interstate Commerce Commission, and all the other institutions that restrict competition and help keep prices up. At the state and local levels, get rid of licensing requirements for lawyers, doctors, taxi drivers, plumbers, and other restricted trades.

The second step is to abolish most of the rest of the government. No more housing programs, food stamps, interstate highways, Medicare and Medicaid. No more bloated Pentagon: cut the Defense Department's budget by 95 percent. (That would still give it about $7 billion, enough to maintain what used to be thought of as a peacetime army.) In states and localities, get along with fewer bureaucrats, teachers, road workers, librarians, sanitation workers, and police. Cut taxes accordingly.

The third step is to restrict the growth of the money

supply. The dollar could be backed by a commodity—gold will do—and the stock of money regulated by the supply of that commodity. Banks should sink or swim on their own: no more restrictions on competition among banks, and no more Federal Deposit Insurance Corporation.

So far, all we have done is to go back to about 1914. We have removed the stabilizing influence of a huge government, and we have rendered expansionary fiscal or monetary policies impossible or ineffectual. We have lubricated the mechanisms that set wages and prices with a healthy squirt of competition. Thanks to all these measures, prices will soon begin to fall as well as rise.

To be safe, though, we should set a firm upper limit, not too big, on the size of business enterprises, then break up any company larger than that. (If the limit were $1 million in annual sales, we would have to break up about 300,000 concerns but could leave about 14 million intact.) Big corporations can't cause inflation all by themselves, as the early years of this century showed us. But they can usually keep prices from falling too far in the parts of the economy where they are dominant. Unless they are broken up, the burden of controlling inflation through falling prices would fall mainly on farmers and small businesses. That would be an unstable arrangement at best. So we had better ensure real competition throughout the economy.

This kind of anti-inflation program is only partly fanciful. The economist Milton Friedman, host of the popular television series *Free to Choose* and coauthor with Rose Friedman of the best-selling book of the same name, espouses some of the proposals outlined above. *The Wall Street Journal*'s editorial page (whose editor, Robert L. Bartley, won a Pulitzer Prize for editorial writing in 1980) would also go along with some. So, in his more private moments, might Ronald Reagan. A large number of Americans read and agree with Friedman and the *Journal*. A larger number voted for Reagan in 1980. The mood of the country, it is said, has turned conservative. There are some who suppose the time is ripe for a return to the past.

But political moods come cheap. Campaign rhetoric notwithstanding, neither the current administration nor any other in the foreseeable future will come close to proposing anything like such a program.* Budget and program cuts, if there are any, will be limited to small fractions of what the government does. No one will suggest abolishing welfare or unemployment benefits, let alone social security, and expect to be taken seriously; and no one, least of all the conservatives mentioned above, will propose a big reduction in the size of the Pentagon's activities. Neither presidents nor Congress will risk the anger of farmers, doctors, home builders, or unions by proposing to do away with the special programs or protections each group now enjoys. And none will seriously attempt to break up the big corporations.

Those who lament this state of affairs frequently blame it on political chickenheartedness. It could more accurately be blamed on political good sense. Most government programs came into being because they served real needs. Many still do. Even those that seem to have grown all out of proportion to the need they once served have active, vocal defenders. A radical reform—abolishing price supports, say —hurts at least one group directly and immediately. If it helps anyone, say by lowering food prices, the effect is felt only gradually and in small amounts. The political calculations, therefore, all point toward not fiddling too much with

---

* Sometimes there is less even to the campaign rhetoric than meets the eye. Two months before the 1980 election, for example, Ronald Reagan made headlines by proposing to slash federal spending by $195 billion. This sounded like a radical cut in the budget. In reality, however, his plan called for only a 2 percent budget reduction in 1981, followed by annual cuts gradually increasing to 7 percent in 1985. They added up to a total of $195 billion on the assumption that federal spending would otherwise climb to about $900 billion by 1985. No mention was made of which programs would be cut, except of course for "waste and inefficiency." If such a plan is ever laid before Congress, it will be interesting to see how far it gets.

the system. American politics *is* fundamentally conservative, but it is the kind of conservatism that seeks to maintain the status quo, not the kind, like Friedman's, that yearns for a different social order.

Fierce political struggles, of course, will be fought over all these issues—over taxes, tariffs, price support levels, health insurance plans, new housing programs, weapons systems, and social security benefits. But nearly all will take place, as economists say, at the margin. Reagan's conservatism, like that of most elected Republicans, is tempered by a healthy dose of pragmatism. Congress will debate budget cuts of a percent or two, probably while increasing military spending. It will consider lopping off one or two of the federal bureaucracy's less important arms. It will cut taxes—but not far below where they would have been if inflation hadn't been driving everyone into higher tax brackets. All these battles will make a difference to those who win or lose jobs, influence, or a few extra budget dollars in Washington. To the rest of us they will mean little. They will have virtually no effect on the major political and economic institutions that have been created over the past fifty years. And they will have virtually no effect on inflation.

Controlling inflation with recession

The middle-of-the-road approach to stopping inflation, and hence the most common one, is not to dismantle the political economy but to control it through fiscal and monetary policies. The typical metaphors for this approach involve automobiles and stoves. Inflation is said to occur when the economy is "going too fast," or when it is "overheated." To stop inflation, the government has to "put on the brakes" or "turn down the heat." The assumption behind both metaphors is that an inflationary economy is operating at very nearly full capacity. Demand is pressing on supply, and prices are therefore tending to rise. Congress can slow it down (or cool it off) by raising taxes or cutting spending, thus removing purchasing power from the economy. The Fed can achieve the same result by raising interest rates or otherwise tightening up the money supply.

In the best of all possible worlds, tightening up the budget or the purse strings a little would dampen inflation without causing any ill effects elsewhere in the economy. In the real world, as all are aware, things are seldom so precise. The economy is an enormous, complex system. It has a momentum of its own, which varies with market shifts, technological developments, investment patterns, and so on. The government's tools to affect this system are at best blunt instruments. Budget cuts require months to take effect. Tax hikes and tight-money policies can work faster, but nobody knows at any point how steep the tax increase should be or how high interest rates should go. Nor do they know to what extent the reduction in purchasing power will show up in the form of reduced production rather than lower prices. If the policies aren't stringent enough, inflation continues. If they are too stringent the economy slips into recession. A government trying to avoid both resembles a drunk walking a tightrope in a high wind.*

Those who propose cutting federal spending without reducing taxes and those who propose get-tough monetary policies are thus proposing that we fight inflation by risking and if necessary enduring a recession. All the discussion of slowing down and cooling off the economy should not be

---

* Economists used to write a good deal about the "Phillips Curve," a line on a graph that seemed to show a predictable trade-off between inflation and unemployment. Increase unemployment a small amount, the curve seemed to say, and you will reduce inflation by a corresponding amount.

For most of the 1950s and 1960s, the curve fit the data pretty well: prices rose a little in good times, when most people were working, and rose scarcely at all in times of relatively high unemployment. In the 1970s, though, devotees of the Phillips curve for the most part folded up their pads of graph paper and began to interest themselves in other things. What had been a comparatively smooth curve now was looking like the doodlings of a creative chimpanzee. Hence the difficulty at present of knowing how much recession is needed to curb inflation.

allowed to obscure this fact. If recessions could be avoided, elected governments would almost certainly avoid them. Yet they occur—provoked, encouraged, or worsened by deliberate governmental policy, carried out in the name of fighting inflation. The recession of 1980 is only the most recent example. It was, wrote economists Martin and Kathleen Feldstein, "the result of a deliberate *and desirable* policy designed to slow the rate of inflation" (emphasis added). Reagan, too, is likely to court recession by tightening up the purse strings.

The policy of throwing recessions at inflation is not, of course, foolish on its face. It was the panics and depressions of the past that once wrung inflation out of the economy. Even in modern times there is little doubt that recessions can change the behavior of some businesses, workers, and consumers in ways that might affect inflation. "In a recession," as business-cycle specialist Geoffrey H. Moore explains it, "businesses try to cut costs, and are often successful. They are forced to shave profit margins and give discounts to get rid of heavy inventories. The cost of holding even a normal inventory—in terms of interest charges—is likely to prove excessive. Some businesses fail, and sell out for what they can get. Overtime work is cut back or eliminated, which not only reduces costs but reduces the incomes of workers who have been earning the high overtime rates. Layoffs occur, wage increases are deferred, and the uncertainty about jobs and earnings makes people cautious about spending for frills, postpone big ticket purchases, seek ways to economize, borrow less. Construction projects get postponed, delayed, or stretched out. Banks take a hard look at new loans, and may urge repayment instead of refinancing existing loans.

"All these factors," Moore concludes, "make it more difficult to raise prices and more difficult to get wage increases. More prices remain steady and some fall."

If everything were so clear-cut, we might glumly decide that a little recession was good for us now and then. But recession's record as a cure for inflation is spotty at best. The reasons for that spottiness are built into our political system as surely as the behavior Moore describes. And because its effectiveness is open to doubt, the hardships recession causes can't be so easily glossed over or accepted. Lost jobs and failed businesses, after all, are easy to accept only when they aren't your own.

The record—and the reasons

Since World War II, there have been seven economic downturns, counting the one that began in 1980.* The rate of inflation, measured over six-month intervals, has turned downward nine times in the same period.† The two phenomena are almost certainly connected. But the connections are not simple, and in recent years they have been growing tenuous.

In theory, the inflation rate should peak during a recession: prices may keep going up for a while as higher costs are passed along, but the factors cited by Professor Moore should make prices rise more slowly than before. That's essentially the way things worked in 1954, 1970, and 1973–75. In 1949, however, prices bottomed out during the recession; the inflation rate had been falling already, and it would soon shoot up because of the Korean War. The recessions of 1958 and 1960 also followed rather than preceded drops in the inflation rate—rather as if medicine were administered after the patient's fever had broken—and in 1966–67 inflation eased a bit without a measurable downturn.

Like a drug used against an increasingly resistant infection, recession doesn't cure inflation as well as it once did. For fifteen years after World War II, prices essentially stopped rising before or shortly after an economic down-

---

* A rule-of-thumb definition of a recession is a drop in real GNP over two successive three-month measuring periods. The semiofficial arbiter of recessions is an outfit in Cambridge, Massachusetts, called the National Bureau of Economic Research.

† Note here that what slowed was the inflation *rate*, not prices. When inflation drops from 6 percent a year to 4 percent, prices are still going up.

turn. In the 1970s, though, with prices going up much faster than they used to, recession never came close to doing away with inflation. The long, deep, and painful slowdown of 1973–75, the worst since the Depression, cut the inflation rate from a high of 12 percent in 1974 to a low of 5 percent in 1976. But the new low was higher than any inflation America experienced between 1951 and 1968. Recession still "worked." But its effects were not what they once had been.

The reasons for recession's blemished record do not bode well for its effectiveness as a cure for inflation in the near future. Essentially, tight-money and tight-budget policies face three obstacles.

One is the uncertainties of timing and magnitude already noted. It is hard to determine what the economy was doing three months ago, let alone what it will be doing three months hence. So no one ever knows how much slowing down the economy "needs." Recessionary measures may come too soon or too late, and they may be too severe or too weak. In either case, the policy is apt to appear misguided, and those who implement it to appear foolish or heartless. When inflation is bad, the risks are magnified by the size of recession thought necessary to curb it.

The second obstacle is the political problem suggested in the last chapter. Anti-inflationary policies—high interest rates, balanced budgets—necessarily remove purchasing power from the economy. Taxes go up, government spending goes down, borrowing gets harder. On paper, this sounds simple enough. In practice the difficulties are enormous. Congress has never been fond of raising taxes. It is even less fond of angering constituencies and federal agencies by cutting back their programs. Even the Fed has problems in maintaining a tight monetary policy. Its governors do not have to be elected, and their terms run for fourteen years, which is supposed to insulate them from political pressures. Still, every Fed chairman in recent memory has worried about how to justify tight-money policies to members of Congress who don't like them. Also, stringent policies may conflict with another of the Fed's purposes, which is to serve as guarantor of the banking system's health and, when the occasion calls for it, lender of last resort. In the 1973–75 recession, the Franklin National Bank in New York failed. In early 1980, the Hunt brothers' speculation in the silver futures market almost brought about the collapse not only of the silver market itself but of some major brokerage firms. In both cases the Fed had a hand in arranging the solution: a takeover of Franklin National, a bailout loan for the Hunts.

The tighter the Fed's monetary policies are, the more banks and big companies are apt to find themselves in trouble, requiring some kind of government help if whole systems are not to collapse. The Fed's dilemma, as the economist Robert B. Zevin has described it, is that in inflationary times it ends up trying to squeeze an egg. It wants to apply pressure to the economy, but it doesn't want to have to clean up the mess when things begin to crack. Again, the dangers are hard to avoid. "Since the mid-1960s," writes Washington University economist Hyman P. Minsky, "the Federal Reserve has been able to force a contraction only as it has taken the economy to the brink of financial crisis."

Because of these political difficulties, nobody wants to maintain a recession too long. Yet it may take a very long time, especially now, for recession to have a noticeable effect on prices. That is the third obstacle faced by the policy of fighting inflation with recession.

If prices responded quickly and accurately to a slowdown in demand, like prices in the stock market, then a recession would rapidly slow or even reverse the rate of inflation. Some prices really do respond this way: spot market prices for industrial commodities, for example, usually fall during a recession. Most prices, however, do not. Some prices fall, but only after six months or a year, when contracts can be rewritten or new deals negotiated. Other prices don't move at all. Most just keep rising. Some go up because the part of the economy in question (government, say, or medicine) doesn't change much during a recession. Others rise because costs are continuing to increase, or because manufacturers are desperately trying to cut losses or protect profit margins. The year 1980, for example, was one of the worst years the domestic auto industry has ever faced; at one point sales were off 25 percent from 1979 levels. Yet average new-car selling prices rose between 6 and 9 percent.

Tight-budget and tight-money policies will always, if they are stringent enough, reduce *spending*. But *prices* will fall only where they are responsive to demand. When prices are going up because of three-year union contracts, because of corporate needs to cover costs or decisions to increase margins, because of external factors like OPEC, or because of governmental policies like Medicare or higher wages for government workers, inflation continues in spite of spending cutbacks, and production drops. That is the recipe for "stagflation."

Is recession worth it?

Even if a recession makes a dent in the inflation rate, its costs are not negligible.

In a recession, production drops off. Businesses fail and workers lose their jobs. Consumers, as economist Moore allows, have to tighten their belts and get by on less. The drop in output, of course, is one reason prices don't fall as far or as quickly as they otherwise might. When people are buying fewer cars, General Motors doesn't cut the price, it just makes a smaller number. The same is true of many manufacturing industries. According to the late Arthur Okun, a member of the Council of Economic Advisers under Lyndon Johnson, "90 percent of the effect [of a prolonged recession] is lost output and jobs, and only 10 percent is diminished inflation." President Carter's Council of Economic Advisers, in their 1980 Economic Report, seemed to agree with Okun. "Unfortunately," the report read, "the overall rate of wage and price increases in the American economy, while not immune to the effects of idle capacity and unemployment, is not highly sensitive to moderate changes in economic slack." Translated from the language of economic policy makers, this means that recession might slow inflation a little but is unlikely to dampen it much. What we get instead is a lot of "idle capacity and unemployment."

Whether recession is worth this cost in lost output and unemployment depends in large measure on whom you're talking to. *The Wall Street Journal* wondered in 1980 whether "the nation now is willing to suffer the degree of economic pain that a substantial reduction in inflation would surely entail." But nations don't suffer pain; people do. Managers of banks and large businesses, academic economists with tenure, most policy analysts and government officials are unlikely to feel a recession's effects personally. Some may even benefit. Hard times tend to squeeze out smaller competitors in an industry, thus strengthening the position of big companies. Hard times may also soften workers' wage demands, thus enabling many employers to maintain or increase profit margins.

The burden of recession, by contrast, usually falls on people who weren't doing so well to begin with. Workers in economically marginal industries and companies suffer. So do workers in highly volatile, boom-and-bust industries like construction. So do those who were last hired and are now first fired. The burden, as it turns out, is borne disproportionately by black and Hispanic workers, by female workers, and by the young.* Those who gain from recession are not all rich,

---

* "Often," writes Lester C. Thurow, "the argument is made that women and children should be more than proportionally drafted into the war on inflation because there are fewer harsh economic consequences when they suffer unemployment since they have families to fall back upon. I have yet to hear this argument made by women or young workers; it ignores a very large number of women and young workers who are family heads or come from low-income families. It also ignores the long-run consequences of having a generation of young people who have either dropped out of the economy or have not gained

and those who suffer are not all poor. But the effects grow considerably less noticeable as you go up the income scale. Not coincidentally, that's where you find most of the people who prescribe recession as a cure for inflation. "In all recorded history," writes management consultant Peter Drucker, "there has not been one economist who has had to worry about where the next meal would come from."

The case for controls

The main cause of inflation, as we have seen, is that a lot of different groups have the ability to make effective claims on how the economic pie gets divided up. Unions demand wage increases. Companies raise their prices without fear of being undersold. Those whose incomes depend on government lobby their representatives for more money, knowing that representatives have an interest in going along whenever they can. When the Fed accommodates all these demands by letting the money supply expand—and it usually has little choice if it wants to avoid a recession—the result is rising prices.

The solution to inflation, however, is not to do away with people's ability to make claims on the economy, abolishing unions, big corporations, government programs, and so forth. Nor is it simply to put a lid on the money supply. Both cures put us back where we started, and wreak disproportionate havoc on those who can least afford it. *The solution instead is to control the claims themselves.* So far we have tried to do this piecemeal, through jawboning, fiscal restraint, and trying to hold down increases in programs like welfare or farm price supports. That hasn't worked well, mostly because a piecemeal approach puts an unfair burden on those who happen to be first in line, or who are politically weakest. Any company, union, or government beneficiary worth its

the work experiences that lead to skills in later life. What do we do when today's unemployed twenty-year-old becomes the next generation's unemployed forty-year-old?"

FIGHTING INFLATION OURSELVES?

"Should We Blame Uncle Sam for All He Spends, or Blame Ourselves for All We Ask?" read the headline on a two-page advertisement that turned up one day in 1980 in *Business Week*. The ad, which was placed by the American Council of Life Insurance, invited readers "to join us in an earnest effort to bring [inflation] under control." All you had to do was fill in the coupon at the bottom of the page; the council would "see that our nation's leaders in Washington hear of your concern."

"I Vote to Self-Control Inflation," the coupon read. "I will not ask for or support government programs that require deficit spending."

Leaving aside the question of which programs are the ones that require deficit spending, the ad called to mind a letter that had appeared shortly before in *The New York Times*. "In this year of high inflation," the letter read, "everyone must sacrifice. The poor will give up food stamps and summer jobs; the rich will give up Federal programs to aid the poor."

SOURCE: This particular ad appeared in *Business Week*, July 7, 1980, pp. 16–17. The letter was written by Paul Rosenbaum and was dated April 18, 1980.

salt will not easily buy the notion that the fight against inflation begins with them, and that others may or may not join later.

The only way to do it is all at once: to control, explicitly, the prices businesses are allowed to set, the wages workers are allowed to earn, and all the other decisions that affect the share of society's resources going to different groups. This does not mean, as we shall see in a moment, that the government has to run the economy. Nor does it mean we have to fight inflation through a wartime-style program of shortages and rationing. It means only that the private sector's freedom to raise prices and wages indefinitely has to be restrained. And it means that the parts of the economy where the government is most involved will have to be restructured so that people's incomes are controlled as well as supported. None of this will be smooth sailing. But the subject at hand is how to curb inflation without causing undue economic distress, not how to make everybody happy. A system of controls, warts and all, is the only anti-inflationary program that seems even roughly fair to all and likely to increase rather than undermine people's sense of security. For just those reasons it seems both potentially feasible and potentially effective.

Political feasibility

Like most proposals designed to curb inflation, wage and price controls provoke a measure of fear and loathing. The economics profession, with only a few exceptions, regards them with about the same affection the Church lavished on the theories of Galileo. Business might accept wage controls and labor might accept price controls, but the standoff between the two ensures that we'll never get one without the other, and neither group is especially happy with that prospect. There is reason for suspicion even on the part of the general public. Controls have traditionally been employed only in wartime, not the happiest of associations. They were last used by a president whose intentions and competence were open to some doubt. And they would be administered by the only institution the public mistrusts as much as Big Business and Big Labor: Big Government.

Nevertheless, opposition to controls is neither as widespread nor as unchangeable as it sometimes appears. Voters generally support a policy of controls whenever inflation gets particularly virulent. A *New York Times*/CBS poll in February 1980, for example, found nearly two thirds of its respondents supporting controls, and other polls have elicited similar reactions. Senator Edward M. Kennedy's espousal of controls during the 1980 primaries did not hurt his campaign noticeably, and indeed may have contributed to his victories in the large industrial states. Even the opposition from business and academic quarters does not seem set in granite. In 1980, before the recession hit and the rate of inflation eased a little, several prominent economists began to debate the case for controls. The magazine *Business Week*, ordinarily a mirror of conventionally conservative views, supported them editorially.

At some point during the next few years it seems highly likely that some form of wage and price controls will be imposed. (Exactly what form is open to question—see box, below.) The reason will not be ideological—Reagan opposes

---

VARIATIONS

This chapter discusses wage and price controls in their classic form—that is, ceiling prices and wages fixed and enforced by a government agency, as in World War II and in the early 1970s. Other, less thoroughgoing forms of wage and price control have been proposed too. "Real wage insurance" would give workers a tax break if the cost of living rose faster than a government-determined ceiling on wage increases. The "tax-based income plan" (TIP) proposed by economists Sidney Weintraub and Henry C. Wallich would tax companies whose total payrolls (blue- and white-collar) rose beyond a certain amount. Either of these, or yet another variation, may be implemented in lieu of comprehensive controls.

We have little way of knowing how effective any such plan would be. The wage-price guidelines of the last twenty years, an even milder form of controls, proved themselves effective in periods of mild inflation (the 1960s) and ineffective in periods of virulent inflation controls—but that other attempts to curb inflation have failed. Suppose, for example, that the Labor Department one day announces that the latest round of collective bargaining will produce record-setting wage increases. An OPEC meeting a week later announces a 10 percent oil price hike. A bad harvest the previous summer begins to show up in higher prices at the supermarket, and mortgage rates again hit 20 percent.

Before long the government announces a monthly jump in the Consumer Price Index of 2.1 percent, translating into an annual inflation rate of over 25 percent. The president announces on television that inflation is expected to abate next month (it is frequently expected to abate next month, at least by the administration in power), but that he will

---

(the 1970s). Today, companies that anticipated sharply rising costs might choose to accept tax penalties rather than forgo their own desired price increases.

The discussion in this chapter focuses on classic wage and price controls rather than variations like TIP for two reasons. Number one: we can assume that strict controls really will hold down prices, and focus on the issue of whether they produce deleterious side effects. With loose controls, both questions are up for grabs. Number two: you don't necessarily gain much by substituting incentives or tax penalties for outright wage and price ceilings. As *The New Republic* has pointed out, to the extent that half measures work, they cause the same potential inefficiencies and problems as full-scale controls. To the extent that they don't cause those problems they aren't working. Lester C. Thurow adds that tax-based incomes plans are "just equivalent to a set of wage and price controls with a predetermined set of financial penalties for violators. Catching the violators and enforcing the rules [are] no less difficult or expensive."

ask Congress for the authority to impose wage and price controls in case it does not. The next month, after a startling round of anticipatory wage demands and price hikes, the CPI again jumps 2 percent and controls are imposed. A few economists wring their hands. The public, rightly recognizing there was no other way out, applauds.

Effectiveness

Will controls work? Economists' opposition to wage and price controls is based largely on the belief that they never have and therefore never can. This view has percolated through the business community and helps account for the policy's unpopularity there. But the case against controls is a little like an old battleship: rusty, leaky, and more appropriate to the last war than the current one. The objections, when scrutinized, turn out to be full of holes.

1. *Controls are like putting a lid on a boiling kettle instead of turning down the heat.* This analogy—back to the cookstove again—crops up repeatedly in newspaper editorials, in statements by political officials, and in the "image" advertisements by which large corporations monger their opinions to magazine readers. Its message is that price controls address the symptom rather than the cause of inflation. The reason for rising prices (in this view) is too much government spending, or maybe too rapid a rise in the money supply, and it is these factors rather than prices that ought to be controlled.

If inflation were solely a case of too much money chasing too few goods, as the government-spending and easy-money arguments imply, then the analogy would be valid. Controls really wouldn't work. Something else would be noticeable too. The economy would be operating at very nearly full capacity. Plants would be running two or three shifts, and jobs would be easily available to all. High demand and high prices, after all, should mean good times for business, and business should therefore be working overtime to sell all it can. Since few businesses are in fact working overtime right now and since the past ten years have not been a period of notably rapid economic growth, something may be wrong with the analogy.

The trouble, of course, is that the argument assumes the economy works much like the stock market, with prices rising only in response to high demand. The real world, as we have seen, is considerably more complicated. Only a small number of prices respond quickly and accurately to changes in supply and demand. Others are raised to protect profit margins—the auto industry, for example—whether or not business is good. Most simply go up whenever costs, especially labor costs, rise.

Controls by definition prevent companies from arbitrarily raising their prices. They also put a lid on most costs, including wages. So in most cases the reason for high prices—the cause of inflation, in effect—simply vanishes. In this sense controls really do turn down the heat; they reduce the upward pressure on prices.

2. *Controls won't work because too much of the economy is outside the jurisdiction of the United States government.* We can't control the price of OPEC oil, for instance, or the world price of wheat, copper, and other internationally traded commodities. If we try, and if the U.S. price is lower than the world price, we simply won't get the goods.

This point is indisputably true. The only economic leverage we have over OPEC is to use less oil and hope that will make prices come down. We have virtually no leverage over the world price of commodities we don't produce ourselves, and little enough over the price of those (wheat, for instance) where we are one producer among several. The price of imported goods will therefore have to rise whenever the world price goes up. Businesses that use these goods should be allowed to pass on part of the cost increases—only part, so as to encourage conservation. Consumers will just have to pay the higher prices. The same may hold true for some goods produced here and sold on the world market. Or we may decide to hold the price down and institute export controls, so that the whole supply doesn't get shipped abroad.

Does this mean that price controls won't work? Obviously not. The fact that we cannot control the price of oil or wheat does not mean we can't control the price of housing, health care, processed foods, coal, secretarial service, or high-school teaching. Rising world prices will inevitably lead to some inflation here at home. A 10 percent jump in the price of oil, for example, might cause one percentage point of inflation in the United States. But the purpose of controls is not to abolish all price increases forever: it is to halt the inflationary spiral. Few would object to paying Kellogg's an extra penny a box for cereal because the price of wheat has gone up, or to paying Blue Cross an extra 1 percent in premiums because hospital fuel bills are on the rise. What we don't like is paying 10, 15, or 20 percent more every year on all such items because the cost of everything else has gone up that much too.

3. *Prices are an important economic "signal." If they are not set by the marketplace, we'll get shortages and black markets. Remember World War II.* To understand this argument, return for a moment to the stock market. Suppose Xerox is selling for 58½, and suppose further that a simple-minded president decides to curb inflation by setting ceiling prices for stock. The Securities and Exchange Commission soon announces that the maximum selling price for Xerox will be 60.

Two weeks later, the company announces a technological breakthrough that promises to improve its profit picture, and investors flock to buy its stock. In normal times, the price would rise sharply—up to a point where the number of shares investors wanted to buy equaled the number that other investors wanted to sell. With price controls on, though, buyers can't bid the price up past 60, and only a few people are willing to sell their shares at that price. At this point one of two things happens. Buyers who obey the law go away empty-handed. The others begin making under-the-table deals with Xerox shareholders, raising the effective price of the stock to whatever the traffic will bear. Thus do shortages and black markets appear when prices are held down below the market level.

Note that in reading this explanation, however, you had to suspend disbelief at a critical point, namely that a president would impose price controls on the stock market. Controls on the stock market are entirely unnecessary, and not only because stock is not a commodity in the usual sense. Stock prices move down as well as up. The market itself is an effective control. Where the economy works like the stock market, controls are similarly unnecessary. The price of most agricultural produce, for example, rises and falls (at least down to the support price) as supply and demand change. So do the prices of manufactured goods in highly competitive industries like clothing, and the prices of some industrial commodities like bulk chemicals. In most of these cases, prices can be allowed to rise as the market permits, because the market doesn't permit much. So no shortages will develop here except those occasioned by real factors like bad harvests.

In other cases, however, the market is largely ineffective. The price of automobiles should be controlled because the Big Three have shown themselves ready, willing, and able to raise prices regardless of market conditions. So with most goods manufactured by highly concentrated industries. The price of health care—doctors' fees, hospital charges—should be controlled because the government has (rightly) interfered so much with the marketplace that competition no longer does its job. And the price of labor—wages—should be controlled not only because it is such an important part of other prices but because the labor market is ineffective in pushing wages down.

In none of these cases are long-term shortages likely to develop. The effect of price controls on highly concentrated industries would be to turn them, in effect, into regulated public utilities, producing at fixed prices for an assured return. There is no shortage of capacity in the regulated sectors of the economy. Where health care is concerned, we already have an overabundance of most facilities and personnel: the problem is that they are poorly distributed. And as for the labor market, there are shortages and bottlenecks already, as with nurses. Would they get worse under a system of wage controls? In fact the opposite might happen: the wage controllers could let the wages of occupations where there are shortages go up while holding others in the same "wage contour" steady.

The widespread shortages that people over fifty remember from World War II were due not to price controls per se but to the fact that there was a war on. Occasionally, peacetime controls might lead to a temporary shortage of something too: no chicken in the supermarket, long waiting periods to buy an automatic washer. That will be a sign that the price schedule needs adjustment. Again, we might get a little inflation. But we would not get an inflationary spiral.

4. *Every time price controls are lifted, inflation reappears.* By this reasoning food stamps must be ineffective too: if the program were terminated tomorrow, poor people would again go hungry. If inflation reappears when controls are lifted, then you lifted them too soon. Unless the economy can be changed in ways that make inflation less likely, or unless a regime of controls itself begins to change people's long-term expectations and behavior, controls may have to be permanent.

5. *But permanent—or semipermanent—price controls will require a huge bureaucracy. And they infringe on our freedom by putting the government in the position of telling businesses how much they can charge and workers how much they can make.* Permanent controls will in fact require a fair-sized bureaucracy. So does nearly everything else that operates on a large scale: the telephone company, the United Auto Workers, the social security system, the Pentagon. The

bureaucracy at times will seem inept. It need not, however, be as large as many government agencies. Nor need it be any more incompetent, ineffectual, and corrupt than, say, the Internal Revenue Service. As with most things political, it depends on who's in charge and on what the governing rules and expectations are. The experience under Nixon was not necessarily a fair test.

The extent to which price controls infringe on our economic freedom is hard to measure. Economic freedom is neither indivisible nor inalienable by anyone's standard. We already pay taxes and submit to extensive government regulation; both are infringements on our ability to get and spend as we choose. The press critic A. J. Liebling once pointed out that freedom of the press is guaranteed to the man who owns one. Similarly, the freedom to determine prices or to set wages, let alone the freedom to determine our own income, is not a freedom most people enjoy. Those who have it will of course give it up reluctantly. The rest of us should not concern ourselves unduly.

There is probably less to wage and price controls than meets the eye. Like other major reforms of the political economy—the graduated income tax, the introduction of social security, government protection for union organizing —controls are an expedient way of dealing with what has become a pressing problem. Like those other reforms, controls will provoke some loud shrieks of agony and a lot of low-grade carping. Eventually, people will get used to them.

Controls will never work perfectly. Nor will they solve many of the various problems that plague the U. S. economy. Nevertheless, they seem worth trying. Inflation may not be the monster it is frequently made out to be, but it does cause a lot of uncertainty and worry, and it always threatens to run away with itself. No other policy has proved effective against it. If we can implement a system of wage and price controls equitably, reasonably, and without unrealistic hopes or expectations, we should be able to curb it.

Other measures

Once price and wage controls are in effect, there are many other ways the government can begin restructuring the economy to prevent recurrent price increases.

• Where the government itself sets wages, prices, and benefits, it can hold them largely constant over time. Thus federal wage levels, social security benefits, or farm price supports would be allowed to rise only after a conscious decision to allocate more of the nation's real income to federal employees, the elderly, or farmers.

• Where the government regulates supply and demand, it can pursue policies aimed at lowering prices. Paradoxically, the policies may sometimes involve using the marketplace. Airline deregulation, for example, has evidently lowered many air fares, and trucking deregulation should have the same effect. In other instances prices will need explicit control. A license to operate a television station, a law firm, a plumbing business or a funeral home, just like a taxicab medallion, should carry a maximum fee schedule along with it. Only if there are no applicants for licenses should we conclude that the fee schedule is too low. If there are many it is probably too high.

• Where the government pays a good part of the bill, as in health care, it needs to set rates more thoroughly and explicitly than it does now. The trick here may be to have the government pay all the bills through some sort of national health scheme, as in England or Canada; it then has an almost inescapable incentive to keep costs in line. Though their systems differ, both nations spend considerably less of their GNP on health care than we do. Yet both Canadians and the English are as healthy as Americans.

• Where the government is drawn willy-nilly into an economic sector, as it has been drawn into energy, it has to pay attention to controlling prices. Gasoline and home heating oil, for instance, should have been rationed the minute it became clear that OPEC could make the new prices stick. Nearly all drivers and homeowners, I suspect, would have preferred a guaranteed allotment of both commodities at a lower price to an uncertain allotment at a considerably higher price. Moreover, the reduced consumption enforced by rationing would have given us a substantial bargaining weapon in negotiations with OPEC.

• Fiscal and monetary policies should not be ignored. The high-employment budget should normally be balanced, the money supply allowed to grow at a modest pace. Levels of spending and money supply growth should be determined pragmatically: avoiding recession on the one hand and the shortages occasioned by high-demand price controls on the other. As at present, this balance will never be perfect. But the dangers on the inflation side will be less, and the chance of avoiding recession that much greater.

Without comprehensive wage and price controls, measures aimed at holding down prices in one part of the economy seem unfair, and the government seldom pursues them. Nor can it easily hold down demand through fiscal and monetary policies without provoking recession, and even then prices may still keep rising. With controls in place, all such policies become possible. Demands from individual groups can be refused because everyone is being asked to sacrifice. And fiscal and monetary policies can be eased a little without risking runaway inflation.

Inflation is a problem that can be solved. The solution, it is true, involves the government deeply in all parts of the economy. This may be lamented by many. But the government is already deeply involved in the economy. Its involvement is a prime reason for the inflation we have experienced for the last thirty-five years. There is little chance of reducing that involvement; nor, in most instances, is there good reason to do so. So we need to proceed to the next logical step, and create the means by which inflation, like so many other aspects of the economy, can be subjected to control.

Epilogue:
After Inflation

In a sense, both inflation itself and the attempts to control it are symptoms of a deeper struggle within the American economy. This deeper conflict is likely to intensify if we succeed in curbing price increases. It is of course the struggle over how the economic pie will be divided up. It used to take place on terms quite different from today's.

In the past, the money pie itself was more or less fixed. Rising prices or wages would, over time, be balanced by falling prices or wages. Then as now, average incomes could rise in real terms only as more was produced. But now money incomes can rise even if real incomes don't.

Also, economic power was in the past distributed quite differently. Economic power is the ability to influence how much of the pie you get. For most of history, essentially the only people who wielded any such power were those who owned land or commanded armies. In the industrial age, the corporations that first capitalized on new markets and new technologies grew large enough to gain economic power, as did the banks and investment houses that provided the capital for all this growth. Eventually other groups, working through the medium of a vastly expanded government apparatus, began to catch up. Today farmers, unionized workers, government employees, doctors, the elderly, and dozens of other groups wield some economic power. The federal government supports or provides a substantial fraction of their income, and they have all won a measure of influence over the government's decisions.

Given these two conditions—a *political* economy, and no firm limit on money incomes—inflation is inevitable. The real economic pie, as always, can grow only as more is produced. But the money pie tends to grow whenever companies raise prices, unions raise wages, and government spends more money. The function of inflation is evident in this context. Every individual act—a price hike, a wage boost, more federal spending—makes somebody think they're getting ahead of somebody else. Since so many people have the power to win such gains and since not everybody can win real increases except to the extent the economy is growing, there has to be a way by which people who think they are winning can turn out to be losing. The way is inflation.

Inflation has a peculiar virtue in this role: it camouflages real changes and thus deflects anger. In an earlier era, when people's incomes were more at the mercy of the elements or the marketplace than they are now, there was no one to blame for economic misfortune and nowhere to turn for economic help. In a political economy the opposite is the case. Any economic agent—a company, an industry, a group of workers, even a region—faced with declining economic fortunes or wanting to increase its share of the pie will look to the government for help. Democratic government, by its nature, is both visible and accommodating. Its actions are a matter of public record and concern. Its officials win popularity, stature, and reelection by granting requests, by spending money, by providing employment rather than by doing the opposite.

Inflation is a way by which the government can appear to be giving out more than it has. It is also a way by which the amount everyone gets can be invisibly reduced, without any particular administration, agency, or member of Congress seeming to be responsible. It allows the struggle over the economic pie to proceed, all the while, as Yale economist James Tobin has put it, "blindly, impartially, impersonally, and nonpolitically" scaling down its outcomes. Inflation is not, of course, wholly invisible, a fact that partially explains the popular outcry against it. But its persistence in the face of widespread opposition suggests that it is a useful veil in maintaining the system as it has come to be. For a while, at least, it keeps people happy.

The imposition of wage and price controls would make explicit what so far has been largely implicit. Some people's wages and prices would still rise, in response to the economic needs and pressures mentioned in the last chapter. But one person's increase would no longer be sufficient justification for another's. Theoretically, for example, a Wage and Price Administration might let hospitals raise nurses' pay in order to alleviate the shortage. It would not then be expected to let doctors', technicians', and orderlies' incomes go up.

The visibility of this governmental intervention in the economy raises the ultimate questions behind the struggle over the economic pie. The questions are these. What is a fair distribution of income? And what distribution of income is consistent with a strong, growing economy? Most political debate revolves around these questions even today. But the questions are answered largely on an ad hoc basis—should wheat price supports be raised this year?—and the apparent answers are then adjusted by inflation into a real gain or real loss for those concerned. A system of wage and price controls requires more explicit choices and makes winners and losers more visible. The struggle over the pie is likely to intensify for precisely this reason.

In a sense, then, the test for the American economy isn't inflation at all, but what happens when inflation is controlled. At that point the role of government will be out in the open, and the struggle begun on a new footing. If the economy grows so rapidly that all remain generally satisfied with their relative shares, then the conflict may never come to a head. If we somehow reach agreement on what constitutes a fair distribution of income, then that agreement itself will define the limits of the conflict. At present, both rapid economic growth and a consensus about income distribution remain elusive objectives.

Our difficulty in reaching these goals, however, does not reflect a lack of knowledge. It reflects the fact that there are several possible solutions to both problems, each one representing different beliefs and different economic interests. The particular path that is chosen will be influenced by philosophic and economic argument, and it will in the end be determined by the way interests clash—by politics. The end of inflation, if it comes, will thus mark the beginning of both a new debate and a new political struggle over how —and for whose benefit—the economy should be managed.

Appendix:
How the Inflation Rate Is Calculated

The most common measure of inflation in the United States is the Consumer Price Index (CPI), a number published each month by the government's Bureau of Labor Statistics.* If the CPI in January is 1 percent higher than the CPI for December, inflation (which is usually reported on a yearly basis) is said to have hit 12 or 13 percent.† When news reports announce last month's or last year's inflation rate or "increase in the cost of living," it is usually the change in the CPI they're referring to.

The CPI does not measure "prices" as a whole. Even if that were possible it wouldn't make much sense: you wouldn't know how much weight to give automobiles, say, as opposed to transistor radios or dental services. Instead, Bureau of Labor Statistics re-

---

* Actually two numbers. The traditional CPI measures the prices of goods and services purchased by "urban wage earners and clerical workers." A broader CPI introduced in 1978 measures the prices of goods and services purchased by "all urban consumers"—in other words, a slightly different market basket, reflecting the buying habits of a somewhat larger group of people. The former is now called CPI-W, the latter CPI-U. So far the two indices have not differed significantly.

† 1 percent monthly increase gives a 12 percent yearly increase if it is not compounded. With compounding, the rate works out to 12.7 percent. Different news reports treat this problem in different ways.

searchers attempt to determine what a typical household spends its money on. The bureau then ascertains the prices of these items from month to month, weighting them according to their share of the family budget. If they cost 1 percent more this month than they did last month, the CPI goes up 1 percent.

Every so often, obviously, the bureau must update the "market basket" that it is pricing. An index that reflects the price of washtubs won't mean much if everyone is buying automatic washing machines. The latest survey of what people spend their money on took place in 1972 and 1973, and it is this basket of goods and services that is "priced" by today's CPI. As it happens, the CPI stood at 133.1 in 1973. (It was arbitrarily set at 100 for 1967.) By 1979 it had reached 217.4. So if you were a typical family and set out to buy the exact same mixture of goods and services in 1979 that you bought in 1973, it would have cost you 63 percent more.

The inflation rate as measured by the CPI is not quite the same thing as an increase in the cost of living. For one thing, the CPI doesn't include taxes. For another, the index measures the price of a specific collection of goods and services over time. Real families, however, don't buy the same mixture of goods and services over time. In 1972 and 1973, for instance, gasoline was still cheap. So our typical family probably owned an Oldsmobile V-8 and took it for a spin in the country every Sunday. Today the same family probably owns a Honda Civic and goes jogging on Sunday instead of driving. Its expenditure on gasoline may have risen only a little, despite the steep price increases. The CPI, however, assumes the family is buying just as much gasoline as before, and the "inflation rate" reflects that assumption.

Also, it is hard for the CPI to separate out inflation—price increases for the same item—from changes in the items themselves. Suppose Sears brings out a newly designed Kenmore dishwasher priced $50 higher than last year's model. Only part of that increase, presumably, is inflation. Another part should represent improvements in the product's quality, attractiveness, or features. The Bureau of Labor Statistics uses various methods to "correct" for quality improvements so that it is always comparing a similar market basket from one year to the next. But the calculations are rough and the judgments sometimes subjective, particularly when a service like medical care is the item in question. Over several years, an apparent increase in the cost of living may represent a higher standard of living (more efficient cars, better medical care) as much as it represents inflation.

Finally, the way the CPI calculates the price of owning a home overstates the cost of living for most families. Housing costs are an important component of the CPI, yet home ownership is a unique kind of expenditure. Part of what the homeowner spends on housing is analogous to rent—current consumption of housing, exactly like the money spent on eggs or hi-fi music systems. Another part represents an investment, like buying stocks or bonds. The price people pay for their homes reflects not only how much they would be willing to pay in rent (if rental housing were the only kind available) but how much they want to invest in real estate. Sharply rising home prices are therefore quite different from sharply rising gasoline prices or clothing prices in their impact on the cost of living. If you're paying a lot for a home, it may be because you have deliberately chosen to do so in hopes your investment will pay off when you sell.

There's a technical problem involved here too. At present, the CPI calculates the cost of buying a home at current home prices and mortgage interest rates. This does not mean, as is sometimes alleged, that the Bureau of Labor Statistics assumes every homeowner is repurchasing and refinancing a home every month. Rather, it assumes that the same number of people who bought homes in 1972 and 1973 are buying them today. And it counts the total of their expenditures—purchase price, financing costs, and so on—as the total home-purchase component of the CPI. All the people who are assumed not to be buying a home are assumed to have no home-purchase expenditures at all. So when current home prices and interest rates are shooting up, the CPI rises rapidly too. Yet most homeowners' mortgage payments—an important part of their cost of living—may not have changed at all.

Other methods of calculating the price of owning a home can easily be imagined, and the bureau has considered adopting one or another of them. It could, for example, try to figure out homeowners' actual outlays in a given month—mortgage payments, taxes, and so forth. That would lump together recent buyers (who are paying today's interest rates) with buyers who are paying interest rates of years past. Alternatively, it could try to figure out what a typical owner-occupied home might rent for, and use that figure as an index of a homeowner's costs. In both cases, rising home prices and interest rates wouldn't push the CPI up so quickly.

Changing the way the CPI is calculated, however, is easier said than done. There is widespread agreement that the index overstates the rate of increase in the average family's cost of living. There is considerably less agreement on whether the index should be changed. Some believe that the index is doing exactly what it was designed to do—measure the cost of a fixed market basket over time. Others believe that meddling with the CPI can become a convenient substitute for doing something about inflation, rather like beheading the messenger who brings the bad news. Most important, the millions of Americans whose wages or benefits are increased whenever the CPI goes up will not welcome changes that threaten to lower the index or slow its rate of increase. At present this group includes not only unionized workers with cost-of-living adjustments in their contracts; it also includes social security beneficiaries, food stamp recipients, and most federal pensioners. Put together, they make up a formidable lobby.

Other measures

Those who follow more specialized accounts of inflation will run into other terms as well.

The *Producer Price Index* (formerly the Wholesale Price Index) is similar to the CPI but measures goods sold at stages of production other than retail. The price of farm produce, steel, lumber, industrial chemicals, and so on shows up first here.

The *Gross National Product Implicit Price Deflator*—GNP deflator for short—is the measure of inflation often favored by economists. Every year the Commerce Department is faced with the task of measuring real GNP—output in constant dollars—as compared with nominal GNP. It solves this problem by breaking down GNP into hundreds of component parts and discounting ("deflating") current production figures by an appropriate price index. If it finds, for instance, that consumers spent $2.2 billion on color television sets, while the Labor Department says that the price of color TV sets has gone up 10 percent, it will determine that "real" production of color television sets is $2 billion. When all the parts are added up, the department will have two figures—one for GNP in current dollars, one for GNP in constant dollars. Figuring the percentage difference between the two gives the GNP deflator.

This measure too has its problems. In particular, it understates the effects of rising import prices. That's because imports are *subtracted* when GNP is added up; rising imports thus give you a smaller apparent GNP and a smaller increase over last year's GNP than you would otherwise get. In an OPEC-dominated world, this can be a serious disadvantage.

The *underlying inflation rate* is the least well-defined measure of inflation. At any given point, inflation may be fed by a variety of fortuitous or uncontrollable events—bad weather, say, or OPEC decisions to raise the price of oil. The notion of an underlying inflation rate is at its best an attempt by economists to remove all these "price shocks" from the calculations and see how bad inflation would be if the wage-price spiral were all we had to worry about. At worst, such calculations are used by administration spokespeople to make the "true" inflation rate seem less than it is. This approach has its ironies. Consumers faced with spiraling food and gasoline prices are told, in effect, that inflation wouldn't be so bad if it weren't for spiraling gas and food prices.

In general, particular measures of inflation don't make much difference. Over time, they tend to follow similar paths. And time is important, for any one index may vary considerably from one month to the next. (In January 1980, for example, the CPI was rising at an 18 percent annual rate; in July 1980 it stood still.) Frequently, attempts to find or use new measures of inflation reflect political desires to make inflation seem better or worse than it is. The Consumer Price Index undoubtedly overstates the inflation that most families experience; nevertheless it is a useful measure of how prices are changing from one period to the next. In any event, the best solution to inflation is not to worry about how it is measured but to do something about the rate at which prices go up

Source Notes

There are three reference books that are indispensable to anyone interested in digging up economic statistics:

The *Economic Report of the President* is issued annually. It includes a report to Congress from the President outlining his economic priorities, and a longer, more detailed report on the state of the economy by the President's Council of Economic Advisers. It also includes more than one hundred pages of statistical tables and is the handiest reference book for aggregate economic figures such as Gross National Product, unemployment rates, and changes in the Consumer Price Index. In many cases the tables go back fifty years.

The *Statistical Abstract of the United States* is issued every year by the Commerce Department. It is a much more comprehensive work than the *Economic Report of the President*, including both detailed economic statistics and statistics on dozens of other subjects.

Historical Statistics of the United States, Colonial Times to 1970 is a massive two-volume compilation of the same kind of statistics found in the *Statistical Abstract* for years past. In most cases, of course, the data relating to the eighteenth and nineteenth centuries are rough by today's standards; the sketchy statistics gathered at the time have had to be supplemented with reconstructions and estimates by present-day historians and statisticians. Still, the historical figures give a broad measure of how things have changed over the years.

In these notes, *Economic Report of the President* refers to the volume issued by Jimmy Carter's administration in early 1980; its tables, for the most part, run through 1979. *Statistical Abstract* refers to the *Statistical Abstract of the United States, 1979,* published in 1980. Its tables ordinarily run through 1978 and sometimes extend into 1979. All these works are available in most libraries. They can be purchased in the U.S. government bookstores to be found in many big cities, or through the Superintendent of Documents, Washington, D.C. 20402.

The "inflation rate" in this book is measured by changes in the Consumer Price Index (see Appendix). The Index and its various components can be found in the *Economic Report of the President,* p. 259ff. (back to 1929) or in the *Statistical Abstract,* p. 483ff. (back to 1950). Month-to-month changes for all the index's components are reported in greatest detail in the *Handbook of Labor Statistics,* issued every year by the U.S. Department of Labor's Bureau of Labor Statistics. Current index figures can be found in the Labor Department's monthly magazine, *Monthly Labor Review.* Historical data on the CPI, including a reconstructed index for the years before 1919, when the Labor Department first began gathering systematic price data, can be found in *Historical Statistics,* pp. 210–11.

In the text, single-year inflation rates for the years after World War II are the so-called December-to-December rates, measured from the end of one year to the end of the next. In all other cases, "inflation rate" refers to the average increase in the CPI during the course of the year. These two numbers differ significantly only when you're looking at what happened within a given year— for example, inflation may have increased rapidly toward the end of a year—not when you're considering what happened over a period of years.

Note: In the citations that follow, omission of an author's name means that the reference was not by-lined. Also, no page references are given for newspaper articles because pagination frequently changes from edition to edition. Full publishing data for a book are given only the first time the book appears in the notes.

Page

6   Opinion-poll lists: The *Newsweek* poll for February
       1980, for example, showed that inflation was once again
       the number-one worry after being displaced briefly by

"international problems." In response to the question "What do you think is the most important problem facing the country today?" roughly half of the poll's respondents cited inflation. See *Newsweek*, March 3, 1980, p. 27.

15   Coffee, record album, automobile, and gasoline prices culled from memory, from newspaper ads of the time, and from components of the Consumer Price Index. New-home prices: *Statistical Abstract*, p. 792; mortgage rates: *Statistical Abstract*, p. 542.

18   Average after-tax income: *Economic Report of the President*, p. 229. The government calculates this figure using the Commerce Department's "personal consumption expenditures deflator" as a measure of inflation (instead of the Consumer Price Index).

   The price of eggs: A "typical worker" in this example means a factory worker. In 1935 factory employees made an average of 54¢ an hour (*Historical Statistics*, pp. 169–70); in 1980 the figure was just over $7.00 (*Monthly Labor Review*, August 1980, p. 76). The price of a small color TV set in 1980 is estimated at $300. In 1970, taking the "television set" price index as a guide, a similar set would have cost at least $290. (Average wages in manufacturing were then $3.36 an hour.) In reality the gap may be even greater; color television sets have almost certainly grown less expensive relative to black-and-white sets, yet the index lists them together.

20n.   The "balance on merchandise trade," which measures imports compared to exports, was $−30.9 billion in 1977, $−33.8 billion in 1978, and $−29.5 billion in 1979 (*Survey of Current Business*, June 1980, p. 33). Gross national product in 1979 was approximately $2.5 trillion; in 1977 and 1978 it was nearer $2 trillion (*Economic Report of the President*, p. 203).

   The "balance on current account" showed a small deficit in 1971, 1972, and 1979, and a somewhat larger deficit in 1977 and 1978.

20   Welfare benefits: Average monthly payments in families under the AFDC program rose from $190 in 1970 to $256 in 1978, an apparent increase of 35 percent. In the same period the Consumer Price Index rose 68 percent (*Statistical Abstract*, p. 352).

Single-parent families account for 19 percent of all families with children living at home, according to the Census Bureau's 1980 estimates, and 90 percent of all single-parent families are headed by a woman. The median income of female-headed families rose 67.6 percent between 1970 and 1978 (the last year for which complete figures are available) while the Consumer Price Index was rising 68.0 percent. See U.S. Bureau of the Census, Current Population Reports, Series P-60, *Money Income of Families and Persons in the United States*, 1970 and 1978.

Minimum wage rates: *Statistical Abstract*, p. 423.

Winners and losers: Industry-wide earnings figures (retail trade, etc.) are from the *Statistical Abstract*, p. 420. The figures on librarians, college professors, steelworkers, and other occupational categories are from Paul Blumberg, "White-Collar Status Panic," *The New Republic*, December 1, 1979, pp. 21–22. Vacuum-cleaner salesmen, Avon ladies, household workers, free-lance writers, and the cowboy all turn up in Edwin McDowell's story "The Big Pay Squeeze: Who Hurts Most," *The New York Times*, April 20, 1980.

21   The elderly: The median income of families headed by a person over sixty-five doubled between 1970 and 1978, for a real gain of nearly 20 percent. The average real gain in median income for all families over the same period was slightly over 6 percent. See Current Population Reports, Series P-60, 1970 and 1978. Note that family median-income figures do not show the same increase during the 1970s as the average after-tax income figures mentioned earlier. The disparity is accounted for mainly by the fact that average family size has decreased since 1970.

Old people living in poverty: *Statistical Abstract*, p. 464. The same point was made by Lester C. Thurow in

"A Government Program with Marks of Success," *The Boston Globe*, April 22, 1980.

Social security benefits account for nearly 40 percent of the total money income going to persons aged sixty-five and over, according to the Social Security Administration. In-kind benefits such as Medicare raise the fraction of total income accounted for by social security to at least half. Cf. Lester C. Thurow, *The Zero-Sum Society* (New York: Basic Books, 1980), p. 159.

Congress raised social security benefits 20 percent in 1972 and at the same time put in place the "machinery for automatic increases starting in 1975." It also raised benefits 11 percent in 1974 ("Social Security Recipients Will Collect 14.3% Increase in Benefits in July," *The New York Times*, April 23, 1980). Average monthly benefits paid to men under social security rose from $131 in 1970 to $292 in 1978, a real increase of 33 percent. For women the figures are $101 and $230, a gain of 35 percent (*Statistical Abstract*, p. 338).

Private pensions: In 1950, only 450,000 people were receiving benefits from private pension plans. By 1970 the figure had risen to 4.7 million, and by 1975 to over 7 million (*Statistical Abstract*, p. 340).

22   Quintiles: From Current Population Reports, Series P-60, 1978. Note that the figures in the text are for families; comparable figures for households of single or unrelated individuals are considerably lower and exhibit greater inequality.

Unionized workers: The gap between unionized workers' wages and nonunionized workers' wages has been growing since the early 1950s, though not in every year and not in every industry. See Daniel J. B. Mitchell, *Unions, Wages, and Inflation* (Washington: The Brookings Institution, 1980).

23   Inflation in other countries: Between 1969 and 1979, U.S. prices rose 101 percent. Over the same period, prices in Canada rose 105 percent; in Japan 137 percent; in France 136 percent; in Italy 219 percent; and in the

United Kingdom 236 percent. The West German inflation rate was only 63 percent (*Economic Report of the
President*, p. 327; data extend through third quarter of
1979).

26   Stock prices: Standard & Poor's common index (500
stocks) in *Statistical Abstract*, p. 543. Bond prices: Standard & Poor's index of corporate AAA bonds in *Statistical Abstract*, p. 543.

Decline in stock prices: "Analysis of declining real stock
prices by two MIT economists indicates that they are
probably related to mistakes in how the financial community evaluates stocks during a period of inflation
rather than to the effects of inflation on income flows"
(Lester C. Thurow, *Zero-Sum Society*, p. 53. The
reference being made is to Franco Modigliani and
Richard A. Cohn, "Inflation, Rational Valuation, and
the Market," *Financial Analysis Journal*, March/April
1979, p. 3).

27   Stock ownership: Slightly more than 25 million individ-
uals aged twenty-one and over owned stock in 1975
(*Statistical Abstract*, p. 544). The adult population of the
United States at the time was 130.8 million.

In 1972, the richest 1 percent of the population owned
15.1 percent of all real estate, 56.5 percent of corporate
stock, 60.0 percent of bonds, 13.5 percent of cash, 52.7
percent of debt instruments (notes, mortgages, and so on),
7.0 percent of life insurance, 89.9 percent of trusts, and
9.8 percent of miscellaneous assets owned by individuals.
All this added up to roughly a quarter of personal wealth
(*Statistical Abstract*, p. 470).

Home prices: The median sales price of an existing
home rose 112 percent between 1970 and 1978 (*Statistical
Abstract*, p. 791), while average prices were rising 68
percent.

Greenspan citation: from Clyde H. Farnsworth, "Loan
Shock: A 16½% Prime," *The New York Times*, February
24, 1980. Senator Cranston as quoted in Robert D.

Hershey, Jr., "Inflation at 13.3%: What is This Rapacious Thing?" *The New York Times*, February 3, 1980.

28   Profits: After-tax profits per dollar of sales for all manufacturing corporations rose from 4.0¢ in 1970 to 5.4¢ in 1978 (*Statistical Abstract*, p. 569).

29   Gains and losses: see, for example, Joseph J. Minarik, "Who Wins, Who Loses from Inflation?" *Challenge*, January/February 1979, pp. 26–31.

30   Lester C. Thurow quote: from "Our Standard of Living Has Not Fallen," *Challenge*, March/April 1980, p. 48.
     Wage figures: The hourly wages are for "production or nonsupervisory workers on [private] nonagricultural payrolls" (*Monthly Labor Review*, April 1980, p. 81).

30n.   Between 1970 and 1978, part-time workers increased from 14 to 15 percent of the labor force (*Statistical Abstract*, p. 397).
     Paul Ryscavage as quoted in Christopher Conte, "The Baby Boom Muddies the Picture," *The Wall Street Journal*, March 27, 1980.

31   Fraction of the population working: The proportion of people considered "not in the labor force"—that is, not working and not looking for work—fell from 38.7 percent in 1970 to less than 36 percent in 1979 (*Statistical Abstract*, p. 394).

32   Israeli inflation rate: reported in *The New York Times*, January 16, 1980. The statistics about Ghana and Peru are from Robert Fuller, "Inflation: The Rising Cost of Living on a Small Planet" (Washington: Worldwatch Institute, Paper No. 34, January 1980), p. 12.

34   Nineteenth-century prices, as explained above, reflect a reconstructed price index (*Historical Statistics*, pp. 210–11). Though the numbers may not be exact the long-term trend is unmistakable. Twentieth-century figures (after World War I) reflect the modern Consumer Price Index.

38   The story of Henry P. Crowell and Quaker Oats, along

with much of the more general information on the emergence of large corporations, is taken from Alfred D. Chandler, Jr., *The Visible Hand: The Managerial Revolution in American Business* (Cambridge: The Belknap Press of Harvard University Press, 1977), p. 293ff. The historian describing the mill (quoted by Chandler) is Arthur E. Marquette, author of *Brands, Trademarks, and Good Will* (New York: McGraw-Hill, 1967).

Quaker Oats's size and rank: from "*Fortune*'s Directory of the 500 Largest Industrial Corporations," *Fortune*, May 5, 1980, p. 274ff. The three largest cereal companies, according to a report in *The Wall Street Journal*, account for 80 percent of the breakfast cereal sold in the United States and have been charged by the Federal Trade Commission with maintaining a "shared monopoly" (Lawrence Ingrassia, "Cereal Firms, FTC Still At It 4 Years Later," *The Wall Street Journal*, June 25, 1980).

39　Figures for 500 largest industrial firms calculated from *Fortune*'s Directory.

41　The account of the cigarette industry is compiled from the following sources: William Bennett, "The Cigarette Century," *Science 80*, September/October 1980, pp. 36–43; Alfred D. Chandler, Jr., *The Visible Hand*, pp. 249–50 and passim; "*Fortune*'s Directory of the 500 Largest Industrial Corporations"; Steve Lohr, "Reynolds Discontinuing Real 'Natural' Cigarettes," *The New York Times*, June 24, 1980; John Koten, "Tobacco Marketers' Success Formula: Make Cigarets in Smokers' Own Image," *The Wall Street Journal*, February 29, 1980; Steve Lohr, "Cigarette 'Tar Wars' Intensify," *The New York Times*, April 15, 1980; Richard Hodierne, "Tastes Like a Chemical Should," *The Boston Globe*, March 30, 1980.

43　Per capita cigarette consumption: *Statistical Abstract*, p. 816. Cigarette-industry profit figures: "*Business Week*'s Corporate Scoreboard: How 1,200 Companies Performed in 1979," *Business Week*, March 17, 1980, pp. 81–116.

44　Price-fixing cases: "Four Gypsum Concerns Settle Price

Case, Agreeing to Pay Taxes on $12.3 Million," *The Wall Street Journal*, March 4, 1980; "Five Firms Charged with Fixing Prices of Packaging Paper," *The Wall Street Journal*, February 29, 1980; Jeffrey H. Birnbaum, "Prospect is Waxing of 2 Crayon Firms Settling Price Case," *The Wall Street Journal*, February 29, 1980.

47   Robert R. Nathan quote: from "Imperfect Markets and Government Policy," *Society*, July/August 1979, p. 15. Price leadership: "U.S. Steel Corp. Follows Price Rise on Sheet Items," *The Wall Street Journal*, March 6, 1980; "Alcoa Lifts Prices of Ingot in U.S. 6 Cents a Pound," *The Wall Street Journal*, March 31, 1980; "GM Raises Auto Prices an Average 2.2%; Ford, Chrysler Are Expected to Follow," *The Wall Street Journal*, April 1, 1980; Reginald Stuart, "Chrysler, VW Raise Prices; Action Follows Other Producers," *The New York Times*, April 8, 1980.

48   Appliance industry: "An Appliance Boom That May Not Last," *Business Week*, March 10, 1980.

49   Chandler quote: *The Visible Hand*, p. 134.

50n. 1   Cf. Chandler, *The Visible Hand*, p. 171.

50   Chandler quote: *The Visible Hand*, pp. 316–17.

50n. 2   Cf. Chandler, *The Visible Hand*, p. 319.

50   Frederick Lewis Allen quote: from *The Big Change: America Transforms Itself, 1900–1950* (New York: Harper & Bros., 1952), p. 74.

51   On the airlines: Winston Williams, "Airlines Encounter Deregulation Snags," *The New York Times*, November 11, 1979; Winston Williams, "Ailing Airlines Blame C.A.B.," *The New York Times*, February 22, 1980; Winston Williams, "Ailing Airline Industry Engaged in a Rate War," *The New York Times*, March 15, 1980; Winston Williams, "Airlines Get Lottery Fever," *The New York Times*, April 15, 1980 (the quote is from this story); William M. Carley, "Losses Jolt Airlines as Fuel Costs Climb and Ticket Sales Drop," *The Wall Street*

Journal, April 23, 1980; "Now the Battling Airlines Try Mass Marketing," *Business Week*, April 28, 1980; Brenton Welling, "A Price War Aggravates the Airline Nosedive," *Business Week*, June 30, 1980.

On the auto industry: John R. White, "The Ford Style on Rebate: 'We Fish Where the Fish Are Biting,'" *The Boston Globe*, March 6, 1980; "GM Increases 1980 Car Prices an Average 1.6%—Similar Boosts Are Expected Soon by Rest of Industry Despite Deep Sales Slump," *The Wall Street Journal*, July 1, 1980. Note that this increase was in addition to the 2.2 percent rise referred to in the text.

52   Robert M. Solow quote: from "What We Know and Don't Know About Inflation," *Technology Review*, December 1978/January 1979, p. 42.

53   Joan Robinson quote: from "Solving the Stagflation Puzzle," *Challenge*, November/December 1979, p. 42.

Arthur Okun quote: from "The Invisible Handshake and the Inflationary Process," *Challenge*, January/February 1980, p. 7.

The price of sugar: "Sugar Price Rise Hurts Consumer," *The New York Times*, June 14, 1980.

Labor Department quote: from "Supply, Demand, and the 'Invisible Hand': Some Prices Still Fall," *The New York Times*, July 13, 1980.

54   On Kodak: "After Silver's Sharp Fall: High Hopes at Kodak," *Business Week*, April 14, 1980; What Goes Up Often Stays Up," *The New York Times*, April 20, 1980; "Kodak Cuts Prices as Much as 28%," *The New York Times*, May 6, 1980; "In Film, Silver Lining is a Cloud," *The New York Times*, August 11, 1980.

55   Firestone cutbacks: Iver Peterson, "Firestone Tire Plans to Close 6 Plants, Idling 7,265," *The New York Times*, March 20, 1980.

The Means memorandum is excerpted in Gardiner C.

Means, *The Corporate Revolution in America* (New York: The Crowell-Collier Press, 1967), pp. 77–100.

60n. Discount oil dealers: Charles Kenney, "Heating Oil Can Cost Less in Cash Deal," *The Boston Globe*, August 29, 1980.

63 Peter Meyer quote: from "Entangled Freedoms," *Harper's*, June 1980, p. 56.

Trucking profits: "Truckers Quietly Get Set for Deregulation," *Business Week*, March 24, 1980.

64 On the New York taxicab industry: "If the Cab Business Is So Bad . . ." *The New York Times* (editorial), March 4, 1980; David A. Andelman, "New York's Taxi Industry Thriving on Some Controversial Economics," *The New York Times*, March 13, 1980; "Hail Not the Taxi Deal," *The New York Times* (editorial), April 5, 1980.

Anesthesiologists, opticians, pharmacists: Michael Pertschuk, "An Inflation Paradox: Business Regulation of Business," *Challenge*, January/February 1979, pp. 57–58.

Lawyer advertising: Linda Greenhouse, "Lawyer Advertising Cutting Fees," *The New York Times*, August 3, 1980.

65 "Industry practices": Isadore Barmash, "Inquiries into Price Fixing: New U.S. Policy More Aggressive," *The New York Times*, September 24, 1980.

Rolf H. Wild quote: from *Management by Compulsion: The Corporate Urge to Grow* (Boston: Houghton Mifflin, 1978), p. 66.

66 Home prices: *Statistical Abstract*, pp. 791–92.

The tax example is calculated from the 1979 Form 1040.

Estimated $14 billion in uncollected revenue: *Statistical Abstract*, p. 261.

67 The specific information on housing in this section draws on the following sources: Paul Starr and Gosta Esping-Andersen, "Passive Intervention: How Govern-

ment Accommodation of Powerful Private Interests Pro-
duces Inflation in Housing and Health Care," *Working
Papers for a New Society*, July/August 1979, pp. 15–25;
Robert J. Samuelson, "Inflation Has Found a Home,"
National Journal, March 10, 1979, p. 402; Brooks Jack-
son, "Costly Mortgages Spur Dire Predictions for Hous-
ing as Big Subsidies Are Sought," *The Wall Street
Journal*, March 7, 1980; Sandy Graham, "Shocked Home-
owners Have Trouble Selling; Some Change Tactics,"
The Wall Street Journal, March 21, 1980.

68   Starr and Esping-Andersen: from "Passive Intervention,"
pp. 21–22, 24.

Medicare spending: Robert Reinhold, "Two Reports
Identify High Cost Patients," *The New York Times*, May
6, 1980.

70   Coffee prices: *Handbook of Labor Statistics*, pp. 434–35.

The general history of U.S. agricultural policy was re-
counted to me by Dr. Wayne Rasmussen of the U.S.
Department of Agriculture.

On specific crops: Richard L. Hudson, "Dairymen
Curdled by Moves to Decontrol Reconstituted Milk to
Quiet Inflation," *The Wall Street Journal*, April 8, 1980;
Seth S. King, "Dairy Prices Rising as Surpluses Mount,"
The New York Times, May 4, 1980; Seth S. King, "Dairy
Aid Reviewed," *The New York Times*, June 5, 1980;
"Dairy Farmer Diets Are a Bit Rich," *The New York
Times* (editorial), June 23, 1980; Blaine Harden, "The
Feudal World of King Tobacco," *The Boston Globe*,
May 5, 1980; Mark Kramer, "The Ruination of the
Tomato," *The Atlantic Monthly*, January 1980, pp. 72–
77.

74   The account of farm economics before the Depression
draws mainly on Lester V. Chandler, *America's Greatest
Depression 1929–1941* (New York: Harper & Row, 1970),
pp. 53–57. The quotation in the footnote on p. 74 is
from p. 65 of this book.

75   New England fishing industry: Bruce A. Mohl, "At Port,

Supply vs. Demand," *The Boston Globe*, June 24, 1980.

78   Nineteenth-century wage rates: *Historical Statistics*, pp 164–65, 172.

The quotation is from Robert Hunter, *Poverty* (New York: Macmillan, 1904), cited in Frederick Lewis Allen, *The Big Change: America Transforms Itself, 1900–1950*, p. 59.

79n.   Philip Taft, *Organized Labor in American History*, 1st ed. (New York: Harper & Row, 1964), p. 408.

79   Depression statistics: *Historical Statistics*, pp. 135, 169–70.

80   The account of Homestead and the Amalgamated comes largely from Philip Taft, *Organized Labor in American History*, pp. 136–45. It also draws on Katherine Stone, "The Origins of Job Structures in the Steel Industry," *Review of Radical Political Economics*, Summer 1974, pp. 113–73, esp. p. 121. The lengthy quote is from Taft, pp. 141–42.

83   The account of union organizing during the Depression draws primarily on Taft, pp. 411–537, and on William E. Leuchtenburg, *Franklin D. Roosevelt and the New Deal* (New York: Harper Colophon Books, 1963), pp. 95–117 and passim.

Leuchtenburg quote: *Franklin D. Roosevelt and the New Deal*, p. 239.

84   Leuchtenburg quote: *Franklin D. Roosevelt and the New Deal*, p. 107.

30-hour week: Leuchtenburg, p. 56.

85   Quote: from Leuchtenburg, p. 106. Union membership figures are from Taft, *Organized Labor in American History*, pp. 419–20.

Leuchtenburg quote: *Franklin D. Roosevelt and the New Deal*, p. 240.

86   Union membership figures: *Historical Statistics*, p. 178; *Statistical Abstract*, p. 427.

88   "Union Accord": *The New York Times*, August 18, 1980. According to the story, 6,000 unionized employees at Uniroyal, Inc., took the "highly unusual step of accepting a 12.9 percent pay reduction this year and a 6.5 percent cut in 1981."

89   Relief spending: *Historical Statistics*, pp. 1120, 1128.

The account of CWA, PWA, and the other agencies follows Leuchtenburg, *Franklin D. Roosevelt and the New Deal*, pp. 118–42. The quote is from p. 129.

90   A summary of modern income support programs can be found in F. Ray Marshall, Allan G. King, and Vernon M. Briggs, Jr., *Labor Economics: Wages, Employment, and Trade Unionism*, 4th ed. (Homewood, Ill.: Richard D. Irwin, Inc., 1980), pp. 455–85.

The figures on transfer payments are for 1979. They are from the *Economic Report of the President*, pp. 226–27, 289–90.

91   Men over sixty-five working: *Historical Statistics*, pp. 131–32; *Statistical Abstract*, p. 392.

92   William Green quote: cited in George Martin, *Madam Secretary: Frances Perkins* (Boston: Houghton Mifflin, 1976), p. 390.

Martin Dies quote: cited in Leuchtenburg, *Franklin D. Roosevelt and the New Deal*, p. 263.

Minimum-wage figures for the 1930s are from Martin, *Madam Secretary*, p. 392. Current figures are from *Statistical Abstract*, p. 423.

94   On wage variations among firms, see John T. Dunlop, "Wage Contours," in Michael J. Piore, ed., *Unemployment and Inflation: Institutionalist and Structuralist Views* (White Plains, N.Y.: M. E. Sharpe, Inc., 1979), pp. 63–74.

95   Wage contours: see Dunlop, "Wage Contours," in Piore, *Unemployment and Inflation*.

On nurses: Colman McCarthy, "Nursing Profession:

An Ailing Patient in Need of Attention," *The Boston Globe*, March 16, 1980; Loretta McLaughlin, "Nurses: Shortage or Rebellion?" *The Boston Globe*, June 16, 1980.

99   The account of the Depression draws on the following sources: Robert L. Heilbroner, *The Worldly Philosophers*, rev. ed. (New York: Simon & Schuster, 1961), p. 214ff; William E. Leuchtenburg, *Franklin D. Roosevelt and the New Deal*, passim; Lester V. Chandler, *America's Greatest Depression*, passim; *Historical Statistics of the United States*, passim. Heilbroner quote: *Worldly Philosophers*, p. 217.

     Chandler quote: *America's Greatest Depression*, p. 45.
     Hoovervilles: Leuchtenburg, pp. 2–3.

100   National Industrial Conference Board study: Chandler, p. 34.
     Chandler quote: *America's Greatest Depression*, p. 51.

101   Hoover quote: cited in Susan Winslow, *Brother Can You Spare a Dime?* (New York: Paddington Press, 1976), p. 17.

102   The account of economic theory and the Depression draws on Heilbroner, *The Worldly Philosophers*, pp. 214ff; on John Kenneth Galbraith, *Money* (Boston: Houghton Mifflin, 1975), pp. 183–234; and on Robert Lekachman, *The Age of Keynes* (New York: Random House, 1961), passim.

103   The Fed's actions: Galbraith, *Money*, p. 185.
     Federal spending: *Historical Statistics*, p. 1114.

104   Leuchtenburg quotes: *Franklin D. Roosevelt and the New Deal*, p. 249.
     1974–75 slump: *Economic Report of the President*, p. 209 (GNP); *Handbook of Labor Statistics*, p. 213 (unemployment). 1919–21 slump: *Historical Statistics*, pp. 226, 126. Note that the text refers to drops in output over the course of a year, rather than the often-used "peak to trough" measure of a recession's severity. Yearly averages are a better measure of a downturn's seriousness, in

my view, because they take into account how quickly the economy recovers from recession.

105   Government employment figures: *Historical Statistics*, p. 1102 (civilian employees); p. 1141 (military); p. 1104 (state and local employees). Current government employment figures are from the *Statistical Abstract*, pp. 277, 313, 373. Estimate of indirect government employment: Lester C. Thurow, *Zero-Sum Society*, p. 165.

106   Unemployment rates for occupational groups: *Statistical Abstract*, p. 407.

107   Figures on transfer payments: *Historical Statistics*, p. 1124; *Economic Report of the President*, p. 289.
Division of transfer payment "dollar": calculated from *Statistical Abstract*, p. 330.

109   National debt (dollar increase and proportion of GNP): *Statistical Abstract*, p. 254.

109n.   The idea of "paying off the debt" is suggested in Robert L. Heilbroner and Lester C. Thurow, *The Economic Problem*, 5th ed. (Englewood Cliffs, N.J.: Prentice Hall, 1978), p. 469.

111   Budget surpluses: *Economic Report of the President*, p. 289. The years were 1960 and 1969. In addition, there were surpluses of less than a billion dollars in 1963 and 1965.

113   On the gold standard, see the entertaining pamphlet by Josephine Polomski O'Brien entitled *Gold*. It is published by the Federal Reserve Bank of Philadelphia and is available for free.

114   Metal dollars: According to a spokesperson for the Treasury Department, the "Susan B.'s" cost about 3¢ apiece to produce (including labor).

115   The account of panics draws heavily on John Kenneth Galbraith, *Money*, pp. 100–15; 183–97; and passim.

116   Bank failures: *Historical Statistics*, p. 1038.

117   On the Federal Deposit Insurance Corporation's recent activities: Richard F. Janssen, "Behind the Signs at the FDIC," *The Wall Street Journal*, April 28, 1980; "First Pennsylvania Bank Gets Assistance of $500 Million from FDIC, 22 Banks," *The Wall Street Journal*, April 29, 1980.

118   On the possibility of another "real depression," see Walter Heller, "Can There Be Another Crash?" *Challenge*, March/April 1980, pp. 31–36.

122   Productivity, real wage, and unemployment figures: *Economic Report of the President*, pp. 247, 244, 237.

123   Troop-level figures: *World Almanac*, p. 715. Defense spending figures: *Statistical Abstract*, p. 364; fiscal years ending June 30, veterans benefits excluded.

124   Budget deficits: Unified budget basis, fiscal years ending June 30.

125   Money supply: *Economic Report of the President*, p. 271.
       Nixon quote: reported in Martin Mayer, *The Fate of the Dollar* (New York: Times Books, 1980), p. 171.
       On the "wrong medicine" argument, see Gardiner C. Means, "Simultaneous Inflation and Unemployment: A Challenge to Theory and Policy," in John M. Blair, ed., *The Roots of Inflation* (New York: Burt Franklin & Co., 1975), pp. 17–19 and chart on p. 20.

126   The McCracken article (*Washington Post*, July 28, 1971) is quoted by John Kenneth Galbraith, *Money*, p. 288. The account of Nixon's New Economic Policy draws on Galbraith, pp. 286–301; on George P. Shultz and Kenneth W. Dam, *Economic Policy Behind the Headlines* (New York: W.W. Norton & Co., 1977), pp. 65–85 and passim; and on Robert Lekachman, *Inflation: The Permanent Problem of Boom and Bust* (New York: Vintage Books, 1973), pp. 21–30 and passim.
       Chickens for broiling: Shultz and Dam, *Economic Policy*, p. 78.

127   Lekachman quote: *Inflation*, p. 28.
          Galbraith quote: *Economics and the Public Purpose*
(New York: New American Library, 1975), p. 190.

          Shultz suggestion: Shultz and Dam, *Economic Policy*, pp.
68–69. The account of international finance draws on
Shultz and Dam, pp. 109–31; on Galbraith, *Money*, pp.
293–301; on Robert Z. Aliber, *The International Money
Game*, 2nd ed. (New York: Basic Books, 1976), passim;
on Irving Friedman, *Inflation: A World-Wide Disaster*
(Boston: Houghton Mifflin, 1973), pp. 237–53; and above
all on Martin Mayer, *The Fate of the Dollar*, passim.

128   Nicholas von Hoffman quote: from "Passing the Buck,"
New York Review of Books, April 3, 1980, p. 16.

129   Paul M. Sweezy quote: from Harry Magdoff and Paul M.
Sweezy, *The End of Prosperity: The American Economy
in the 1970s* (New York: Monthly Review Press, 1977),
p. 1.
          Figures on foreign dollar reserves and gold supply:
Aliber, *International Money Game*, p. 39.

132   Nixon quote: reported in Mayer, *The Fate of the Dollar*,
p. 202. Aliber has Nixon calling it "the most important
agreement in history," *International Money Game*, p. 45.
          1970 exchange rates: *Statistical Abstract*, p. 915. 1980
exchange rates: *The New York Times*, October 1, 1980.

133   World money supply: Aliber, *International Money
Game*, p. 23.
          World commodity prices: Reuters index, cited by
Mayer, *The Fate of the Dollar*, p. 209.
          Martin Mayer quote: *The Fate of the Dollar*, p. 209.
          Dan Morgan quote (and additional information on
grain buying): Dan Morgan, *Merchants of Grain* (New
York: Viking, 1979), pp. 156–58.

134   Adam Smith quote: from "Oil's No Problem," *Esquire*,
April 1980, pp. 19–20.

135   Figures on oil use: from Steven A. Schneider, "International Rivalries and the Oil Price Revolution," Ph.D. Dissertation, University of California at Berkeley, 1980, chapter 4. This discussion of oil use and OPEC draws heavily on Schneider's work.

137　　*Business Week*, quote: "How Price Tactics Feed Inflation," *Business Week*, March 10, 1980, p. 36.

Real interest rates: Tom Herman, "Even Today's Steep Interest Rates Appear Low if Taxes and Inflation Are Taken Into Account," *The Wall Street Journal*, April 3, 1980.

Business debt: Alfred L. Malabre, Jr., "Debt Grows at Same Pace as Postwar Economy, But Spurt in Private Borrowing Worries Some," *The Wall Street Journal*, February 26, 1980. See also *Business Week*'s special issue, "The New Debt Economy," October 16, 1978, p. 76ff.

Credit and mortgage figures: *Economic Report of the President*, pp. 280–82.

Money supply: *Economic Report of the President*, p. 271. The growth figure refers to M_3, a relatively broad measure of the money supply. Narrower measures—M_1, M_1+, and M_2, all since redefined by the Fed—grew somewhat more slowly.

138　　On Eurodollars and other financial instruments, see Robert B. Zevin's newsletter, *U.S. Trends* (issued by the United States Trust Company's Boston office), Volume III, Number 4 (November 23, 1979). The growth of financial assets that are largely outside the Fed's control has led some analysts to conclude that the Fed can no longer effectively manage the money supply. ("Has the Fed Lost Hold of the Money Levers?" *Business Week* columnist Lewis B. Beman asked in the March 10, 1980, issue.) It also led President Carter to extend the Fed's jurisdiction—to include credit-card lending, money market funds, and the like—by invoking the Credit Control Act of 1969 (March 14, 1980).

Robert L. Heilbroner quote: from "Inflationary Capitalism," *The New Yorker*, October 8, 1979, p. 134.

142   Calvin Coolidge: "When people are out of work," the taciturn president is alleged to have said, "unemployment results."

Government regulation: Mark Green and Norman Waitzman, "A Challenge to Murray Weidenbaum," *The New York Times*, October 28, 1979; Murray Weidenbaum, "Mr. Weidenbaum Answers His Critics," *The New York Times*, November 4, 1979. See also Green and Waitzman, "Cost, Benefit, and Class," *Working Papers for a New Society*, May/June 1980, pp. 39–51.

142n.   Nicholas A. Ashford quote: from "In Many Cases, Regulation Pays," *The New York Times*, June 15, 1980.

Detroit and small cars: "The automobile industry might be smarting further beneath the wave of economic Japanese and European imports had the environmentalists' call for fuel efficiency not helped force domestic changes in Detroit" (Anthony J. Parisi, "Utilities Have Cause to Thank Their Critics," *The New York Times*, September 7, 1980).

144   Minimum wages: The federal minimum was scheduled to reach $3.35 an hour on January 1, 1981, just as this book was going to press (*Statistical Abstract*, p. 423). The minimum wage fell from about 50 percent of average manufacturing wages in 1970 to about 45 percent in 1980.

Robert Gough and Robin Siegel: cited in Lester C. Thurow, *Zero-Sum Society*, p. 47.

145   Petroleum industry net income: *Statistical Abstract*, p. 607.

146   Oil imports rose from 811 million barrels in 1972 to 2,275 million barrels in 1978: *Statistical Abstract*, p. 206. They started to decline in 1980.

Robert L. Heilbroner quote: "The Inflation in Your Future," *The New York Review of Books*, May 1, 1980, p. 6.

147   Alfred L. Malabre, Jr. quote: from *America's Dilemma*:

Jobs vs. Prices (New York: Dodd, Mead & Co., 1978), p. 105.

148   Lloyd J. Dumas quote: from "Economic Conversion: Cutting the Defense Budget without Sacrificing Jobs," *Working Papers for a New Society*, May/June 1979, p. 52.

151   High-employment budget figures: *Economic Report of the President*, p. 50.

Arthur Schlesinger Jr. quote: from "Inflation: Symbolism vs. Reality," *The Wall Street Journal*, April 9, 1980.

Washington's role in the government sector: both Lester C. Thurow and Robert L. Heilbroner have made this point repeatedly. The figures for 1979 are from *Economic Report of the President*, pp. 288–89.

153   Milton Friedman: see, for example, Milton Friedman and Rose Friedman, *Free to Choose* (New York: Harcourt Brace Jovanovich, 1980), p. 257.

155n.   See Martin Feldstein and Kathleen Feldstein, "The Fed Shifts Monetary Policy Aims," *Boston Globe*, July 8, 1980.

158n.   Lester C. Thurow argument: *Zero-Sum Society*, pp. 62–63.

160   Administrative inflation: Gardiner C. Means, "Simultaneous Inflation and Unemployment," in Blair, ed., *The Roots of Inflation*, p. 11ff.

165   Figures on firm size refer to proprietorships, partnerships, and corporations (1975 data rounded upwards): *Statistical Abstract*, p. 555.

169   Martin and Kathleen Feldstein quote: from "Policy to Combat Inflation Gives Strength to Recession," *Boston Globe*, August 19, 1980.

Geoffrey H. Moore quote: from "A Truism: Recession Slows Inflation," *The New York Times*, November 18, 1979. Not everyone, it should be noted, accepts this "truism." Herewith a sample of article titles, all written by economists or business journalists:

"Recession Isn't Cure for Inflation, Study for Congress Says," *The Wall Street Journal*, April 28, 1980;

Michael K. Evans, "Recession Stalls Inflation But It's No Solution," *Boston Globe*, May 6, 1980;

Edward Cowan, "Can a Recession Slow Prices?" *The New York Times*, June 13, 1980.

172 The Fed and the Hunt brothers: "The Fed was so worried that the giant Hunt silver debacle could damage the commercial paper market, and thus the entire U.S.—indeed, international—financial system, that it was willing to endorse the billion-dollar underwriting of the Hunt brothers' enormous silver losses." *Business Week*, May 19, 1980.

Robert B. Zevin reference: from *U.S. Trends*, Volume IV, Number 1, February 22, 1980.

Hyman P. Minsky quote: from "The Federal Reserve: Between a Rock and a Hard Place," *Challenge*, May/June 1980, p. 35.

173 Auto prices: *Business Week*'s adjectives for the auto companies' price hikes were "nervy" and "aggressive." *Business Week*, August 18, 1980, p. 27.

Arthur Okun quote: cited in Edward Cowan, "Can a Recession Slow Prices?" *The New York Times*, June 13, 1980.

Council of Economic Advisers: from *Economic Report of the President*, p. 101.

174 *Wall Street Journal* quote: Alfred L. Malabre, Jr., "Shadows in the Promised Land," May 5, 1980.

174n. Lester C. Thurow quote: *Zero-Sum Society*, p. 65.

175 Peter Drucker quote: from Laurence J. Peter, *Peter's Quotations: Ideas for Our Time* (New York: Bantam Books, 1979), p. 470.

177 Economics profession: The most notable exception is, of course, John Kenneth Galbraith, and a cogent case for controls can be found in *Economics and the Public Purpose*, especially chapter 30, pp. 292–305. See also Galbraith's *A Theory of Price Control*, reissued in 1980 by Harvard University Press (Cambridge).

New York Times/CBS poll: reported in E. J. Dionne, Jr., "The People Want Controls," *The New York Times*, February 3, 1980. Shortly before, Yale economist James Tobin had written in the *Times*, "Mandatory controls are unthinkable now; only the people support them" ("Why the Fed's Cure Won't Work," *The New York Times*, November 11, 1979).

178   The debate on controls:

Shlomo Maital, "Inflation: It's Time for Controls," *The New York Times*, January 13, 1980;

Leonard Silk, "Uncertainty on Controls," *The New York Times*, February 22, 1980;

"Time for Controls?" *The New Republic* (editorial), February 23, 1980, pp. 5–9;

Leonard Silk, "Price Controls Gaining Friends," *The New York Times*, February 27, 1980;

Walter Heller, "The Case for Wage and Price Controls," *The Wall Street Journal*, February 27, 1980;

"Shock Treatment for Inflation," *Business Week* (editorial), March 3, 1980, p. 96;

Paul Samuelson, "The Case for Controls," *Newsweek*, March 3, 1980, p. 57.

178
(box)   Sidney Weintraub offered a short account of his plan in "The Human Factor in Inflation," *The New York Times Magazine*, November 25, 1979, pp. 116–19ff. It is presented in greater detail in his book *Capitalism's Inflation and Unemployment Crisis* (Reading, Mass.: Addison-Wesley, 1978), pp. 121–63.

The New Republic reference is to the editorial "TIPsy over inflation" in the magazine's issue for March 15, 1980; Lester C. Thurow quote: *Zero-Sum Society*, p. 67.

180   Lid on a boiling kettle: Or, as *New York Times* writer Robert D. Hershey put it, "corking a whistling teapot instead of turning down the heat" ("Inflation at 13.3%: What Is This Rapacious Thing?" *The New York Times*, February 3, 1980).

186 England and Canada: The idea is from Paul Starr and Gosta Esping-Andersen, "Passive Intervention," pp. 24–25.

187 OPEC: Or, as Rutgers economist Alfred S. Eichner has proposed, the United States could pursue "an agreement between the major commodity-producing countries and the major commodity-consuming countries to stabilize the price of basic commodities (including oil)." "Combating Inflation," *The New York Times*, July 8, 1980.

APPENDIX

The Appendix draws on the following sources:

The Consumer Price Index: Concepts and Content Over the Years (Washington: Bureau of Labor Statistics, May 1978);

Measuring Price Changes: A Study of the Price Indexes, by William H. Wallace and William E. Cullison, 4th ed. (Richmond, Va.: Federal Reserve Bank of Richmond, April 1979);

Revising the Consumer Price Index (Washington: Bureau of Labor Statistics, 1978);

Revising the Consumer Price Index: A Brief Review of Methods (Washington: Bureau of Labor Statistics, 1976);

The Consumer Price Index Revision—1978 (Washington: Bureau of Labor Statistics, 1978);

Janet L. Norwood, "The Consumer Price Index Puzzle," *Challenge*, March/April 1980, pp. 41–45.

Index